UNCHARTED

A SURVIVAL LOVE STORY

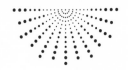

JULIE JOHNSON

JOHNSON INK, INC.

Subscribe to Julie's newsletter:
http://eepurl.com/bnWtHH

Cover Design by: One Click Covers

*This one's for the **ocean**...*
for teaching me not to fear the deep.

That's often where the best treasures are hidden.

"I must be a mermaid. I have no fear of depths and a great fear of shallow living."

ANAIS NIN

CHAPTER ONE

DEPARTURE

"Do you have your passport?"

"Yes."

"What about your neck pillow?"

"Yes."

"What about your sunscreen? Honey, you know how you burn..."

I sigh. "For the thousandth time, *yes*. I have everything. I promise."

"What about—"

I cut off Mom's next question by inflating my cheeks and unleashing a series of rapid whooshing noises as my arms rotate around my head in my best impression of chopper blades. The family of four unloading their station wagon a few feet away stare at me perplexed, but Mom just shakes her head, all too familiar with my antics.

"Yes, yes, I get it. I'm being an unbearable helicopter parent. No need for sound effects, Violet."

I cease whooshing and shoot a grin at her. She doesn't return the gesture. Instead, her face wrinkles into a familiar mask of concern — the same one she's been wearing for the past two weeks, since I broke the news of this trip. "Honey…"

I brace myself.

"Are you sure you want to do this? It's not too late to back out, you know."

"Mom!"

She holds her hands up in defense. "Okay! Okay. Just checking."

"You've *checked* about a zillion times already."

"Well, you could've changed your mind."

"Between now and the last time you asked, approximately twenty minutes ago?"

"You're seventeen. You change your mind every twenty *seconds*."

"Way to perpetuate a flagrant, reductive stereotype about teenagers, mother."

Her eyebrows lift in amusement. "Flagrant? Reductive? Where was this vocabulary when you torpedoed your SATs last year?"

I roll my eyes. "Now I'm *definitely* getting on the plane."

"Honey…"

"Mom! Stop. It's only three months. You'll barely have time to miss me."

"But then you're straight off to college in the fall." Mom's bright green eyes — twins of my own — gloss over with tears, and suddenly there's a catch in her voice. "I just thought… I guess I thought we'd have one last summer together before everything changed. I wasn't planning to lose you so soon."

"Careful, Mom, you lay on that guilt any thicker and I'll suffocate."

Her forehead crinkles. "I'm sorry. You know I'm proud of you for taking on this new opportunity. But... the house will be awfully quiet without you."

"After all the yelling you've done over the years about me blaring loud music, I'd think that would be a selling point."

She forces a laugh, but I can tell she's barely keeping it together. In an unfortunate show of solidarity, my own throat begins to clog with emotion. I blink rapidly to keep tears at bay. Clearing my throat has little effect.

As much as I want to go, I hate the thought of leaving Mom alone. For as long as I can remember, it's just been the two of us — a bona fide mother-daughter-best-friend duo, much like the titular Gilmores of our favorite TV show, albeit a slightly less caffeinated version. I don't know what she'll do without me around this summer. Frankly, I don't think she does either. She has a few close friends, but she's never been one for boyfriends, despite the fact that she's a total catch. Dad died when I was seven, and she hasn't shown a flicker of interest in another man in the decade since. All efforts to set her up — with the sexy science teacher at my old high school, with the cute waiter at our favorite diner, with the adorable golden retriever owner who visits her veterinary practice every few months — have gone to utter waste.

I already had the love of my life, honey, she'd say with a rueful smile. *You're young, but one day you'll understand. Anything after that kind of love would be a cheap imitation. Like wine after whiskey.*

It still seems ludicrous to me — the idea that your heart could beat so utterly for another person, if they walked out of your life someday it might cease to beat at all. That the right someone could make all the other someones look like weak knockoffs, in comparison.

I've never had anything — any guy — come close to inspiring those feelings inside my chest. I seriously doubt I ever will. That kind of love is for fairy tales and cheesy romantic comedies.

Whenever I say this, Mom just smiles in that annoying, knowing way and shakes her head.

He'll show up when he's meant to, honey. Don't rush it.

I usually laugh off her words, but I can't help wondering... Do I even want a love like that? The kind that burns so bright, you spend the rest of your life blinking away sun spots, half-blind from the experience?

That doesn't sound particularly appealing, if you ask me. Mom may be resigned to a life of single-motherhood and celibacy, but I'm not. Not yet, anyway.

Maybe that's why it was so easy to say yes to this trip. It's my one chance at a detour outside the path that's been set for me since day one. *The Life of Violet Anderson*: pre-written and choreographed like the script of some cliché teen movie I can't escape. Ballet lessons and soccer practices and student council meetings and prom queen tiaras. A high school sweetheart named Clint, who just so happens to be both homecoming king and the quarterback of the football team. And me at his side, just another pom-pom waving brunette with above-average looks and below-average test scores. Destined not for greatness, not for adventure, not for anything at all, really, except the sort of mind-numbing mediocrity only those unplagued by imagination embrace with wholehearted enthusiasm.

Even at seventeen, I know that won't be enough for me. To never taste adventure on my tongue... never color outside the lines of a socially-acceptable suburban life... never amount to anything except the status quo everyone else in my tiny hometown always seems so content to charge toward with blinders on, like racehorses on a track.

If I stay, I'll never acknowledge the dull ache inside my chest that screams out in the small hours of the night that there must be something *more*, something *different*, something that will make my stomach fly up into my throat and my fingertips lose circulation because they're squeezed so tight into fists of anticipation.

So, I'm leaning into the winds of change. I'm walking away

from that life, and I'm not looking back at the things I'm leaving behind.

A tiny town, with sun-dappled streets.

A farmhouse full of memories.

A promise ring from Clint on my bedside table.

And, most of all, Mom's face, etched with incalculable worry on the curb of the Departures drop-off zone.

Reaching out, I grab her hand and squeeze. I strive for a light tone, knowing if I let a single tear trickle out, I'll set off a show of waterworks to rival Niagara Falls.

"You're not losing me, Mom. It's a nannying job in the South Pacific, not a colonization mission to Mars."

"I'd feel safer with you on Mars. Astronauts are very honorable. We barely know anything about this family you'll be working for. They could be drug lords for all we know."

I snort. "Dramatic, much?"

"Violet, I'm serious."

"So am I! You have to relax. Mrs. McNally never would've suggested I work for crazy people."

"Well. Maybe *Mrs. McNally* didn't tell you the full story," Mom says in a decidedly un-neighborly tone.

My eyebrows shoot up to my hairline.

"Don't give me that look, Violet. She could have an ulterior motive, you don't know!"

"The woman runs the church bake sale every year. She's not a criminal mastermind."

"...or so she wants you to believe."

"*Moooooom.*" I groan. "Come on. The Flints are a normal family."

"Normal families don't spend their summers island-hopping around the South Pacific, or hire an au pair for their five-year-old."

"Did you swallow a bitter pill with your coffee this morning?"

"I'm just saying." She tosses her chestnut hair, one shade lighter than mine and twice as glossy. "What's the point of having children at all if you're just going to hire full-time help to raise them for you?"

"Mom, don't you think you're being a bit judg—"

"And, anyway, I can't fathom why they have to go all that way for a little sunshine. Florida has perfectly lovely beaches."

"As we've discussed *several times* already," I say slowly, summoning composure. "Mr. Flint is a resort developer. His company is scouting potential building locations on a few different islands. There's a whole team going — a handful of execs from The Flint Group, plus a photographer, the architect, a few marketing people..." I shrug. "Rather than leave his wife and daughter home for three months, Seth decided to bring them along. In my book, that makes him a pretty decent dad."

Mom's mouth presses into a firm line as she tries to formulate a counter-argument to change my mind. Even now, standing on the curb outside Boston Logan International Airport with my bags packed and my ticket in hand, she's still half-sure she might somehow convince me to stay. I pull a deep breath in through my nose and remind myself that this overbearing, overprotective show she's putting on comes from a place of love. She's not deliberately trying to annoy me.

I don't think so, anyway.

"Listen, I'm going to miss my flight." I sling my duffle strap a little higher over my shoulder. "I have to get going."

"Call me during your layover."

"I will if I have time."

Her worried look returns. "You're sure they're sending someone to meet you at LAX?"

"Yes, outside the baggage claim area. Mrs. Flint's personal assistant emailed this morning to confirm."

"I still don't like the idea of you on one of those tiny chartered jets across the Pacific. Why can't this family fly commercial like the rest of America?"

"It's the Flint *company* jet, mother. I think, once you invest in one of those, you're pretty much obligated to use it." A wicked grin spreads across my face. "Plus, think of all the free inflight champagne they'll be serving!"

She glares at me. "Violet, so help me—"

"Joking!" I interject hurriedly. "Just joking. I'm going to be babysitting, not joining the mile high club." I pause. "You know I've never been one for organized group activities."

"How did I ever raise such a smartass?"

"In your exact image," I point out.

Even as Mom nods in agreement, her bottom lip begins to tremble. I think she's going to dissolve into a puddle of tears but instead, she reaches out and hauls me into a crushing embrace. For such a petite woman, her hug is impressively rib-cracking.

"Can't... breathe...." I joke-wheeze, hugging her back equally hard.

"You be safe, you hear me?" she whispers forcefully.

I nod, wishing my eyes weren't pricking. "I will."

"You email twice a week."

"I promise."

"You take lots of pictures to show me when you get back."

"Of course."

She grabs my face in her hands and plants a kiss on my forehead like she did when I was barely more than a baby, heading off to kindergarten for the first time.

"I love you, Violet."

"I love you too, Mom. See you in September."

I brush tears from my cheeks as I turn and walk away from her, scolding myself for being silly as I pass through the sliding glass doors and hike my bags a little higher on my shoulder.

Maybe if I knew I'd never see her again, I'd have taken a second glance back, in those final moments on the sidewalk. Maybe I'd have memorized her a little better, so conjuring up the slope of her nose or sound of her laughter wasn't so hard later, when it really counted.

But how could I possibly know what would come to pass? How could I know that the summer job I'd foreseen as a free adventure in paradise would blow up my life more effectively than a block of C4 thrown into my path? How could I know that, in seeking change, I'd courted my own demise more doggedly than a suicidal bridge-jumper?

I couldn't have.

So... I didn't look back. Not even once.

I guess it's true what they say about hindsight.

That bitch is twenty-twenty.

CHAPTER TWO

BAGGAGE

SIX HOURS and three thousand miles later, I walk into LAX deflated like a piñata at a children's party. After the cross-country voyage, my once chic, travel-savvy outfit is rumpled beyond recognition, my carefully-curled mahogany waves have flattened into a hopeless tangle of frizz, and my neck is aching fiercely from a seemingly endless flight crammed into the middle seat between a bickering couple who refused to relinquish either window or aisle, instead preferring to argue across me for the duration of our trip.

I'm due to meet the Flints in an hour, but I can't show up looking like this. I can almost hear Mom's voice in my head.

You never get a second chance to make a first impression, honey. How you're dressed determines how you'll be addressed.

I heave a sigh, adjust the grip on my backpack, and head to the baggage claim to retrieve the duffle I checked before leaving Boston. Seth, his wife Samantha, and their daughter Sophie are at the swanky private terminal across the concourse, where all privately chartered flights depart Los Angeles. It caters specifically to celebrities, VIPs... and, evidently, my new employers. A flutter of nerves zips through my veins as I realize I'll be face to face with them in mere minutes.

We conversed by email and video-chat after I accepted the position two weeks ago. They seemed nice enough from the relative obscurity of a laptop screen, but... I'd be lying if I said I wasn't nervous. I've been so eager to get out of my hometown, I barely considered the fact that this family isn't like mine. Not in the slightest. Anderson mother-daughter trips involve pitching a tent on the Saco River every summer, or hiking to the summit of Mt. Washington to see the view of the famed White Mountains that belt our state.

We're campfire songs and roasted marshmallows...

They're caviar and company jets.

My pace increases as I make my way through the maze that is LAX, jostling around other travelers and keeping my eyes fixed on overhead Baggage Claim signs. The air here is saturated by a frantic sense of urgency. Everyone's in a rush — searching for gates, running to make connections, shuffling doggedly through gridlocked security lines. Impatience is tangible. With each minute that ticks by, I feel my heart kick into higher gear, a mad tattoo of nerves jangling inside me like wind-chimes in a hurricane. It's a potent medley of anticipation and anxiety.

Breathe, Violet. Just breathe.

My grip tightens on the straps of my backpack, fingers squeezing until the canvas cuts into my palms. I scan the faces around me — a sea of strangers rushing from one terminal to the next, their travel-weary eyes checking flight listings, their bare toes flexing against security line floors. Thousands of humans headed hundreds of places, jetting off from a single runway like branches of a tree reaching across the sky in all directions. Just being here, in their midst, is the most exciting thing that's ever happened to me.

Ever.

I can't decide if that's cause for excitement or self-pity.

Even though I'm here — three-thousand miles from home and only halfway to my destination — it still seems like a daydream. Like some elaborate inside joke between me and the universe. When Mrs. McNally cornered me in the produce aisle of our local supermarket two weeks ago and presented me with the *opportunity of a lifetime* — working as a nanny for her son's former Dartmouth fraternity brother, Seth— I thought she was screwing with me. When I realized she was serious, the word *yes!* popped out of my mouth before she could fill me in on so much as a single detail.

Frankly, the details didn't matter.

I didn't care why their other nanny had suddenly become unavailable for the summer, or that they'd barely pay me anything except a small living stipend during the twelve-week trip, or that she'd already taken the liberty of telling the Flints all about my years of babysitting experience for the many families in our hometown. None of that concerned me. Not when there was a free trip to paradise on the table.

But now, minutes from meeting the Flints, all those concerns I've been so determined to push aside are clanging around inside my head so loud, it's hard to think about anything else.

In twelve hours, I'll be in a bikini on a beach, I remind myself. *Focus on that.*

With a renewed bounce in my step, I finally locate the BOS-LAX carousel in the baggage claim area. I wait with several dozen strangers, eyes trained on the unmoving luggage chute. It seems an eternity before the orange strobe lights begin to pulse, assaulting my weary eyes with rhythmic flashes. A few seconds later, there's a grind of gears and a metallic groan as the carousel churns into motion. My ability to filter out the many sensations occurring around me is all but gone. Every sound and smell feels like an assault — the piercing scrape of metal against metal, the pungent medley of too many sweaty, perfumed bodies crushed together.

When the first suitcase slides from the chute, everyone presses inward in an impatient wave, all eager to get their bag and then get the hell out of here. My nose twitches as a woman wearing a heavy dose of Chanel presses against my right side. I catch an elbow to the collarbone when an aggressive man yammering into a cellphone spots his black rolling bag and staggers forward to retrieve it. I don't know how he recognizes it — those rectangular rolling suitcases all look identical to me. Black on black, without so much as a sticker or a luggage tag to distinguish them from the rest.

Bags disappear one by one, and their owners along with them, eventually thinning the crowd until I can breathe again. Mine must be in the bowels of the plane because by the time it finally appears, I'm one of the only people left gathered around the carousel. The green duffle is well-worn, made of sturdy canvas with thick padded straps — a relic from my father's days in the army. It survived a war zone; let's hope it'll outlast a few weeks with me in the South Pacific.

Mom wanted to buy me a flashy new rolling set for the trip, but I wouldn't budge. Even though he's long gone, carrying Dad's duffle somehow makes me feel like I'm carrying a small piece of him with me, wherever the journey leads.

Rushing forward with my eyes fixed on the bag, my arm lifts from my side on auto-pilot. I'm eager to finally be on my way. So eager, in fact, I don't notice I'm on a crash-course with something that — when I look back later — I'll have no choice but to ascribe to fate.

My hand closes around the right strap. I'm already turning on my heel to walk away when I hit unexpected resistance. A sharp, opposing tug stops me in my tracks, jerking me back like a puppet on a string. For a second, I think a strap must've gotten stuck in the carousel, but when I whip around, I see it isn't caught in a metal gear.

It's trapped inside a hand.

A big, callused, *male* hand.

What the hell?

Reflexively, I yank at the right strap still curled in my fist; at the same instant, the stranger attempting to steal my stuff gives a sharp tug from his side. The duffle jerks into the air as we pull in opposite directions, the bag suspended between us in the strangest game of tug-of-war I've ever participated in. No matter how hard I pull, he doesn't relinquish so much as a single finger's grip.

"Hey!" I squawk, eyes flashing up to his face, fully prepared to unleash a string of less-than-polite accusations. "What the hell do you think you're—"

The words dissipate on my tongue mid-sentence, because the man attached to my bag, the one who owns that massive, callused hand currently wrapped so firmly around my duffle's other strap, is simply...

Breath-stealing.

I feel like I've been sucker-punched as my eyes roam over his features. He's not handsome — the word doesn't do him justice. He's far too rough around the edges, with stubble peppering that strong, square jaw and a thin scar bisecting one of those dark, slanted brows. An aristocratic nose sits squarely above a set of lush lips that, it must be noted, are currently pursed in an impatient scowl as he meets my gaze.

I suck in a much-needed breath.

He's glaring down at me from an impossible height, a wall of muscle in faded jeans and a black v-neck. In his late twenties or early thirties, he looks like a man accustomed to things I can barely fathom: fine meals and fast cars and gorgeous, glamorous women with loads of experience — sexual and otherwise. I feel like a little girl standing here beneath his gaze. Sloppy and naive and impossibly young.

There's a rhythmic ticking in his jaw that tells me his patience is about to expire. It takes all the willpower I possess not to drop my hand from the bag and simply give it to him, such is the effect of those intense eyes scorching into mine.

Honestly, I've never had a grown man glare at me before, besides the time I crashed Clint's sit-atop lawnmower into the pond after one too many post-graduation wine coolers and incurred his father's — much deserved — wrath. Call me crazy, but I just don't get what most girls find so attractive about total assholes. I'm not submissive. I don't have authority issues or daddy issues or whatever other issues usually make the fairer sex swoon over that gruff smolder adopted by blockbuster action heroes and angsty teen dystopian bad boys.

Or... I didn't.

Until this moment.

Because, while I'm perfectly aware I should *not* find myself thinking that this glaring stranger is the most magnetically attractive man I've ever laid eyes on...

Damn.

I repeat: *damnnnnnn.*

Swallowing harshly, I banish the thoughts to the back of my mind. Drooling over him won't help me get my bag back.

"Sorry," I prattle breathily after a pause that's dragged on far too long. "I think there's been a mistake—"

"I should say so." He cuts me off, a fissure of displeasure furrowing his forehead until the small white scar bisecting his left eyebrow stands out starkly against his tanned skin. His voice is sandpaper — full of grit. The stranger's dark green eyes flicker to my toes and back in the space of a single, thudding heartbeat. I get the sense that despite the brevity of his assessment, he could describe every article of clothing on my body right down to the unfortunate coffee stain sitting just above my boob from a bout of turbulence on my last flight. Whatever he sees, it's clearly not worth a second look. His eyes return to mine without lingering longer than an instant. "What do you think you're doing?"

My spine straightens at the anger in his tone. "Excuse me?"

His eyes flash with impatience. "I'm going to need you to let go of my bag."

"*Your* bag?"

He nods sharply, patience dwindling. "Listen, I'm in a bit of a hurry, so unless you're going to pull out a pamphlet and sell me some Girl Scout cookies..."

"Did you just call me a Girl Scout?" I snap, feeling my temper rise to meet his.

His eyes never shift from my face. "If the sash fits."

What a dick!

"I think you're having a senior moment, grandpa, because this is *mine*," I hiss, tugging back. "This isn't funny."

"I agree, it's not funny at all." His jaw ticks. "*Let go.*"

"I don't know what game you're playing, but you can just back the hell off."

I yank again, to punctuate my words.

The bastard yanks right back.

I gasp at his audacity.

He glares at my pig-headedness.

The bag swings comically between us.

"What the hell is your problem?" I snap.

"*My* problem?"

"Yes!" I gnash my teeth. "You clearly have a problem, because normal people don't insult strangers they've never met in airports for no reason at all!"

"I'd say I have a pretty valid reason."

"I'd say you're an asshole!"

His lips twist. "Aren't you a little young for that kind of language? Careful or mommy's going to come wash out your mouth with soap."

"You unbelievably arrogant *asshole*," I say again, with added emphasis.

His brows arch sardonically. That look says more than a thousand jeering words.

Little girl, little girl, little girl.

My tone is seething. "Just leave me alone!"

He snorts. "Leave *you* alone? You're not the one being mugged!"

My arm is starting to ache from the effort of keeping the bag aloft between us, but I ignore it. I can hardly believe this is happening — that I'm engaged in a battle of wills over my belongings. I don't know why he's chosen me as the target of his theft. All I do know is... he will *not* win. This was my dad's bag. One of the only things I have left of him. Damned if some asshole is taking it from me.

Our strange stalemate has begun to attract a crowd. In my peripheral, I spot a middle-aged woman eyeing us with concern, clearly considering an intervention. I keep my focus on the pissed-off stranger, hoping he can't see the way my pulse is pounding in my jugular from four feet away. It takes all my resolve to keep from shrinking back when he takes a purposeful stride into my personal space.

Shit.

For a moment, I think he's going to rip the bag right out of my grip — which, let's face it, he definitely could, judging by the impressive bicep muscles I can see peeking from his sleeves. My heart pounds madly as he lifts his free hand. His eyes burn into mine, green clashing with green, stealing all the oxygen from my lungs. I'm paralyzed as his hand extends closer. The quivering voice of self-preservation inside my head is screaming, *Run, you idiot, it's just a bag!*

I ignore it, with effort.

In a calculated show of intimidation, the stranger's strong fingers clasp the luggage tag affixed to the zipper and flip it over with one deft movement. His lips twist in a self-congratulatory smirk that makes my stomach thud to my feet like a bowling ball. My reluctant eyes drop to scan the tag and I feel all the blood drain from my face. Because there, etched in neat, masculine lettering, is a name. And… it's not mine.

B. UNDERWOOD

For a crazy instant, I allow myself to contemplate what that first initial stands for.

Blaine?

Blake?

Ben?

No. None of those sound right to me. I wish, in spite of his curt attitude and clear contempt for me, that I wasn't too chicken-shit to ask his name.

"I…" I gulp. "That's…"

"My bag," the gruff stranger finishes, his tone suggesting I'm a few screws short of a set. "As I've been trying to tell you."

"I… I'm…" My mouth is too dry to speak.

His lips twitch in what looks like amusement. His tone gentles a bit as his eyes scan my burning cheeks, noting my deep embarrassment. "I'm going to need you to let go now."

My hand drops from the strap like I've been scalded. I'm abruptly mortified. I've made a total, complete fool of myself in front of the hottest man I've ever seen in real life. I can't meet his eyes, so I mumble something in the ballpark of *I'msorrymymistake-Ididn'trealize* before turning on my heel and bolting like a shame-less coward.

I make it only a handful of steps before I realize that my bag — my real bag — is still going round and round the baggage claim. So much for my great escape. Clinging to the shreds of my dignity with shaky fingers, I slam to a stop and stalk, cheeks ablaze, back to the metal conveyer belt. Sure enough, another army green duffle is slowly chugging along the track.

I chastise myself for ever mixing it up with B. Underwood's —

now that I'm paying attention, the differences are clear as day. Years of sun have bleached my Dad's canvas from true army green to a lighter olive shade, and then there's the small black LIVE FREE OR DIE patch Mom sewed on the right side years ago, to cover a tear.

Nice work, Violet.

I could spontaneously combust with shame as I speed toward the bag, but I refuse to give B-Is-For-Bastard Underwood the satisfaction. I don't dare risk a glance back in his direction, but as I haul the strap up over my shoulder, I'm nearly positive I hear someone laugh in a gritty, entirely-too-recognizable voice.

Asshole.

I practically sprint away, eyes smarting with infuriating tears as I round a corner and dash into the first restroom I come across. The stall door slams behind me and I fall back against it, panting hard. I'm pissed at myself for allowing a total stranger to get so far beneath my skin, for pushing my buttons until I'm teetering on the edge of a total meltdown.

It was an honest mistake!

He didn't have to be such a jerk about it.

Pushing thoughts of B. Underwood — and his distractingly full mouth, chiseled jaw, and dark eyes — from my head, I force deep breaths in through my nose until my heartbeat has returned to its normal tempo. There's no time to be embarrassed. I have a flight to catch and employers to impress.

After a quick rummage through my duffle, I locate a pretty blue sundress in the depths of my bag and pull over my head. The coffee-stained blouse and black skinny jeans are banished to the bottom of my backpack, alongside the three travel-sized bottles of SPF50 suntan lotion Mom forced on me. Staring into the fluorescent-lit bathroom mirror, I yank a brush through my curls to give them some volume, swipe some sheer gloss across my lips, and straighten my shoulders.

I look composed — on the outside, at least. I barely resemble the flustered girl at baggage claim, except for the slight red blush still tinging the apples of my cheeks. Or, so I assure myself as I gather my bags and head for the door, my gauzy skirts swishing around my legs with each step.

Anyway, I think, walking from the bathroom with my head held high. *It doesn't matter. It's not like I'll ever see that jerk B. Underwood again.*

Looking back, I can almost hear fate laughing at me.

That bitch.

CHAPTER THREE

TAKEOFF

A CHAUFFEUR in a smart black suit is waiting for me at the curb, holding a sign bearing my last name. He barely says a word to me except to confirm that I am, in fact, the ANDERSON he's been waiting for as he holds open the back door of a sleek silver town car that says PRIVATE SUITES across the flank in crisp capital lettering. I scramble gracelessly inside, somehow managing to bash both my forehead and my funny bone in the process. The vehicle is fancier than any I've ever been in, including the limo my friends rented for prom. There are creamy leather seats, customizable air settings, and complimentary French seltzers in every cup holder. I feel markedly out of place as we pull away from the curb and head for the private terminal.

Chartered flights leave LAX from a special runway across the road, designed to prevent celebrities and other VIPs from having to mingle with us common folk.

The horror!

I ignore the thudding of my heart as I'm ferried away from the main airport. It's a quick trip to the terminal — no more than a five-minute drive across the tarmac. I have a front row seat to a superb airshow directly outside my window. Flights taxiing down the labyrinth of runways, silhouetted against the blazing red-orange sunset as they take off for destinations unknown. We weave through a maze of hangars and gates, the aircrafts shrinking from jumbo 747s to sleek, jet-propelled private charters as we leave the commercial gates behind.

As we pull up, I see instantly that the private terminal is a far cry from the frenetic energy of the main concourses. It's all glass and exposed wood, angular furniture, and polished marble surfaces. I've barely made it two steps onto the curb before my duffle is whisked away by a competent bag handler. I keep my small, carry-on backpack with me as a woman in an immaculately pressed black blazer leads me through a nondescript security checkpoint, then down a hallway to a private suite.

The tagline they push on their website — *just seventy steps from your car to the plane!* — is no mere marketing tool. When the door swings inward, I see a small fleet of shiny jets parked just beyond the wall of floor-length windows. A quick glance around the lavish waiting area reveals a set of pristine white sectionals and a stocked buffet area, laid out to accommodate the rich and famous before they board jets bound for exotic locations.

There are about ten people already gathered inside the room, most of them men in their early forties, huddled at the conference table with their faces poised over phone screens and tablets. They glance up when I enter, but otherwise pay me little attention, returning to their calls and private discussions without missing more than a beat.

A woman with a shiny fall of blonde hair rises from the couch in a single, smooth motion. Her long limbs are concealed by wide-legged white linen pants — the kind you see on the glossy pages of

21

fashion magazines but never in real life, because surely no one is elegant enough to pull them off. Except, apparently, Mrs. Flint.

"You must be Violet," she murmurs, friendly but reserved as she slides her hand into mine with a firm shake. My palm feels like a pumice stone against hers. I marvel at her ageless skin — she looks barely older than I am, though I know she's nearing forty. "Welcome. We're so glad to have you."

"Mrs. Flint, it's wonderful to meet you."

"Please, call me Samantha."

"Samantha, then." My eyes shift downward, to the small blonde shadow hovering a step behind her mother's wide-legged pants. "And this must be Miss Sophie."

I catch a flash of platinum pigtails and hear a muffled giggle before the little girl ducks behind her mother, so she's fully hidden from view.

"She's a bit shy," Samantha says apologetically. "We're hoping this trip will help her get over that."

"I was pretty shy myself, when I was her age." I smile as the little girl sneaks a peek at me from behind Samantha's hipbone.

"She'll warm up, once she gets to know you," Samantha assures me. "Isn't that right, sweetie?"

In response, Sophie gives a small nod and twines her fingers with her mom's. A pang shoots through my chest as I think of my own mother. With all the drama at baggage claim, I haven't even had a chance to text her. She'll be worried.

"Come, sit with me and chat," Samantha says, leading Sophie to the sectional and gesturing for me to follow. "We're still waiting on one more person before takeoff."

I follow hurriedly, sliding my backpack to the floor by my feet. My ungainly plop onto the cushion is a stark contrast to Samantha's elegant motions. She doesn't walk; she *glides*, barely disturbing the air. I wonder if that kind of grace is something that can be learned, or if you're simply born with it.

Her smile is warm. "How was your flight from Boston?"

"Oh, it was fine." *Besides a bickering couple and a coffee-boob stain.* "Somehow, I have a feeling it won't compare to this one." My eyes travel to the private jet, parked on the runway outside.

Samantha's gaze follows mine. "Ever flown private before?"

"Actually, I'd never even been on an airplane until about seven hours ago."

Her smile widens. "Well, you're in for a treat, then. Flying private puts first class to shame."

I think it's best not to mention the fact that I spent my first leg of this voyage sandwiched in a middle seat in steerage.

"Any problems with your luggage?" she asks.

"They took it from me at the curb." I pause. "Some rude guy did try to swipe it at baggage claim earlier, though."

"Really?" Samantha's eyebrows lift in two perfect blonde arcs. Her nose wrinkles, as though she can't fathom a world in which one might handle their own luggage, let alone have it nearly snatched off the conveyer belt.

Okay, so technically I was the one doing the snatching.

Whatever.

"He was extremely rude." I flush again at the memory of his intent green eyes. "I thought he was going to rip the bag right out of my hands."

"Oh my," she murmurs, shaking her head. "Did you talk to airport security about him?"

"No, it wasn't worth going to all that trouble. In the end, I got my bag. That's really what counts." I shrug. "And... he wasn't violent, just—" An *utter ass.* "—a bit hotheaded. Thankfully, I'll never see him again."

"Still, I'm sorry to hear your trip started on such strange footing! I promise, it'll all be downhill from here. You're going to adore the South Pacific."

"I really can't wait."

After another moment of pleasantries, Samantha excuses herself to go speak with her husband, who's still fully entrenched in a business meeting with his co-workers from the Flint Group. My eyes move to Sophie. She's sitting directly across from me, studying my every detail with narrowed, periwinkle blue eyes. Her cute-as-a-button face cants at an angle as she considers me.

I hold her stare and await her judgment.

Aside from dogs and horses, I've always thought kids are the best judges of character on the planet. Tiny bullshit detectors — they can see through you in an instant. Generally speaking, if you don't like kids... it's probably because kids don't like *you*.

"What's in your backpack?" she asks, breaking her silence as curiosity finally gets the best of her. I hide a grin as I pull the bag up onto the coffee table.

"Want to see?"

She nods.

I slide over on the cushion until I'm right beside her. Yanking open the drawstring of my backpack, I pull out a coloring book and a massive pack of crayons. "Do you want to color with me?"

Sophie's eyes light up. She doesn't respond audibly, except for an excited intake of air which I take as a resounding *yes*. After much deliberation, she settles on a garden scene in the middle of the book. I work on the flowers at the edge while she meticulously applies various shades of brown to the squirrel centerfold.

Watching her color from the corner of my eye, I find myself somewhat taken aback. I've never seen such concentration in a five-year-old. She's so very serious. Almost... somber. It's an eerie trait, in a child. She's more self-contained than most adults I know.

I study her perfectly groomed pigtails, not a hair out of place. Her pale pink dress looks freshly ironed. There are no runs in her tights, no smudges on her shoes. Not a single stain or trace of wear anywhere, so far as I can tell. Her white sweater has pearl buttons, for god's sake. I don't doubt for a minute that they're real. She looks more like a china doll than a little girl.

I can't help but wonder about her life.

Do they ever let her play? Run through the dirt? Splash in a puddle? Roll in the grass? Skin her knees? Jump in a pile of fresh-raked leaves?

I can't see Mrs. Flint, with her perfectly manicured fingers and high-fashion ensembles, condoning such behavior.

When Samantha walks back over a few moments later, we've nearly finished our picture.

"Look, Mama," Sophie says, holding up the book for her to see. "Isn't it pretty?"

"Mmm." Samantha's eyes are trained on her cellphone. They dart up for a nanosecond, scan the work of art, and drop back to the screen. "Lovely job, sweetie."

I swallow down a scoff of disbelief as Sophie slowly lowers the picture book. Our eyes meet across the coffee table. I smile at her as I pass her a purple crayon.

"Hey, Soph, can you show me how you made your flowers so pretty? Mine don't look half as good."

She blinks gravely. "That's because you're not using two colors."

"*Two* colors? Pink *and* purple?" I gasp. "I didn't think of that!"

She sighs deeply, as if I'm a total idiot. "Okay, I'll show you. Pay attention."

I salute her and am rewarded as she cracks her first smile.

Maybe there's a little girl beneath all those manners, after all.

We color for a few more moments in silence, until Samantha's sound of displeasure makes me look up.

"What could be taking so long…" she murmurs, crossing one leg over the other. Her eyes lock on mine. "We're supposed to take off in a few moments and we haven't even boarded."

"Are we still waiting on someone else?"

She nods. "The photographer Seth hired. He takes brilliant shots, but you know these artistic types — they're always a loose end in need of tying."

I nod, as if I know anything about *artistic types* or their habits. The only real photographer I've ever met was the man who took my senior portrait for the yearbook last summer, and I'm pretty sure it wasn't his day job since a few weeks after our photoshoot I saw him working as a barista at the one fancy coffee shop within a twenty-mile radius of my hometown.

"More trouble than they're worth, if you ask me," Samantha mutters. "I don't know why we couldn't just take our own photographs. You know, I've built quite a strong social media following with just my iPhone. No need for a telephoto lens and some overrated National Geographic shutterbug who charges an astronomical fee just to take some snapshots. So, he won a Pulitzer or two. I don't see what the big deal—"

Her stream of words is cut off by the pointed sound of a throat clearing. Before we can even turn our heads to the door, a wry male voice fills the air.

"Three, actually."

I go totally still at the sound of that sarcastic tone.

No. No. No.

It can't be...

A low chuckle reverberates from his throat. "Three Pulitzers, that is. But, by all means, if you think your iPhone can outperform my Nikon, I'll save myself eleven hours on a plane with you."

Glad I'm not the only one he's rude to — even if she does deserve it.

Samantha looks rather ruffled as she turns to face the man she's just spent the better part of five minutes deriding. Her face is pale as she rises to her feet in greeting. I tell myself to follow suit, but I can't. Here on the floor, half-hidden by the coffee table, I'm safe. Maybe if I stay down here, I can pretend the man attached to that voice — that incredibly gritty, incredibly familiar voice — isn't the one person I most dread ever laying eyes on again.

"Mr. Underwood," Samantha drawls, dashing my hopes to dust. "Thank you for finally joining us. I apologize if you misinterpreted my earlier words. It was a joke in poor taste. I certainly didn't mean to insult you—"

He snorts.

"Anyway." She swallows audibly. "Shall we get underway?"

Without waiting for his response, she turns and flees across the suite to her husband's side. Unfortunately, I have no such escape route. I keep my eyes on the coloring book, but all my attention is honed on *him*.

There's another amused snort, which quickly turns into a scoff of disbelief. "You again? This just gets better and better..."

He's spotted me.

This alarming realization is accompanied by the sound of heavy male footsteps crossing the room. Moving closer... closer... and still closer, before coming to a definitive stop at the edge of the coffee table, mere inches from where I'm sitting on the floor like a child. Maybe if I squeeze my eyes shut and pretend he's not there, he'll disappear.

Don't look up, don't look up, don't look up.

He waits for a moment, then lowers his duffle bag down into my line of sight, until it's nestled beside my backpack. My eyes lock on the green canvas. My fingers have grown so clammy I can barely keep hold of the crayon in my hand. Sophie colors on, unaware of the adult drama unfolding around her.

The silence grows so prolonged, the air between us turns stale. I hardly dare to breathe, let alone move. I can feel his eyes on me, waiting for me to glance up. My heart hammers like a blacksmith with an anvil.

"Watch that bag for me, will you?" he asks the top of my head in a strangled voice. "Last time I left it unattended, some girl tried to steal it from me."

He turns on his heel and walks off without another word.

The sunset orange crayon snaps in half in my hand.

Suddenly, my perfect trip to paradise is beginning to resemble hell on earth...

CHAPTER FOUR

TURBULENCE

"Can I get you anything? A snack? Something to drink?"

"No, thank you." I hold up my diet soda can. "I'm still working on this one."

...and I've already stockpiled two in my backpack for later.

The cute male flight attendant nods and moves on through the cabin, checking to see if anyone else needs a cocktail refreshed. I turn my eyes back out the nearest portal.

I'll admit, I was upset about not having the window seat on my first flight. Unnecessarily so, it turns out — there's not all that much to see at thirty-five-thousand feet. Just a whole lot of billowy cloud-tops and an endless spread of ever-darkening horizon. The Pacific is somewhere far below us, growing dimmer with each passing hour as we chase the sunset across the sky.

I've been monitoring the growing darkness with keen attention, since I don't dare cast my gaze elsewhere. Not when there's a certain undesirable character who shall-not-be-named sprawled in the seat directly across from mine, just waiting for another chance to mortify me.

I sigh and rub my sore neck. It may have a permanent crick from craning away from *him* for the past five hours. When we boarded the small jet, I was hopeful I could avoid him. I thought there'd be a seat at the back, far away from the rest of the passengers, where Sophie and I could continue coloring in peace.

No such luck.

The jet is much smaller than I'd anticipated. After my inaugural voyage on a 747, it seems more like a levitating tin can than an actual aircraft. It can't be more than forty feet long, and most of that space is taken up by the cockpit at the front, the flight attendants' galley at the back, and the two bathrooms. What little space remains for our group of ten was designed with social passengers in mind — rather than standard row seating, an open plan of couches and comfortable bucket chairs line the walls of the plane, clustered together for maximum fraternization and in-flight networking.

As soon as we stepped aboard, Seth and his fellow Flint Group executives dispersed in the main lounge section at the front. They all look so similar I can't keep them straight — five carbon-copy men in their mid-forties, with standard haircuts and forgettable names.

The rest of our party was relegated to the section by the tail, a cozy arrangement of four recliners around a communal coffee table. Much to my horror, as I strapped Sophie into the seat beside mine, Samantha settled across from her daughter...

Leaving just one open seat.

Directly across from me.

One guess who's sitting in it.

Perhaps the arrangement wouldn't be so bad, if Samantha hadn't sucked down a sleeping pill along with her glass of chardonnay about ten minutes after takeoff. She's been drooling onto her neck pillow ever since, a sleep mask fixed firmly over her eyes. Sophie is out cold as well, curled in a small ball with a fuzzy white blanket cocooned around her. The anti-nausea supplement she swallowed knocked her out almost as soon as we boarded.

Like mother like daughter.

Even the Flint Group drones eventually give their business ventures a rest — a few hours into the flight, I spot Seth snoozing in a benzo-induced stupor, his face pulled tight with stress even in sleep. His colleagues bear similar expressions. They probably dream about profit margins and business mergers.

I know I should get some rest but, try as I might, I can't force my eyes to close, even when the sky outside my window falls dark and the flight attendants dim the cabin lights. I almost wish I'd taken Samantha up on her offer when she extended an extra sleeping pill in my direction, so casual you'd think it was a breath mint.

Every so often, I hear the sound of the man across from me shifting in his seat or sighing lightly. The faint illumination of his laptop screen is the only light in the entire jet. I haven't turned my head forward in five freaking hours, for fear he'll strike up another oh-so-unpleasant conversation, but even ignoring his presence can't remove the odd currents running through the cabin. There's something strange about being the only two left awake, trapped together in strained silence. A charge of lingering animosity from our earlier interaction still buzzes between us, along with something else, something I can't quite define. A tangible tension.

The darkness forces my other senses to overcompensate, until every sound he makes — from the small sighs that slide from his lips to the muffled shift of his black jeans against the leather — hits my eardrums like a mallet on a gong.

He's captivated me and he's not even trying.

How annoying is that?

I change positions in my reclining chair, arching my back as I stretch my arms above my head. It feels so good, a tiny sound of pleasure escapes my mouth as stiffness unfurls from my spine. The moan is barely audible, yet there's a slight pause in the persistent clicking of Underwood's laptop keys, as though it has shattered his focus. By the time my hands fold back in my lap, his keystrokes have returned to normal and I've convinced myself the lapse was all in my head.

Just because you're attuned to his every move, doesn't mean he's attuned to yours, Violet. Your sleep deprived brain is imagining things. Get it together.

With effort, I shove him from my head and squeeze my eyes shut. The jet's plush recliners are infinitely more comfortable than the narrow middle-seat I was crammed into on my flight from Boston to Los Angeles. My eyes are finally growing heavy when a sudden jolt of turbulence rocks the cabin.

I'm instantly awake.

There's a crash from the kitchen galley as a tray goes tumbling. My eyes snap wide as my fingers curl into the armrests like talons, an automatic reflex to combat the sensation of sudden free-fall. I can't even form a screech of dismay as we plummet — there's no air left in my lungs. My stomach has shot up into my chest cavity and taken up residence inside my throat.

Contrary to popular near-death-experience lore, my life does not flash in front of my eyes. There is no montage of watercolored high school memories — graduation and the homecoming game, prom and my first kiss with Clint as the center console dug into my ribs after he drove me home from cheerleading practice in his truck last fall. The only thought in my head is, *Mom is going to kill me if I die in a plane crash!* which may well be the dumbest thing I've ever fathomed in my seventeen years of life.

Not exactly an eloquent end-of-existence sentiment.

Thankfully, the pilot, who is clearly far cooler under pressure than I am, corrects our course so fast, the sleeping passengers barely have time to blink awake before we're gliding smoothly once more. Through the window, I watch the wings level out and tell myself to stop preparing for demise. It was only a bump.

Planes don't just fall from the sky, Violet.

Breathe.

In and out.

"Sorry about that, folks." The captain's voice crackles over the speaker system. "We've run into a patch of rough weather, but we're going to do our best to avoid the worst of it by diverting our course about fifty miles. Don't worry, we shouldn't touch down in Fiji more than a few minutes past your scheduled arrival. In the meantime, keep those seatbelts securely fastened. There may be some turbulence for the next hour or so."

I pull in a deep breath as I reach over and check Sophie's seatbelt is snug across her stomach. She's still sleeping soundly, hands pillowed beneath her head. I brush a strand of hair off her cheek, then sit back and tighten my own belt. It feels painfully ineffective, this thin tether against gravity, especially when we hit another jarring bump a few moments later. My soda can rattles on my small side table as my heart leaps inside my chest. I watch a bolt of lightning slash the dark sky outside the portal. It seems far too close for comfort.

My fingers tighten against the leather of my seat as we jolt through the air with all the grace of a wheelbarrow on a dirt road. Despite the luxe accommodations of, as Samantha would say, *flying private*, I can't deny I'd feel a whole lot safer in a jumbo jet right now.

I glance around the cabin for a distraction. Samantha's so drugged she hasn't stirred, despite the frequent bumps of turbulence. The Flint executives are all silent and still in the darkened front section. The flight attendants are strapped into their jump seats in the galley. Which just leaves...

Him.

Over the desperate thudding of my pulse, I hear a metal cap twist open. Unable to stop myself, I allow my eyes to shift to the man sitting across from me for the first time since we boarded. Those chiseled features are half in shadow, but I can feel the weight of his tractor-beam emerald eyes on my face as he lifts the flask to his lips and takes a lengthy swig. I watch him swallow, mesmerized by the way the muscles in the strong column of his throat contract as the alcohol slides downward. The silver container flashes in the semi-dark as he holds it out across the space between us.

"Here."

My brows shoot up. I don't move a muscle.

"Take a swig," he says softly, eyes locked on mine. "It'll soothe the nerves."

I don't know what comes over me, in that moment. Maybe it's the fact that I'm scared out of my head. Maybe it's the dark, quiet cabin. Maybe it's simply the fact that, for the first time since our paths crossed this morning, he's not looking my way with total disdain, or chiding me for daring to breathe his air.

Whatever the reason, I bite back a snippy retort about plying underage girls with alcohol and allow my eyes to flicker down to the silver flask clasped in his strong fingers. Those hands hold so much power. They've won three Pulitzer Prizes. Looking at them now, though... all I can think about is how they'd feel cuffing my throat like a necklace.

Bending me to his will.

I've never felt this way before. I barely recognize these strange desires swimming inside my head. It's entirely out of character for me to be unhinged by the mere sight of a man's hands, and yet... I want to trace their tendons, want to study every callus and learn every line.

His throat clears softly, drawing my gaze up. I feel my cheeks heat, embarrassed by the strange course of my own thoughts. My heart thuds against my ribs like a wild animal trying to escape its cage.

"No," I force out, breathing too hard. "N-no thank you."

"Suit yourself."

He shrugs and settles back against his seat. A few seconds later, we hit another dreadful bump of air, strong enough to jostle my entire body sideways. Biting the inside of my cheeks to suppress a squeak of fear, I watch as bolts of lightning streak the clouds just outside our windows. Planes may be engineered to survive a strike, but the thought of being hit with that much electricity sends a shiver down my spine.

I close my eyes to shut out the view and turn my focus inward, counting down in my head until the turbulence subsides.

One Mississippi

Two Mississippi.

Three Mississippi.

When the shaking ceases, I open my eyes and look straight into the stranger's. He's watching me again with that all-too-perceptive gaze. A true photographer, he takes inventory of every detail, from my white-knuckled grip on the armrests of my seat, to the tension in my ramrod spine, to the lack of blood in my complexion.

"What?" I snap thinly, annoyed by the implication in his eyes.

"I didn't say anything."

"Just because your mouth didn't open, doesn't mean you weren't communicating."

"Oh?" His eyebrow quirks. "And what, exactly, was I saying? Since you seem to be an expert in the matter."

My teeth grind together. "You were judging me for— for being afraid."

His dark brows pull inward. When he does respond, his voice is uncharacteristically soft. Almost like he's talking to himself. "Nothing wrong with fear. When you're afraid, you know you're alive."

I'm unsure how to respond. Every thought in my head seems painfully childish, every opinion inadequate.

"Anyway." He seems to snap back into himself. His eyes refocus on mine. "What I was *actually* wondering..." His lips twist in a smirk as he turns the flask over in his hands. "Was how many bumps you'd last before you change your mind."

"I don't—" My words turn to a wince as we hit more turbulence. I bite my lip and ride it out. "I don't make a habit of drinking with strangers," I say, when I've finally gotten ahold of myself. "Especially while I'm on the clock."

His gaze moves to Samantha, who's slackened face is half-concealed by a sleep mask. He doesn't say a word, but I can read his thoughts like a billboard.

Your boss wouldn't notice if you did a keg stand, let alone took a single sip from the flask.

I grimace as the whole jet jostles once more. This time, it takes five full *Mississippis* before we level out — and another five after that for my breathing to return to normal.

He notices.

"Nervous flyer, huh?"

I clench my jaw. "I'm fine."

"You don't look fine," he says bluntly, eyes scanning my bloodless face. "You look like you're about to pass out."

"If anything, my nausea is inspired by present company," I say sweetly. "It has very little to do with the turbulence."

He laughs, a flash of white teeth in the darkness of the cabin. My stomach clenches at the sight of his chiseled features smiling instead of smirking or scowling in my direction. Asshole or no, he remains the most attractive man I've ever seen, let alone had a conversation with.

Taking one final swig from the flask, he twists the cap back on and tucks it away in the side pocket of the duffle bag beneath his seat. When he straightens, he catches me watching.

"Can I help you, oh judgmental one?"

I scoff. "You do realize one of the perks of flying private is that you don't have to BYOB?"

He shakes his head. "Afraid blue label Johnnie doesn't come in airplane nips."

"Johnnie?"

"Walker." He assesses my blank look. "It's a scotch whisky."

"Oh. I've never had whisky."

He's studying me carefully across the half-dozen feet that divide us. "How old are you?" he asks softly, as though it's just occurred to him that I might not be of legal drinking age.

My mouth opens to respond but the word *seventeen* never leaves my throat because, out of nowhere, the whole world flips on its axis. A brilliant flash of lightning envelops the plane as we pitch left, then start to plummet. I know instantly that this is far worse than the other times — infinitely worse. This is no mere bump, no small pocket of air pressure that makes the plane wings rattle.

This is a nosedive.

A plunge.

A *crash*.

There's a blood-chilling creak from outside as the plane struggles to right itself — a groan of metal, as though the whipping winds of the storm raging outside are strong enough to tear us apart. The lightning flashes seem closer than ever, or maybe that's just the cabin interior lights flickering, a terrifying strobe. My ears pop painfully, an explosion of pressure going off behind my eyes as we lose altitude too rapidly to compensate.

Between the light flashes, I watch things unfold in a series of disembodied still frames. The flight attendants scrambling for emergency rafts in the overhead bins. Half-empty drinks careening toward the ceiling and shattering on impact. Glass shards whipping through the cabin like razor-sharp raindrops. Air masks deploying from the ceiling like yellow plastic piñatas.

The intercom crackles on, filling the cabin with terse orders from our captain that cut in and out every few seconds. Despite the static, I recognize the strain in his voice.

"Ladies and gen... unexpected turbul..."

The words of the captain are drowned out by the loudest bang I've ever heard. It sounds like a bomb has gone off. The entire vessel jolts violently sideways in the air as we're thrown off course by the force of the engine exploding. My body slams to the left like a rag doll in a twister, the canvas belt across my lap cutting harshly against my waist but mercifully keeping me in my seat.

Some aren't so lucky — with growing horror, I watch as the male flight attendant is hurled into the air and slammed against a storage compartment. He crumples to the floor with a sickening thud, blood gushing from his temple. He does not get up again. The emergency raft rolls from his limp hands, far out of reach.

I pray for the plane to level out again, as it has before, but this time...

We simply keep falling.

Half-convinced I'm dreaming, I operate on auto-pilot, yanking my mask over the lower half of my face then grabbing the one swinging in the air beside it.

Sophie.

She's crying — cheeks red, snot streaming from her nostrils. I want to tell her it'll be okay. I want to take her in my arms and promise we're all going to be fine. But I can't. Not only because she can't hear me over the screaming storm splitting our fuselage in two... but because I know it would be a lie.

"Emergency... left engine..."

The captain's panicked words cut out as the plane loses all electrical power. The lights flicker one final time, then never come back on. I hear someone screaming — I think it's Samantha, but more voices join in as we continue to free-fall through the air. A chorus of terror, harmonizing with the shrieking wind.

I'm going to die, I think ludicrously, hyperventilating into my air mask. I wish I could force my eyes to close. I don't want to see what comes next, but I can't stop watching. It's like a bad horror film, the kind you can't tear your eyes from even when you know it'll end horribly for the heroine.

Except this isn't a movie.

I *am* the doomed heroine.

Or... maybe not the heroine at all. Certainly not a hero. No more than a cowardly side character, who dies before the audience can become too emotionally invested.

In the imaginary crises I sometimes allow myself to conjure up while lying in bed at night, I'm always brave. Smart. Strong. Leaping through fire, charging toward danger. I thought, in an emergency, I'd save the world — or at least my own life. But here I am, living a nightmare, and I'm paralyzed with fear. I watch my own demise unfolding around me and can do nothing to stop it except stare straight ahead, hope slipping through my shaking fingers.

Waiting to die.

The green-eyed stranger in the seat across from mine is gesturing wildly to get my attention, the whites around his irises flashing like surrender flags on a battlefield. He's scared, too. I can't see his mouth beneath the mask, but his eyes are screaming indecipherable instructions at me. When I see him pulling a neon bundle from beneath his seat, his message clicks.

He's telling me to put on my life vest.

Panting hard, I pull the deflated plastic over my head. I do my best to get one over Sophie's blonde pigtails, but it's hard to control my limbs, the plane is jerking so much.

The stranger is gesturing again — this time at my feet. In the turbulence, the compressed life raft has rolled my way, coming to rest just beside my backpack.

Grab it! The stranger's eyes are flashing. *Grab the raft!*

I watch my hands like they belong to someone else as they

close around the straps and pull the thick roll of yellow fabric up into my lap. It's surprisingly heavy. I cling to it with desperation, afraid another bump might make me lose my grip. When we hit — because, in these horrid, frozen instants, it has become increasingly clear that impact is not a matter of *if* but *when* — it may be the only salvation from the crushing embrace of dark water.

I should be crying, by my tear ducts refuse to cooperate. I cling to the emergency pack, my mind empty except for a single thought I repeat over and over, a prayer to any god who happens to be listening.

I don't want to die.

I don't want to die.

I don't want to die.

I want to go back — back to that curb at Boston Logan international Airport, to wrap my arms around my mother one last time. Back to before I got on this plane. Back to that simple town I couldn't wait to escape. Back to that picture-perfect future I dismissed with such disdain.

But I can't.

The only thing I can do, here and now, is adjust my grip on the raft and reach out for Sophie. I feel her small fingers slip into mine, and squeeze hard to tell her I'm here with her.

You're not alone.

Looking straight ahead, my gaze locks on a steady sea of green within the chaos. It's strange that the last thing I'll ever see are the eyes of a stranger, burning into mine.

My final moments, shared with an utter asshole I met at the airport.

If I could muster any sense of humor, I'd have to laugh at the absurdity of fate.

We approach the Pacific with all the optimism of a bug on a crash course with a car windshield. And in that free-fall, his eyes are the only thing holding me steady. They never shift away, even as our descent picks up speed. Even as I discover that I was wrong — my tear ducts are perfectly capable of producing moisture.

A single tear streaks down my cheek.
One Mississippi.
Two Mississippi.
Three Mississippi.
I never make it to four.

CHAPTER FIVE

UNDERTOW

I LOVE THE WATER.

I spent six summers teaching sailing lessons — instructing New Hampshire youth on the finer points of wind direction, tying square knots, capsizing two-person SunFish. You don't take on a job like that voluntarily if you don't enjoy getting wet.

I lived for those salt-skin summers. Bronze limbs, sun-bleached hair. Fingertips turned to prunes from too many hours in the ocean. Each morning, I'd swim from the dock to my small sailboat in under a minute, half across the harbor in the same time it would take anyone else to affix oars to a dinghy. Submerged beneath the surface, my strokes effortless, I'd imagine myself a mermaid, or a selkie from the Irish fairy tales Mom used to tell me.

I love the water.

Correction: I *loved* the water.

...until the moment we crash into it.

I'll never forget how it knocks the breath from my lungs like a punch to the gut. How it pulls at me with aqueous fingers, dragging me to the depths along with the fragmenting fuselage. We hit with a force that rattles my bones and steals every molecule of air from my lungs. Sophie's small hand is snatched from my grip. The only reason I'm able to hold onto the emergency raft is the strap looped tight around my wrist.

The plane fills so instantly there isn't even time to catch a proper breath before water rushes in from all directions. I grapple with my seatbelt buckle as my head whips sideways, searching for Sophie and Samantha.

They're simply... gone.

The cabin has cracked down the middle, sheared clean in two like a soda can on one of those late night infomercials for expensive knives. I hear metal tearing as the front section of the plane falls away, sucked down to the bottom of the ocean. There's a flash of silver, like light catching the scales of a fish, before it sinks out of sight, into the dark depths of the Pacific. It's only a matter of time before the tail follows suit.

I have to get out of here.

The life raft's pressure gauge goes off — with a hiss of compressed air, it inflates and shoots upward. The strap, still wrapped around my wrist, threatens to tear off my arm as I'm pulled after it, a helpless fish on a hook. I'd kick for the surface if I could tell where it was. There's no light, no air, no indication of up or down. I am a meteor in space, drifting without direction, my course set by the gravitational pull of the raft.

My lungs are on fire inside my chest, screaming for oxygen. Black spots explode behind my eyes. If I don't get a breath soon, I'm going to pass out. My lips open, desperate for air, and salt water rushes into my mouth. I know a single gulp will seal my fate, but there's nothing I can do to stop it. My limbs aren't cooperating. My body is no longer under my command.

I think I see some light, a flicker of the storm at the surface, but it's too late. Water pours down my throat, into my lungs. It sweeps away my last thread of consciousness, stills my legs from kicking, slows my heartbeat down to nothing. I feel myself lose the fight for survival as that faint flicker of hope above fades out of view and my eyes drift shut.

And then...

I'm gone.

"BREATHE, DAMN YOU! *BREATHE!*"

There's a mouth on mine, blowing air into my lungs. Hands on my chest, pounding down on my ribcage in even beats.

"Come on! You don't get to die on me!"

His lips are warm. So are his hands as they cradle my face, pinching my nose closed as he breathes me back to life.

"Stay with me. *Please.*"

Choppy pants of air hit my cheeks as he shoves at my chest with renewed efforts. He is a one-man life support system, keeping me alive through sheer force of will. His words are punctuated by the rhythm of his hands.

"Stay. With. Me."

The voice is ragged. Laced with desperation.

I know that voice...

I choke as briny water rushes up my throat and explodes from my lips. Half the Pacific streams from my nose as wet coughs wrack my body. I heave and wheeze until my throat is raw, until every drop has been expelled from my lungs. Consciousness creeps back slowly. I feel dazed, still half-dead. And frankly shocked that I am not a waterlogged corpse at the bottom of the ocean.

Gradually, I become aware of my surroundings. The half-inflated life vest, lying limp against my chest. The strange sensation of the raft beneath me, sloshing with each wave like a massive waterbed. The chill of my damp skin, soaked through from the sea and the rain still pouring down. The strong arms around me, cradling my head and shoulders, warm and sturdy and alive.

I'm alive.

My eyes flicker open. I look up into a set of green irises, narrowed with shock and fear. His fingertips flex against my skin, digging in hard enough to bring feeling back into my numb arms. *B. Underwood.* My stranger from the plane, my asshole from the airport.

My salvation in the storm.

"I've got you," he assures me, voice low with worry. "You're okay."

I want to laugh.

I'm not okay. None of this is okay.

He sees the panic in my eyes. "Just breathe. *Breathe.* In and out."

It's not a request — there's a steel undercurrent in his words. An unmistakable order. I find some comfort in the authority he's exerting. Staring into his eyes, at the pretense of composure he's arranged on his features, some long-ingrained childish instinct kicks in, the same one that suggests I seek out an adult in a crisis because, surely, an adult will know what to do.

Of course, I've known since I was ten years old that it's bullshit. Truthfully, adults rarely know what to do any more than the rest of us — they usually just hide their panic a little better. But, in this moment, I don't care. Staring up into the eyes of the man who singlehandedly tore me from death's clammy embrace, I can almost pretend things haven't totally fallen apart at the seams. That my life hasn't begun to resemble the opening act of my least favorite Tom Hanks film.

He knows what to do. He'll fix it.

Rain falls steadily on my face as I pull in a shaky breath, throat still burning from the seawater, and watch lightning flay the sky. I flinch when thunder shakes the air a few seconds later. The storm is still raging all around us. A wave crashes over the side of our raft, dousing us both. A terrified bleat bursts from my bruised throat as I contemplate what will happen if we flip.

I can't go back in that water.

"Hey," he murmurs, recognizing my terror. "I've got you."

His hands move from my arms to my face, brushing wet strands of hair from my eyes. I don't shift from his lap, where I'm cradled like a child after a nightmare. Under any other circumstance, I'd be embarrassed to be this close to him. But now, still reeling from the crash, all I feel is numb terror.

"I've got you," he repeats, a fervid promise. "We're going to survive this."

I hold his eyes and pull in another jagged breath.

"Do you understand me?"

"I..." The word catches in my sore throat. I clear it and try again. "I hear you."

"Good. Can you sit up?"

My head bobs in his hands, an affirmation.

He's infinitely gentle as he maneuvers me into a sitting position with my back braced against the inflatable wall. I bite back a protest when he releases me, feeling far safer in his hold. He's my only touchstone in this maelstrom.

I press a hand to my aching temple. "I... I don't remember..."

"You were passed out when I got to you, so you might've hit your head, but I don't see any blood..." He's crouched close by my side, scanning me intently for further injuries. "Your wrist was still wrapped in the raft lines. If not for that, and your life vest..." He trails off.

I'd be dead.

I clear my throat. "I don't think I hit my head. I just... ran out of air. When we crashed, it was so dark beneath the surface. I couldn't tell which way was up. I couldn't—" I bite down on my lip to contain my words — words I don't dare let myself speak, about the small hand that was ripped from mine. I can almost still feel her tiny fingers, the ghost of a grip lingering.

The grip of a ghost.

I couldn't hold her.

"Is anyone else..." I can't ask, but I must know. My eyes move around the expanse of empty raft and I think I already have my answer, horrific as it may be.

There were fifteen people on board, including the crew. Surely, others made it out. Surely, it's not just the two of us...

"You're the only one I found." A crease appears between his eyes and he seems to steel himself. "So far."

He scrambles back to the edge of the raft, clutching the life-lines when a massive wave threatens to capsize us. I grab hold as another hits, pitching us violently sideways.

My stomach turns inside out.

I focus on my savior instead of my own panic. He's leaning against the inflated wall, eyes squinting into the darkness. There's no sign of the jet in the water, nor any of the other passengers. It's hard to see anything at all, except during the brief moments when a bolt of electricity lights up the world.

Adjusting my grip on the safety lines, I pull myself to his side and help him look. At first, there's nothing. Nothing but rain and relentless swells of ocean, foaming white at the crests. But then, a flash of color in the distance — something yellow. A single daisy petal floating in a vat of ink.

"There!"

My voice breaks on the word as my hand flings out, pointing madly as thunder booms overhead.

"What?" he yells, over the howling wind.

"I think I saw someone!"

"Where? I can't see anything."

"Wait for the lightning!"

Another bolt streaks across the sky a few seconds later. My heart leaps inside my chest when I locate the flash of yellow, maybe fifteen feet from us in the thrashing waves. A life vest. There's definitely someone out there.

This time, he sees it too. We call out, but there's no response. If they're still alive, they're either unconscious or unable to reach us on their own.

Which means... one of us has to go get them.

I feel him tense at my side as the same realization jolts through him.

"I'll go."

I suck in a breath. "But—"

I cut off my own objections as my gaze creeps over to his. I see fear and hope warring in his eyes — the possibility of another survivor, weighed heavily against the prospect of leaving the raft to save them. I'm sure there's a similar war waging inside my own eyes. As I watch, he clears his face of all emotion and loops one of the emergency lines around his midsection. He attempts a hurried knot with shaking fingers.

"No."

He goes still when I speak, eyebrows lifting.

"Not like that. It won't hold."

I lean forward and pull the rope from his hands. I hook the end through the closest belt loop on his black jeans, then string it through the others, one after another. I have to lean in and loop my arms around him to reach the ones at his back. We're practically embracing as my hands work, my head pressed so close to his chest I can feel his heart hammering beneath my cheek. I barely breathe until his whole waist is circled and I've pulled back out of his space.

Able to breathe once more, I fashion a proper bowline. I've done it a million times — taught a million campers. Still, my fingers shake as I tug the knot tight.

47

"There." My eyes lock on his. "That'll hold you."

He nods stoically.

"You..." I swallow. "When you reach..." I can't bring myself to say *the body*. "Call out. I'll pull you back in."

Another nod.

I bite the inside of my cheek, trying not to let the fear show on my face. Fear for him. Fear for myself. Fear that he won't come out of that water again, once he goes in.

"If you're not back in five minutes..."

"Start pulling," he murmurs, eyes on mine. "But I'll be back."

I can't help myself. I reach out, grab his hand, and squeeze. "Promise me?"

He doesn't promise. He doesn't even nod. But his hand tightens on mine, a white-knuckled grip, and in that instant I feel something forge between us. A bond. Not of love or friendship or respect, not even of compassion or civility... but of survival.

If politics make for strange bedfellows, plane crashes certainly create the most unlikely allies.

His pulse is pounding in his jugular. Tick, tick, ticking like a bomb set to self-destruct. He's afraid. I can feel it in his grip, see it in the depths of his stare. I want to tell him to stay with me, in this flimsy floating shelter. To be selfish. To let whoever is out there find their own way to salvation.

Don't leave me here alone!

I bite back the words.

He swallows down his fear.

We drop our hands at the same time and turn, side by side, to face the raging water. Barely breathing, we wait for another bolt of lightning to show us the way. When it comes, I throw my pointer finger out to guide him, but he's already airborne. He hits the water with a splash and starts swimming, his strong strokes cutting like a knife. A wave crashes and I lose sight of him for a moment. Panic sluices through me.

Where is he?

I can only make out his form during the lightning flashes. I feed out the line bit by bit as the ocean swallows him up. My fingernails cut crescent moons into my palms as I wait, eyes straining in the dark, ears alert to every sound. For a long time, there's nothing but the howl of the wind, the rasp of the rope against my damp palms, the whipping waves that drench me, the rain that fills the raft with several inches of water. The high, tubular walls keep most of the ocean spray out, but there's still a considerable amount sloshing around my folded legs. The hem of my blue summer dress ebbs around me, translucent as a jellyfish. I feel a bolt of shock move through me as I spot my bare feet. I've lost both sandals in my frantic swim to the surface. I hadn't even noticed, which says something about my state of mind.

A giggle of hysteria bubbles up from my stomach. I can't help it — the sight of my pink-painted toenails shoves me over the edge of shell-shock on which I've been dangling.

Can it really be less than twenty-four hours ago that I sat in a massage chair, chatting with Mom as two technicians applied tiny dollops of magenta polish to our toes? That girl — the one who was so concerned with making a good impression on her new employers, who cared about things like taming frizzy airplane hair and finding the perfect pair of stylish-but-sensible sandals to match her outfit — seems galaxies away. Just the thought prompts another chortle of hysteria.

Logically, I recognize that I'm experiencing a certain amount of shock. But knowing something and changing it are vastly different feats. I don't know how to overcome the strange, detached sensations coursing through me as I wait for Underwood to return with the other survivor. If someone had told me at the LAX baggage claim that a handful of hours later, I'd be praying for a glimpse of his brooding eyes and pursed lips, scowling in my general direction, I'd have laughed my head off.

Funny how fast the world shifts.

The longer I wait for him, the tighter my grip grows on the

line. I hold so tight I'm worried it'll fray apart in my hands as I shiver in the darkness with my eyes on the sea.

I've always thought the ocean was beautiful. The way it eternally kisses the shore, the most persistent of lovers. The sound it makes as it skims over sand dunes and rocks. The ocean is a place for skinny dipping on summer nights; for long walks at sunset, ankle-deep in warm shallows. Powerful, to be sure, but restrained. A slow-eroding force, graceful even in its destruction.

But now, as I watch it claw at the raft, as I see the unadulterated fury in its every ebb and flow, I realize I have judged a beast by the tip of its smallest talon. The seashore of my summer sailing days was the merest hint of this wild creature, thrashing thousands of miles from the nearest point of land. This, here, is the true heart of the ocean. The beast of Poseidon, unleashed.

Doing its damnedest to tear us to shreds.

"Well, go ahead and try," I hiss, staring down the monster as another wave hits me in the face. "You can't have us." I tighten my grip on the rope in my hands. "You can't have *him*."

I've more than likely gone mad, because here I am, yelling into a hurricane… but I don't care. The defiance emboldens me.

I don't even know his first name, I realize ludicrously, eyes locked on the dark horizon. *If he dies, I'll spend the rest of my life wondering what that goddamned B stands for.*

Over the howl of the wind, I think I hear him cry out, but the sound is snatched away so quickly I'm half convinced my ears have deceived me. But then it comes again, a shout in the night, calling for help. With aching arms, I heave him in inch by inch, foot by foot, until the rope coils on the bottom of the raft. When he finally comes into view, I see instantly that he's not alone. There's an unconscious man in his arms — one of the flight attendants, judging by the uniform beneath his life vest. I recognize him from the preflight safety demonstration he gave before takeoff.

If there is a drop in cabin pressure, panels above your seat will open, revealing oxygen masks...

A water evacuation is unlikely, however, life vests are located under your seats...

At the time, I thought it was a useless piece of protocol. I never imagined, a few hours later, we'd be here.

Living the emergency demonstration.

"Is he alive?" I yell as they reach the side of the raft. The flight attendant's body is limp, his youthful features ashen white. I can't tell whether or not he's breathing.

"I think so." Underwood treads in place, straining to hold the man above water. "Can you grab his arms?"

Careful not to fall in, I reach over the edge and grab the flight attendant by the lapels of his uniform, beneath his life vest. Together — Underwood pushing from below, me pulling from above — we attempt to maneuver the sodden body into the raft.

He's so heavy. Deadweight.

My muscles throb with the effort of holding him as we pitch sideways, knocked off course by another large wave. He nearly slips from my grip.

"He's too heavy," I gasp, feeling tears sting my eyes. "I can't—"

"Yes you can," Underwood growls, glaring up at me. "You can and you will. Now *pull.*"

I bite my lip and heave with all my might. Mercifully, the flight attendant flops forward, the inertia of his fall knocking me backwards. I'm already struggling to breathe from pulling him in; when he lands squarely on my chest, two hundred pounds of waterlogged male flesh, I cease breathing altogether.

Thankfully, Underwood scrambles nimbly up after him and quickly rolls the man off me.

"Is he breathing?" I wheeze as air returns to my lungs, crouching over the prone form.

Green eyes meet mine. "Faintly. I'm just hoping we can keep him alive until help arrives."

I startle.

Help.

In the chaos, I haven't let myself look ahead to anything beyond the next few seconds. When the plane crashed my future, once so solid beneath my feet, dissipated entirely — like stepping out on a frozen lake expecting thick ice and finding slush instead.

But as I watch a set of lush lips form the word *help*, that future freezes back into something tangible beneath my heels. Of *course*, help will be coming. Helicopters and search parties and rescue missions full of well-trained macho men, to pull us from the waves and return us to dry land.

Rescue — even just the *possibility* of rescue — lifts a heavy weight off my chest. Dread falls away and something else takes its place. It's fragile, hardly more than a flicker, but it's there.

Hope.

A low curse makes me look up. Underwood is frowning mightily, his eyes locked on the flight attendant's left leg. It's bent at several angles that are anatomically impossible, if the bones are still intact. Through the dark fabric of his pants, I see a sharp fragment of metal protruding from his flesh. A jagged piece of plane debris has punctured deep into muscle and bone. My stomach clenches at the sight.

"If you're going to be sick, do it over the side," Underwood snaps.

My eyes fly to his face. I feel my jaw clench in sudden anger. "I'm not going to be sick."

"Then make yourself useful and grab the emergency kit over there." He jerks his chin to the left.

My gaze swings in that direction and I spot a small black bag lashed to the side of the raft. A built-in supply kit. I'm floored to see my canvas backpack sitting beside it, along with a familiar green duffle bag — the one I accidentally snatched off a conveyer belt a million years ago.

"You brought my bag?" I ask, reaching for it with shaking fingers. I thought it was lost in the crash. "I can't believe—"

"Wax poetic about my acts of kindness later; find the first aid kit now."

I bite back a retort and fumble for the emergency bag. "What do you need?"

"Gauze, alcohol pads, anything we can use to pack the wound. I don't want this metal shifting around and doing more damage."

"Okay." I open the heavy plastic zipper and sort through the contents, muttering aloud as I take inventory. "Compass… two emergency flares… raft patches… whistle… aluminum blankets… ration packets…" I swallow hard. "I'm not seeing a first aid kit."

"Look harder."

I stiffen. "Don't snap at me!"

He grunts — apparently, that's as close to an apology as I'm going to get. I decide to ignore him as I continue my search. I'm nearly at the bottom of the bag, now.

"Plastic bailor… knife…" My hands close on the last item, a flat white box with a red cross on top. I yank it impatiently from the depths. "First aid kit."

I crawl back to the men. Underwood is bent low over the flight attendant's leg to examine the wound. He's ripped the man's pants apart around the metal, to better see the damage. My heart fails when I see the blood gushing out. There's a lot of it. Too much. It's saturating the fabric, dripping into the bottom of the raft where it mixes with rainwater to form a macabre cocktail.

I know just enough about anatomy to recognize that the shard of metal is dangerously close to piercing the femoral artery, if it hasn't already. The bones in the lower half of his leg look completely shattered. He must've been crushed by a heavy piece of debris during the crash. The skin is badly bruised already; I can only imagine what it'll look like in a few hours.

"Fuck," I whisper, wiping rain from my eyes with my forearm as I watch blood flow from the wound.

Underwood grunts. "My thoughts exactly."

"It's a good thing he passed out. He's got to be in unbearable pain…"

Busy applying pressure to the wound, Underwood grunts again. Apparently, that's his main form of communication.

As I get a look at the damage up close, dread washes over me. There's no way we can set a fractured femur, no way to cure a knee pulverized into dust. I wouldn't know how to fix this man in a state of the art operating room with all the surgical instruments in the world at my disposal; my chances of mending such an injury on a raft in the middle ocean, without access to more than the most basic medical supplies, are dire indeed.

I glance down at the kit in my hands.

Band-Aids. Gauze. A pair of shears. A scalpel. A suture kit.

For all intents and purposes… these items are useless.

Blinking back tears, I yank a bandage out and press it against the worst of the bleeding, aligning my hands beside Underwood's. When the flight attendant moans in agony, I have to bite down on my lip to keep the tears at bay.

You cannot cry, Violet.

Keep it together, for his sake.

Blood saturates the thin cloth in mere seconds.

"Shit!" I exclaim, watching the dark stain spread. "I can't get this bleeding to stop."

Underwood glances up sharply. "We need to tourniquet the wound or he's going to bleed to death."

"Tell me what to do."

His eyes dart left and right as options whirl through his mind. A belt would be the obvious choice, but neither of us is wearing one.

"My shoelace," he says finally, sticking out a booted foot in my direction. "Pull it out."

I do as he says, unlacing the thick black string with trembling hands. When I tug it free, I look up at Underwood for guidance. I see my own fears reflected back at me, bright on the surface of those emerald irises.

"If you can't do this..." He trails off.

"I can do it," I snap.

After a second, he nods. "Tie it tight, just above my hands, where the bone is still intact," he instructs, jerking his chin toward the flight attendant's thigh. I keep my hands as steady as possible as I wrap the shoelace around the muscle, trying not to look too closely at the mangled limb mere inches from my face. The damage is catastrophic.

My fingers move deftly, looping and twisting and tugging tight enough to stop the bleeding. Once the tourniquet is in place, I exhale a faint sigh of relief as I watch the bleeding subside from a steady flow to a trickle. Underwood's eyes move from the staunched wound to my blood-stained hands to my pale face. There's grudging respect etched on his expression.

"Help is coming," I whisper, more to myself than him. "They have to come."

He nods.

"We just have to hold on till then." I dunk my hands into the shallow water at the bottom of the raft and watch dark blood flow off my skin in rivulets. When they're clean, I reach out and gently brush a strand of blond hair from the flight attendant's face. Even unconscious, I can read the pain on his features. When he wakes, he'll be in absolute agony.

"You have to hold on," I tell him, throat thick with unshed tears. "Just a little while longer. Help is coming."

Help is coming.

Help is coming.

Help is coming.

Stroking a stranger's forehead, I whisper it over and over under my breath, like a witch weaving a spell that might summon a fleet of search and rescue helicopters from the skies above. I repeat it for hours, until my voice goes hoarse and the lightning ceases, until the rain gentles from a torrent to a patter, until the sky is streaked with the first pale pink traces of the coming dawn.

Help.

Is.

Coming.

It must.

Because the alternative...

That's simply unfathomable.

CHAPTER SIX

ADRIFT

AT SOME POINT OR ANOTHER, the thought crosses all of our minds.

If I disappeared one day, would anyone bother to notice?

The truth is, no matter how confident or self-assured you appear on the surface, deep down we all wonder what would happen if we inexplicably vanished off the face of the earth. Without a note, without a trace, without any explanation as to how or why you've blinked out of existence. Just a slew of memories and a thousand questions.

Are they looking for me?

Mourning me?

Missing me?

Is there a tombstone engraved with my name on it, sitting atop an empty grave?

I think it's natural to wonder. We're all human — predisposed to experience the same existential crises every now and again. But few people ever have a chance to put those abstract musings into practice. Few actually *do* disappear.

I definitely never thought I'd be one of them.

That first day on the raft, we keep a vigilant watch — still full to the brim with blazing conviction that, any moment now, our rescuers will arrive. With the rising sun come rising temperatures. On a positive note, my sundress dries completely for the first time since the crash; on the negative, while it's nice not to be damp, I quickly find my pale skin begins to crisp like a piece of bread beneath a broiler.

Underwood struggles to unfurl the overhead tent — a bright orange canopy affixed with plastic rods, that covers half the raft. As he fiddles with the straps, I pull a tube of SPF50 sunscreen from the bottom of my backpack and slather my arms, face, and bare legs. I send up silent thanks to my mother for her persistence in protecting me from melanoma. I can practically hear her.

I told you you'd need it, honey!

"Here," I say, extending the bottle out to him. It's the first word either of us has spoken in hours.

He glances at the tube, grunts unintelligibly, and begins applying.

No *thank you.* Not even an acknowledgement that I've spoken.

I bite my tongue to stop the torrent of words poised on its tip. I'd like nothing more than to unleash all my frustrations on him — all the pent up anger and hopelessness and fear that we're never getting off this raft. That rescue isn't coming. That my last few moments will be spent watching a man die in agony in the middle of the ocean, with only a total jerk for company.

I refuse to give him the satisfaction of watching my meltdown.

He looks as guarded as ever as I glare at him. Nothing I say or do seems to provoke a response from this man. I can't read a single emotion in his eyes, in his expression. Never in my life have I encountered someone so self-controlled. Either he's a sociopath, or he's the best actor I've ever met.

Or... maybe he's known so much pain in his life, the only way he can manage it is to shut out every other feeling along with the heartache. A total emotional blockade.

I bury that thought in a fortified box at the back of my mind and dump a half-ton of concrete on top, in case I'm ever tempted to revisit it. Mom always says having damage isn't an excuse for being a dick. Rationalizing a man's rudeness is a slippery slope to romanticizing all his less-than-reputable characteristics. Just ask Jane Eyre. Or Catherine Earnshaw. Or any other woman who's ever swooned over a Byronic hero.

The silence lingers between us as our gazes lock. This close, I can see our eyes are almost the same shade, except for those tiny rings of hazel around the edges of his irises. I'm breathing too hard, barely able to keep my rapidly fraying emotions in check... and he's a brick wall, a solid edifice of composure. My total counterbalance.

A chatterbox and a curmudgeon, I think. *Fate definitely has a sense of humor.*

One of us needs to break this growing silence. The longer it stretches out, the more charged the air becomes. The charge between us — two polar opposites, trapped together like repelling magnets — is so potent, I can practically taste it on the tip of my tongue.

Say something.

Say anything.

Just stop looking at him like that.

Thankfully, the tension snaps when the flight attendant moans. We trade another glance and somehow, without speaking a word, come to an agreement. In silent tandem, we drag the injured man beneath the canopy, moving slowly so we don't jostle his broken leg overmuch. I wish we had something to splint it with, but there's nothing. My eyes linger on the mottled purple flesh below the tourniquet, then move up to his face.

It's a starling contrast — the ugly wound, the handsome

features. At the moment, they're contorted in acute agony, but there's no denying he's an attractive man. In his early twenties, he has a full head of sandy blond hair, the slim build of a soccer player, and — if I recall correctly from his preflight demonstration — a pair of dimples that offset a megawatt smile.

I wish I could do something, *anything*, to help him. In truth, he's in worse shape than I thought when we first pulled him from the water. In addition to his shattered leg, there's a pretty serious laceration by his temple. I force myself to unbutton his uniform shirt — once so crisp and white, now streaked with blood and grime — and find a slew of angry purple skin streaking over his ribs. A surefire sign he's bleeding internally.

Hold on.

Just a little while longer.

I wipe his damp brow with a gauze pad from the first aid kit, pillow his head on my backpack, and carefully remove his shoes so he's more comfortable. Digging one of the silver foil space blankets out of the survival kit, I tuck it around his body to keep him warm, hoping a bit of heat might stave off the clammy shock of blood loss.

Everything I do feels woefully inadequate. I am ill-equipped for this scenario: a glorified babysitter, for goodness sake. I assumed the only skills I'd be utilizing this summer included sand-castle construction and water-sport supervision. The only shoelaces I planned on tying were on a little girl's pink sneakers — not emergency leg tourniquets. I never could've imagined I'd be dealing with something like this.

Defeated and dehydrated, I crane my head back to look up at the sky. It's endlessly blue, not a single cloud in sight now that the storm that brought down our plane has finally passed. For hours we drift along in silence, our raft borne miles from the crash site by swift ocean currents. Without any landmarks to gauge our distance, it's hard to tell how far we travel. Only the sun provides an indicator for the passage of time, inching east to west across the sky in torturous increments.

It's been a single day, but I feel as though I've been awake for an eternity. My eyelids grow heavier than anvils as I strain to keep them open. My very bones ache with exhaustion. The lulling rhythm of the waves doesn't help matters; I fight the strong lure of sleep with every ounce of energy I have left. I can't allow myself to doze. If a ship appears on the horizon, someone needs to be awake to fire a flare.

I mean...

When a ship appears.

Not *if.*

As the hours drag on, it becomes increasingly difficult to hold onto my positive attitude. When the sun takes her final bow and the moon makes his debut, a blanket of brilliant stars appear one by one in the night sky. During yesterday's storm, we couldn't see them at all. With a blank canvas, in the total absence of light pollution, the constellations create a work of art most people go their whole lives without ever glimpsing. And yet, peering up at them, I feel no awe. Despair has crept in with the shadows, chipping relentlessly at my stalwart optimism until rescue more closely resembles a shimmering mirage on a distant horizon.

The moon is nearly full, big as my fist. It seems far closer from this vantage than it ever did from my bedroom window in New Hampshire, and it basks us in a balmy white light. I stare at the face on its glowing surface, formed by craters and crags a quarter million miles away, and feel a strange kinship with that lonely man in the moon, so far removed from life and civilization in the cold reaches of outer space.

I'd cry, if I could spare the water. My tongue skims my parched lips, dry and cracked as desert adobe. I can't afford to waste a single drop of moisture on something as useless as tears.

Besides, I remind myself. *Compared to the others, I don't have it so bad.*

Sophie. Samantha. Seth.

All the others from the plane.

After we pulled the flight attendant from the water, we continued to search for them. For hours, we stared into the hurricane, weary eyes watching the waves, hoping against all odds we'd spot another flicker of life in the roiling surf. Praying someone else survived.

But prayers went unanswered.

I tell myself that there's a chance another raft deployed — that the rest of the passengers are safe and sound, floating in their own garish yellow inflatable hexagon. But in the darkest corners of my mind, I acknowledge the truth. If another group of survivors was out there, they'd be trapped in the same ocean currents. Floating alongside us.

The others…

They didn't make it.

I shove the thought away and distract myself by bailing the shallow puddle of remaining seawater from the bottom of the raft. It's still tinged red with blood from the flight attendant's seeping leg wound. I grimace as I work, gripping the plastic bailer with fingertips that have long since shriveled to raisins. It's a Sisyphean task: every few hours, the waves replenish what I manage to remove. Still, the ritual — scoop, dump, scoop, dump — gives me something to do other than stare at the dying man beneath the canopy on my right, or the brooding one propped against the wall on my left.

"You should save your strength." His voice is gruff as ever in the darkness. Hours of silence followed by terse orders. What a surprise.

I keep bailing, pointedly ignoring him.

"Fine." He sighs with exasperation. "Wear yourself out just to spite me. That's smart."

My hand stills. I glance up, glaring at him. "Are you this rude to everyone, or am I special?"

"Oh, I'm sorry," he drawls, voice thick with sarcasm. "Do my manners need work?"

"Manners?" I roll my eyes. "*What* manners, exactly, are you referring to? Because I haven't seen any in the few words you've bothered to exchange with me since we met."

"This isn't a fucking tea party, in case you haven't noticed."

"Trust me, I've noticed." My voice cracks. "But since we're stuck here together in the middle of the godforsaken ocean, at the very least you could be civil!"

"*Civil* isn't going to keep us alive." His words are intent. "Neither will wasting strength on non-vital tasks."

"And I suppose screaming our heads off at each other is a good use of energy?" I ask, fingers tightening on the bailer.

He holds his hands up in a defensive gesture and settles back against the side of the raft. His black jeans and v-neck are streaked white with dried salt and ocean spray. In the pale moonlight, I can make out the deep circles beneath his eyes. He's just as exhausted as I am. Maybe more so — he did pull two people from the ocean. He saved us all.

Still, I think haughtily. *That doesn't give him license to be such a jerk.*

A groan of pain from the flight attendant makes me discard the bailer and scramble to his side. His eyelids flutter, but he doesn't wake. I lay the back of my hand against his forehead. It's burning with fever. Sweat coats his skin and he shivers with cold.

"He needs water and antibiotics," Underwood says lowly. He's moved to the prone man's other side, his bleak gaze lingering on the ghastly leg wound. "Without them, he won't last another day."

My eyes narrow. "That's a rather callous assessment."

"It's a realistic assessment. You need to prepare yourself. If he—"

"Ian," I interject, jerking my head at the brass name tag still affixed to his white button down. "His name is Ian."

There's a heavy pause. Finally, with great effort, he echoes, "Ian."

As if acknowledging him as a person, with a name and a family and a life, is a burden he'd rather not shoulder.

I shake my head, dumbfounded by his indifference. "Unbelievable."

"What was that?" he asks sharply.

"Nothing."

A muscle ticks in his tight-clenched jaw. "Believe this — if he doesn't get treatment soon, that wound will start to fester."

"You think..." I curse myself for the tremor in my voice. "You think he'll lose the leg?"

"The leg? He'll be lucky if he doesn't lose his life." His head shakes. "He isn't going to last much longer."

"Stop saying that!"

"What? The truth?" His eyes narrow. "You may not like the situation we're in, but that doesn't change a damn thing. You need to prepare yourself for the possibility that this story might not have a happy ending."

"You think I don't know that?"

His eyes scan my face, my pretty sundress, the long tendrils of hair falling in a curtain around my shoulders. "I think you still believe life is a fairy tale, because it hasn't disappointed you yet."

"This may shock you, since I'm getting the sense you're pretty much in love with yourself, but being here with you?" I lean in. "*Big* disappointment."

"Don't be a child."

"Don't be an ass!" I shoot back. "What does it cost *you* if I decide to stay positive? Holding onto hope isn't a crime, except maybe in the totalitarian society you're trying to institute here."

"You want to be in charge instead?" he snaps. "You want to make all the tough decisions? Ration the water and food packets so we survive this? Make the call when Ian here is too far gone to continue wasting limited resources on?"

I gasp.

Wasting resources. As if his death is a foregone conclusion.

My hands curl into fists. "I'm not giving up on him, even if you have."

"I'm not telling you to give up. I'm just saying... I wouldn't get attached."

"I know *you* wouldn't," I practically spit, suddenly seething with rage. "You don't ever get attached, do you?" Before I can stop myself, words are pouring out. I don't even know where they're coming from, let alone how to stop them. "No need for names! No personal details! No small talk! Certainly no comfort or kindness, even in the bleakest fucking circumstance!" I'm shaking so hard, salty strands of hair fall into my eyes. "Because *god forbid* you let anyone inside that fortress you've put up around yourself — you might actually start to give a shit about them!"

"You don't know the first thing about me," he growls.

"I know nothing affects you," I retort hotly. "I know you're a fucking *robot*, who apparently feels nothing about the fact that we're in this mess together. From where I sit, it seems like you'd rather be alone on this damn raft! Hell, I bet you regret pulling me from that water!"

He flinches at the accusation. "Don't be ridiculous."

"What's *ridiculous* is this! Me and you! The twisted fate of ending up stranded with the last man on earth I'd ever choose as a companion!"

"Trust me, sweetheart, you wouldn't be my first choice either. You're not exactly Lara Croft."

Ugh!

I'm burning with rage and righteous indignation. I don't let myself look too deep at the source, for fear of what I'll find. Because, even as the vitriol pours fourth from my lips, I've begun to suspect this man — this gruff, grumpy, heroic, handsome, infuriating man — is not actually the reason I'm so steaming mad.

But I can't be mad at a storm in the sky.

I can't be mad at a plane for crashing.

I can't be mad at a little girl for letting go.

I can't be mad at a man for dying.

I can't be mad at rescue for not coming.

He's all I have left. He's the only one here. The only outlet for my rage and terror and guilt. So, it doesn't matter that none of this is his fault. I bottle up every ounce of emotion raging inside me and blast it at him without remorse.

"The minute I met you I knew you were the worst kind of man!"

"And what kind of man would that be?" he fires back, just as pissed off at me as I am at him. Maybe I'm not the only one who needs to release a little rage. "Since you're apparently so well versed in the subject of men and their shortcomings."

"Arrogant. Rude. Impatient." I'm panting. "Bossy. Manipulative. Condescending."

And entirely too good looking, I add silently.

He scoffs. "You got all that in the first minute?"

"The first bloody second!" I snap.

His eyes narrow on mine. "Well, I could tell as soon as I clapped eyes on you that you were a pampered little princess. Believe me, baby, of all the women I could've ever envisioned myself marooned with... I never once imagined I'd end up with a *child.*"

I swallow down a scream. "If I'm a child, you're a cantankerous old man!"

"Does someone need a time out?" he mocks.

I do scream, this time. My hand curls around the bailer and before I can stop myself or think about the repercussions of my actions, I crank back my arm and chuck it full-force at his head — forgetting, in my rage, that it's fastened to a short tether line. The plastic bucket arcs perfectly toward his face, a straight shot, before jolting to a stop at the end of its rope and falling to the empty span of raft between us.

For a moment, it's totally silent as we stare at each other. I think he's stunned I tried to bean him in the head. Frankly, I'm a bit stunned myself.

His eyes flicker from my face down to the bailer and back again. I see a glimmer of humor flash in their depths, but it's gone so fast I convince myself I'm hallucinating.

Of all the things that might make him laugh, surely me screaming insults and attempting to maim him isn't at the top of that list...

Shame swamps me. He was right to call me a child — I've behaved worse than a toddler throwing a tantrum. I open my mouth to apologize for my outburst, but he beats me to the punch.

"You should rest," he says carefully, as though navigating a minefield blindfolded and barefoot. "I'll keep watch for a while."

"You're just as tired as I am," I point out quietly. With the tension finally abated between us, the fight has gone out of me, replaced by such intense exhaustion I fear I'll pass out before the protests leave my lips. The stress of the last twenty-four hours has officially caught up. I've been reduced to a hollow shell of my former self.

"I can hold out a little while longer," he murmurs, those unreadable eyes burning into mine once more. "We'll take shifts. There's no point in both of us staying awake all the time."

My lips twitch as my eyelids droop closed. "Plus, there's probably less of a chance I'll toss you overboard, if one of us is asleep..."

"True enough."

I'm half-dreaming when a throat clears roughly, pulling me back from the precipice. His voice is uncharacteristically soft when he asks a question that makes my heart clench.

"Your name." He pauses a beat. "What's your name?"

I keep my eyes closed, unable to look at him as I answer. The syllables feel strange on my tongue — like a secret I hadn't realized I was keeping.

"Violet." My pulse pounds faster. "My name is Violet Anderson."

He's silent for so long, I don't think he's going to reciprocate. When he finally does, his voice isn't full of scorn. It's achingly sincere. Alarmingly sincere.

"Violet," he rasps softly, sending a shiver down my spine. "I'm Beck."

Beck.

The name wraps around my mind, smooth as silk sheets, and I tumble mercifully into oblivion.

CHAPTER SEVEN

LANDFALL

ANOTHER DAY SLIPS by without fanfare.

I doze in short spurts, often jolting out of sleep at an unfamiliar sound: a pained moan from Ian, a particularly large swell crashing against the side of the raft, Beck sorting through his duffle bag and the emergency pack, taking stock of our limited supplies. The only sounds I want to hear — the whirring of helicopter blades, the rumble of a ship engine — never manifest. No salvation appears on the horizon, despite the constant vigil we keep.

Trading shifts, Beck and I are rarely awake at the same time. Even when we are, we speak infrequently. Our conversations are limited to such scintillating topics as *how many more sips of water are in the canteen* and *is Ian still breathing* and *pass the sunscreen.* I think we're both afraid any further attempts at communication will devolve into another screaming match.

The truth is, we both made assumptions. We held trial and passed judgment before giving the benefit of the doubt. And now, having convicted each other without a shred of evidence besides our own snap judgments, having screamed and raged and mocked one another...

It's difficult to go back. Hell, it's difficult to look his direction.

Princess.

Asshole.

You still believe in fairy tales.

You're a fucking robot.

The barbs still slice and tear, embedded deep in the walls of my heart. I can see my own words reflected at me every time I catch his eyes. If I could take them back, I would.

I spend my waking hours by Ian's side, stroking his damp hair and squeezing his hand with a reassurance I don't feel. I do my best to soak up the blood around his wounds with a damp piece of gauze, wringing it out over the side until my hands are streaked with red.

When several large, pointed gray dorsal fins begin to stalk us through the water, I decide I don't mind the sight of blood pooling in the bottom of the raft. Not if the alternative is a nine-foot long sea monster with rows of razor-sharp teeth tearing the inflatable into shreds and the limbs from our bodies.

My heart hammers double-speed inside my chest the entire time the sharks trail us. They swim with a predatory, prehistoric aggression, circling like wolves hungry for blood. It's a few endless hours before they finally slink out of sight, and even after they're gone, I'm haunted by the knowledge that they're out there. Lurking in the depths beneath us. Waiting.

The thought is enough to make me shiver in the intense heat.

Hunger gnaws at my stomach lining, relentless and rumbling. Hours ago, Beck and I split one of the vacuum-sealed meal packets from the emergency kit — a paltry portion of granola that did little to tide me over. Blessed with a naturally fast metabolism, I've never been one to count calories or restrict my carb intake, never a fan of fad diets or juice cleanses, unlike so many of my friends on the cheerleading squad. Back home, I used to wake up an hour early each morning, so I'd have time to make a full breakfast before school. French toast, a frittata, an omelet, pancakes, you name it.

Enjoy it while it lasts, Mom used to say, shaking her head at me over a bowl of plain bran cereal. *After you turn thirty, I swear you can just glance at chocolate and gain five pounds.*

If she could only see me now — cursing the hearty appetite I've always prized. I'm so hungry I'd eat the glue off an envelope and award it a Michelin Star.

Still... ravenous or not, I can survive without food. But water?

That's another story.

The two cans of diet soda stashed in my backpack are gone, split between us sip by sip until they were sucked dry. Beck's stainless water bottle is nearly empty now. A gulp, maybe two, is all that remains. It's not enough to keep even one of us alive in this relentless heat, let alone three.

I look from Ian's feverish pallor to Beck's gaunt face as my sandpaper tongue scrapes the inside of my arid cheeks, wondering if today will be the day dehydration wins its slow war of attrition.

Which one of us will die first?

"I will," Beck whispers in a cracking voice, extending the bottle out to me. "Here. Take it."

It's only then I realize I've spoken my delirious thoughts aloud. I shake my head with the last dregs of energy, my movements sloth-like. Someone's shoved a wad of cotton between my ears, muting every sound and color. The world swims before my eyes, out of focus.

"We'll split it," I insist weakly.

"Only enough for one." He flips his wrist and sends the bottle rolling toward me. "You're smaller. You need less. If you drink it, you might be able to hold out until…"

"Until rescue comes?"

"Rescue? Hell, I'd settle for a single raincloud."

A laugh snags in my throat. "Your standards are too low. I'm holding out for a cheeseburger. A big, fat, juicy one with a pile of extra salty fries on the side."

He groans. "Don't torture me."

"Sorry, it's my only real pastime on this raft."

"Talking about food is cruel and unusual punishment."

"Would you rather I throw a bailer at your head again? I'll untie it this time."

"Honestly?" he asks, attempting a light tone. "*Yes*. A concussion sounds preferable to dying of thirst."

My chapped lips crack as a smile tugs at them. I can't bring myself to comment on the irony of us finally getting along, now that we're about to die. Come to think of it, perhaps that's the only reason we're getting along. We no longer have any need for pretense, nor the energy for verbal sparring.

I'm happy he's ten feet away. I'm so delirious, if he was close I might find myself doing something stupid, like twining his fingers with mine, or begging him to wrap his arms around me. I don't want to die, but if I have to… I definitely don't want to do it alone.

"What's that look?" he asks, eyes locked on my frowning lips.

"What look?"

"The one on your face right now."

I sigh deeply and force myself to say it. "They're not coming."

He stares at me blankly.

"The search party. The rescue mission. They're not coming, Beck." My voice catches on his name. "We were hundreds of miles off course when the plane went down. We've drifted hundreds more. If anyone is looking for us… they aren't looking in the right place."

The words trail off into a depressing silence.

There it is.

The truth, laid out for us both to swallow. It's a bitter pill.

I've known from the beginning, but it's different to acknowledge it aloud. It feels somehow like a defeat. Like admitting failure, though I'm not exactly sure how we failed.

Can you fail a situation you have no control over?

"Violet."

It's the first time he's ever used my name, and it moves through me like an electric shock. My eyes open to focus on him. I didn't even realize I'd closed them.

"Drink the water," he says intently. *"Please."*

My mouth opens. I'm not sure whether I'm going to accept or reject his offer, but it doesn't matter because the words don't make it past my lips. My eyes go wide as saucers as I stare at the horizon.

"Hey, princess, did you hear me?"

I'm trembling, half convinced I've gone mad, half hopeful that my eyes aren't telling lies.

"Would it kill you to listen to me for once?" Beck grumbles. "Grant a dying man one final request. Drink the damn water. It's the least you can do."

"No." I shake my head. "Afraid I can't do that."

"Why the hell not?"

"Because..." I hardly dare to believe my own words. "Beck... look behind you."

He goes totally still. "Why?"

I press a hand to my stomach, but it does nothing to calm the explosion of butterflies that have just hatched inside my gut. I stare at the small patch of green and gold, growing clearer as the currents sweep us toward it. If I squint beyond the rough break of reef... I can just make out the shape of palm trees lining a white sand beach along the shore.

It's real.

It has to be real.

"It's... it's an island."

MY FEET HIT THE BEACH, wobbly and weak. I can barely stand upright, but I don't care. I dig my toes into the white sand to ground myself in reality. Part of me still thinks this must be an elaborate delusion brought on by intense dehydration. But no hallucination could ever be this detailed. My brain could never dream up the crystalline sparkles on the water's surface in the small inlet where we've washed ashore, the brilliant blue of the sky overhead, the riot of dense green rainforest twenty yards up the beach.

The waters here, in the shelter of the reef, are still and so clear I can see straight to the bottom. Curious fish dart in and out of the aqua shallows, lured close by the bright colors of our raft. I watch crabs scurry under rocks, their hard-shelled claws clicking like castanets. Small shorebirds gather on the jagged rocks to our left, where coral and algae grow in abundance.

We made it. We survived.

I could kiss the sand beneath my feet, but I'm afraid I might not have the strength to get back up. Plus, there's Ian to think about. We're so exhausted, we can't lift him from the raft. Instead, we drag the entire vessel, Beck grabbing a handle on the right side as I grab one on the left. We both grunt with the effort as we pull it from the shallows onto solid sand. The grains slip and slide beneath my feet, so fine it's hard to walk a straight line. The sun beats down so strongly against the white beach, my retinas are scorched by the refracted beams. I grit my teeth and keep pulling.

Before the atoll came into view, I thought I'd reached the absolute bottom of my energy stores, that one more move would land me at rock bottom. It seems I still have some unforeseen stamina left, though, because I stagger stubbornly onward, running on gasoline fumes from an empty tank. I can't let Beck and Ian down — not now that we've finally found sanctuary. Or... at least some semblance of it.

Our odds of survival have to be better here on land than in the middle of the damn ocean.

We move with the alacrity of octogenarians; it takes an eternity to pull the raft a half dozen yards. By the time we come to a stop, my head is pounding, my eyes are swimming with sunspots, and my limbs are barely cooperating with executive orders. I tug a line from the raft and secure it to a fallen palm tree, embedded in the sand halfway up the beach. Tying the rope around the trunk saps the last sliver of strength from my bones. I can feel myself hovering on the precipice of unconsciousness as I stare down at Ian's pale face, swaying on my feet. I wish I could help him but right now, a rogue gust of wind could carry me away.

At least he's covered by the canopy and — I think — far enough from the water's edge that he won't float out to sea with the swells. The inlet is so calm that seems unlikely, but I'm not sure how far the tide rises here. I'm not even sure the South Pacific *has* tides the way we do at home.

Home.

The thought is nearly enough to break my remaining resolve. I shut it out before it cripples me completely.

There'll be time to fall apart later. On the rescue boat. Because, surely, now that we've made it to land...

They'll find us.

Someone has to find us.

I try to move toward the shade, but my body finally gives out beneath me, a paper doll folding in on itself. My knees hit the sand beside the raft, my back hits the beached driftwood trunk. For a long while — it could be minutes or hours or eons — I lay there in the sun, unable to focus on anything except the foreign sensation of solid ground beneath me for the first time in days. My body still feels like it's moving, swells of vertigo crashing regularly through my system like the rhythmic waves that ferried us along to this atoll. I wonder vaguely how long it will take my sea legs to fade, if I'll die of thirst before I'm able to walk straight again. I can't summon enough energy to truly care. About water, or walking, or even the hot sun scorching down, baking me like Mom's famous spinach-artichoke dip, the longer I lie here exposed to the elements.

"Come on."

Beck's voice.

I crack open one eye, but otherwise don't respond. He's collapsed against the tree beside me, so close I can see each individual grain of sand coating his forearms, but still not touching. His breaths are just as labored as mine, though his eyes remain razor-sharp with intensity.

"We can't stay here." His chapped lips form words it takes my sluggish brain far too long to piece together into thoughts. "We have to get out of the sun. Find some water."

"Ian... We can't just leave him here..."

"He's covered by the canopy. And we can't help him if we're dead."

He has a point.

His hand stretches toward me, each finger creating a divot in the sand. I watch with detached fascination as it comes to a stop beside mine. My eyes lift to his, wide with wonder.

"Let's go." His jaw locks. "Time to get up."

My dry tongue attempts a rebuttal, but before I can say a word he closes that last shred of distance and laces our hands together. They fit like two perfect puzzle pieces. I suck in a sharp gasp of air as the sensation of his callused palm slides against mine, sandy and strong. I feel the tendons flexing in his fingers as they envelop mine, and nearly cry as I realize how much I have needed to feel human touch. How, more than water or shelter or rescue, I have longed for someone to take me into their arms and tell me it will all be okay. That I'm not alone in this nightmare.

"Together," he whispers, hand squeezing mine tight.

"Together," I echo.

He pulls me to my feet and supports me when I nearly stumble off balance into the sand. I stare up at his face, haloed by the sun like some angel sent down to save me, and cannot think of a single thing to say to him. I know I should drop my hand from his, should pull out of this half-embrace that's brought inconsequential parts of our bodies into contact, but I cannot make myself do that either.

Instead, inexplicably, I find my hand squeezing ever tighter as he leads me toward the tree line. One careful step at a time. Connected in a way I haven't even begun to understand.

Not quite enemies.

Not yet friends.

Something... indefinable.

THE GRACEFUL PALMS that bow like swan necks at the edge of the beach soon yield to a dense canopy of forest. The temperature drops about ten degrees as soon as we step into the shade. I'm glad to give my bare feet a break from the burning sand and my eyes a rest from the glaring sunbeams as we venture a few yards inland. The wild jungle looks untouched by time. It calls to mind images of the Jurassic Period in my old science textbooks — massive ferns, creeping mosses, hanging vines thick as my fist. Every verdant inch teems with life, utterly unmolested by human influence. Devoid of any traces of development.

My heart clenches.

In the most desperate corners of my mind, I was holding out hope that perhaps we'd fortuitously washed ashore just around the bend from a five-star resort, where we'd be welcomed with open arms and free buffet access. In actuality, I suspected otherwise the moment the island came into view.

This place is deserted.

Uncharted.

One square mile at most and, from the looks of it, entirely uninhabited. Just one of a million small atolls that span Polynesia, Micronesia, and Melanesia. Too small for major foreign enterprises, too isolated to lure in local residents. To be sure, there's a certain dark twist in the knowledge that, had the Flint Group stumbled across it under different circumstances, we might've ended up here at some point anyway — Beck taking photographs of potential building sites for Seth's luxury property, me making sandcastles and exploring tidal pools with Sophie.

Funny, the games fate likes to play with us.

The air here is heavy with moisture. It sings with the persistent buzz of insects, punctuated by the occasional chirp of a songbird in the branches overhead. Thick foliage grows in a riot across the ground. Lizards rustle through the underbrush as we pick a path along; I watch them scurry away on tiny legs, their tails flicking madly.

I bet we're the first humans they've ever seen.

With no path to follow, our pace is glacial. We pick our way through the dense forest, hands still entwined. I keep my eyes on the ground — sharp-edged palm fronds and rough coral rocks are abundant; one misstep could easily puncture the thin skin of my bare feet. I glance at Beck's boots with a fair amount of envy. He doesn't notice my discomfort as he tugs me along, focused on forging a way through the thicket.

The farther we venture, the more humid the atmosphere becomes. Each breath feels too-thick inside my lungs. It's a far cry from the crisp New England air to which I'm accustomed. When we step into a sun-filtered glade of massive elephant ear plants and I spot the beads of condensation collected like glittering diamonds in their leafy boughs, I drop Beck's hand and rush forward, uncaring whether I tear my feet to shreds in my haste. I'm too desperate to sate my thirst to think about anything else.

Falling to my knees, I fold a leaf larger than my torso into a crude funnel and pour the droplets onto my arid tongue. It's the sweetest thing I've ever tasted. I grab another and slurp it dry, then another and another, until I've lost count. I'm sure I've drunk from every leaf in the glade when I finally cease feeling like a dried out sponge left too long in the sun.

My senses return one by one as I push to my feet. The unique, earthy smell of the rainforest — dirt and decay, greenery and growth. The gorgeous sight of dappled sunbeams all around me, filtering through the thick canopy above my head. The soothing sound of...

Hacking?

My gaze follows the incongruous noise to Beck. He's a few dozen feet away, biceps straining as he slices his way through a thick hanging vine with a tiny utility tool blade. I think he's going to pull a Tarzan and start swinging but when the ropey end falls free, he catches it in one hand and inserts it into the wide mouth of his water bottle, filling it drip by drip. A natural hose.

Smart.

I was so busy sucking down leaf droplets, I didn't even consider there might be an easier water source hanging right overhead.

Sensing my eyes on him, Beck glances my way. He gives a small start, as if caught off guard by something.

My brows lift.

He clears his throat roughly and lifts the slow-filling bottle. "For Ian."

I nod and wipe my damp brow before glancing down at myself. I suck in a breath of mild alarm as I realize the humidity has coated my limbs in a thin sheen of sweat and moisture. My dress clings to my body like a second skin, hugging my chest and hips in a way that leaves little to the imagination. With each labored breath, the white crests of my breasts rise and fall too rapidly to ignore, straining against the confines of my neckline.

The feeling of two green eyes lingering on my exposed skin only makes my heart pound faster — especially when I look up to meet them.

Even from across the glade, he towers over me. We've spent so many hours horizontal in the raft, I'd almost forgotten how tall he is. How powerfully built, even without the benefit of proper sleep or sustenance. How magnetic those eyes can be when they lock on yours, learning your every detail, memorizing your every curve...

We both avert our gazes at the same time.

I cough to break the sudden tension. "We shouldn't leave Ian for much longer."

He grunts in agreement.

"We'll have to drag the raft up to the tree line."

Another grunt.

I stare at the chipping polish on my toes, still afraid to look at him directly. Now that I know what his hand feels like in mine, my fingers itch to twine once more. The desire is unwelcome, but unshakable. My need for human contact burns violently within me. My fingernails cut crescent moons into my palms as I do my best to curtail it.

"It'll be dark in a few hours. We need to find somewhere to spend the night together." My eyes widen as I realize my suggestion, while innocent in intent, has conjured an unexpected question in regard to sleeping arrangements. "I mean we— I didn't mean *together*—" With effort, I bite my lip and put an end to my babbling.

His brows arch in amused speculation.

"Shelter. We need to find *shelter*," I clarify needlessly, feeling blood rush to my cheeks.

He doesn't answer.

With a huff, I turn on one heel and stalk back in the direction of the beach without waiting for him. I'm not sure what I expected — another grunt, perhaps, or a chiding remark. Instead, his tone is full of barely-leashed laughter as he calls after me.

"You're going the wrong way, you know."

My cheeks blaze ever brighter as I pivot a hundred and eighty degrees. I don't look at him as I stomp toward the beach, but I can feel his eyes lingering on me the whole way back.

Ass.

CHAPTER EIGHT

SPARKS

I SPONGE water between Ian's sunburned lips with a wet cloth, supporting his head so fluid doesn't collect in his lungs. Pneumonia is the last thing he needs to deal with, right now. His leg wound has worsened greatly over the last few hours. Angry red streaks of infection stretch from his shattered femur down to his toes. I recognize them.

Sepsis.

Blood poisoning.

Gangrene.

Ugly names for an even uglier reality.

Cut off from blood flow, the tissues in his leg are dying. If there's any chance left at saving the limb, we have no choice but to take action — and soon. I know that. I just wish I felt more confident about actually doing it.

Thankfully Ian is still unconscious; I hope that means he's been spared most of the pain of this ordeal. He looks paler than ever in the shadows of the small shelter we've set up at the edge of the trees. The raft is suspended at an angle several feet above our heads in a makeshift lean-to, one flank resting on the ground, the other tied to the highest branch we could reach on a nearby palm tree. It doesn't offer much in the way of cover, but night will be here soon. Until we can rig up something more permanent, it's better than nothing.

Ian shivers violently despite his proximity to the small fire we built using twigs, coconut husks, and the waterproof matches from our emergency pack. The temperature has dropped several degrees in the past few hours. As the shadows grow, so do my worries about hypothermia and exposure. If my years of hiking and camping have taught me anything, it's that even the warmest summer days can drop off to become the coldest of nights. Especially if you're sunburned, malnourished, injured, or dehydrated.

Not to mention all four at once.

I ignore the goosebumps covering my own chilled skin and focus on Ian. I've already layered both foil blankets over him, along with the sweatshirt from Beck's duffle bag. Still, he shakes and shivers with fever.

"Come on," I murmur, stroking his damp forehead. "Don't give up on me now. Don't leave me alone with *him.*"

My eyes move to the tall male form a few yards away. He's cutting branches from one of the low-hanging palms, working like the devil himself has a whip to his back. He hasn't spoken a word to me since our strange moment in the woods this afternoon, nor have I attempted another conversation. Even as we cleared debris, strung up the raft, and stoked the fire from sparks to a steady flame, we worked in total quiet.

Silence feels safest between us at the moment. I wrap it around me like a protective shield.

Every so often, he returns to dump a fresh load of fronds on the pile beside me. I avoid his eyes as I arrange them into a pallet beneath the lean-to, spreading the plant cuttings flat like a mattress before maneuvering Ian's prone form onto it, one limb at a time. It's not exactly a top of the line TempurPedic, but it should keep the sand out of his wounds and the rain off his face if we're hit with another weather system in the night.

He lets out a small sound of pain, forehead furrowing as another violent spasm shakes his body. Guilt lumps in my throat as I tuck the thin blankets more securely around him, careful not to put pressure on his mangled leg. If he's this cold now, what will happen when the sun goes down? Judging by its ever-sinking position over the water, that will be rather soon.

It's odd — we spent two nights on the raft, shivering in the darkness, dozing on and off as we drifted. I was thirsty, I was cold, I was downright miserable... but, somehow, the prospect of our first night on the island feels infinitely scarier. I wrap my arms around my knees as I sit by the fire, listening to lizards rustling in the trees and wondering what other animals inhabit our new home. Hopefully, nothing with teeth or talons.

Or a taste for human blood.

Then again, the most dangerous predator of all may not be a creature in the forest. My eyes slide over to Beck like a moth drawn to an intoxicating flame. He's walking back to me, the setting sun casting him in silhouette, his powerful arms flexing as he lugs another stack of branches. He sets them down, then sprawls out on the opposite side of our small fire with his shoulders braced against a tree trunk, a groan of fatigue rumbling deep in his chest. His eyes close as his head cranes back, exposing a tanned column of throat and a bobbing Adam's apple.

A few days ago, I would've sworn this man didn't experience emotions... but there they are on his face.

Exhaustion. Hopelessness. Anger. Sorrow. Hunger. Pain. Regret. Fear.

He has been pushed past his breaking point and perseveres regardless. It's hard not to respect him for it. An irrepressible pang of sympathy clangs through my chest as I stare at him.

Reaching into the black bag, I pull out one of our remaining ration packs and toss it in his direction. His eyes open when it lands in his lap.

"Eat something before you expire," I suggest quietly.

He doesn't argue. I notice his fingers shake as he tears open the foil and shoves a helping of trail mix between his lips. My own mouth fills with saliva. I'm so hungry I could cry, but we need to save the rest of our food packets. There are only a handful left.

As the sun slowly sinks toward the water's surface, he savors his small meal. I feel his eyes on my face occasionally, studying me, but I distract myself by rooting through my backpack. There's not much inside — what remains of our sunscreen tubes, a laughably large pack of crayons, a children's coloring book, a small bag of toiletries, two empty soda cans, the coffee-stained outfit I wore in Boston, and my smartphone — now considerably less smart after a thorough dunking in the Pacific. Our first day on the raft, I'd foolishly hoped it might still power on. Even if it hadn't been destroyed in the crash, I doubt there are any cell towers on this deserted island.

I layer the stained button-down blouse over my sleeveless summer dress for extra warmth, then pull the coloring book into my lap. I hold my breath as I flip open the cover. The pages are water stained and wrinkled. They crackle beneath my fingers as I turn to the only page in color. A cheerful squirrel stares back at me, meticulously shaded by a five-year-old who stayed inside the lines better than her babysitter.

Hey, Soph, can you show me how you made your flowers so pretty? Mine don't look half as good...

I flip the book violently closed.

"It's not your fault, you know."

His voice hits me like a shockwave. I glance up to find him staring at the book in my hands.

"What?" I ask, barely audible.

"The little girl. It's not your fault, what happened to her."

I blink hard to keep tears at bay. "I could've tried harder. I should've held on tighter."

"Maybe." He shrugs. "Or... maybe then you'd be dead too."

"It was my job to keep her safe and I failed. I failed her—" The words break off on a half-sob.

"You didn't fail her." He runs a hand though his dark hair, mussing it instantly. "You can't save everyone."

I allow my eyes to move to Ian's gaunt face, the only part of him visible above his thin blanket. As I watch, he spasms again.

"His infection is getting worse," I force myself to say, hardly daring to broach the topic.

"I know."

"We have to do something."

He pauses. "I'm not sure there's anything we *can* do."

My tears win the battle I've been waging; they fill my eyes and spill down my cheeks. "We have an obligation! We can't just watch him die, Beck!"

Ever-guarded, he watches me weep for a few long seconds. When he finally breaks the silence, there's an odd look in his eyes, like he's bracing for the worst.

"How, exactly, would you have me deal with him?"

I breathe deeply, summoning composure. "Tomorrow, once it's light enough to see clearly, that metal shard has to come out and the leg has to be splinted as best we can manage. I thought maybe we could leave it in until help arrived, but now that we're here..." I heave in a breath and brush the tears from my face, trying to remember everything I learned in the mandatory first aid courses I took a few years back, during my sailing instructor certification. "If we can restore blood flow to the leg, we'll have to sterilize the wounds to stop the infection, then suture them closed as best we can. If we can't get blood flowing again..." I shake my head. "No. I don't want to even consider that possibility until we absolutely have to."

Some of the tension eases from his shoulders. Relief flashes across his face. "You want to try to fix him."

"What? Of course." I pause, head tilting as I consider him in the growing darkness. "What did you think I was asking?"

He shakes his head, a dismissal.

"Tell me," I insist.

"I thought..." He blows out a sharp breath. "I thought you were going to ask me to... put him at peace. At *rest*."

My eyes widen. "I hope you don't mean the *eternal* rest."

He pauses, then nods reluctantly.

"What kind of person do you think I am?" I explode in disbelief. "You think I'd ask you to kill a defenseless man?"

"No! Christ. I didn't know *what* you meant!" he growls. "Don't look at me like that."

"How am I looking at you?"

"Like I'm talking about murdering a man in cold blood." His eyes are blank orbs of green, so hard you could bounce quarters off their surfaces. "You can wave around your righteous indignation all you want — it would be *mercy*, not murder, and you know it."

I feel my face go pale. "Why are we even talking about this? It's not happening. *Drop it.*"

"I'm not the one who brought it up."

"Well, I'm not the one who took it to *Lord of the Flies* levels!"

He snorts. "I don't know if I'm more surprised that you can read, or that you're still living in such a state of optimistic delusion, despite our current circumstances."

"Oh, read *this*!" I flip him off with my middle finger.

He smirks without humor. "Cute."

"Why can't you ever just be nice?!"

"Says the girl who just told me to go fuck myself."

"I—" I flush, marginally chastised. "I—"

He holds up his hands. "Spare me the false apology, will you?"

"Gladly," I sneer with every ounce of disdain I can summon.

"Can we go back to not speaking, now? I'd prefer frozen silence to this conversation any day."

"Fine by me, princess."

"Don't call me that!"

"Then stop acting like some valiant prince is going to ride in and rescue you any minute now. This isn't a fairy tale. There is no happy ending here. And I'm sure as hell not your prince."

"You've made that abundantly clear."

"Good."

"Good!"

Fuming with anger, we're both leaning forward into the fire, drawn together by the heat of our argument. I'm so close to the flames, I'm surprised my hair hasn't gone up in smoke. With effort, I settle back against my tree and slow my breathing to a normal tempo. He leans back against his at the same time, slinging one arm across his knee and staring at me with something like amusement. I'd like nothing more than to smack that expression right off his face.

His smug, superior, annoyingly attractive face.

Ugh! How does he manage to get under my skin so quickly?

Turning my back to him, I shove my backpack into a ball and plunk my head down on top of it. It's barely dark outside, but I don't care. If sleep is the only option for escaping his company, I'll gladly close my eyes and surrender. I just hope I don't find myself dreaming of green eyes and lush lips and infuriating sparring sessions that leave me breathless with rage and something else.

Something I'm afraid to look at too closely, even in the dim firelight.

I STIR awake to the sensation of my frigid body being repositioned against the hard-packed earth. The first thing I become aware of is the biting cold. Every inch of exposed skin feels frozen to the bone. Icy winds whip strands of hair across my face. My eyes sliver open to the dark sky overhead. The stars are concealed by a dense cloud-cover, blanketing the world in pitch black. The fire's burned out in the gale. Still half-asleep, a weak sound of discontent slides from my lips as large hands shift me onto my side.

"Shh. It's me." A familiar male voice hits my ears as a body moves closer. "I heard you shivering."

"Beck?"

"Christ, you're colder than a glacier."

"The fire..." I murmur.

"I can't build it any higher. In this wind, there's no way to keep it contained. One spark could send our whole camp up in flames."

Another mewl of discomfort slips out as a gust blows cold sand into my eyes. I close them and duck my head to my chest, curling in on myself for warmth.

"It's so cold," I whisper, teeth chattering.

"I know. I thought..."

He breaks off, clearly torn about something. A second later, a huge, hesitant hand lands on my hipbone. I hear a sharp intake of air from his lips as soon as he makes contact. Half-asleep, I can barely fathom what it means.

Slowly, so slowly I think it might be a fragment of a dream, the hand moves from my hip to my stomach and pulls my body backward. My spine hits a solid wall of muscle and warmth.

Abruptly, I'm very awake.

"...Beck?"

His name is a question and a plea, all rolled into one.

"It will be warmer this way." His voice is rougher than usual. Laced with a new edge I've never heard before. He's so close, I hear him swallow against my ear. I'm sure he can hear my heart beating. "Unless..." He takes a breath. "Unless you'd rather tough it out alone."

I open my eyes again and stare into the dark. I can feel every indentation of his warm chest against my back, every strong plane of his thigh muscles pressed against mine. We fit like we were made to lie together, his larger frame tailor-made to complement to my slighter one.

In his arms I feel that same, strange sensation that commandeered my system the moment he first said my name on the raft, and again later when he laced our hands together on the beach.

Somehow, when he's touching me, all our simmering animosity falls away and what's left behind is...

Something good. Something right. Something real.

"Do you want me to go?" he asks, voice muffled against my hair. I feel his fingers flex on my stomach.

Fighting the urge to snuggle closer to his chest, I ball my hands into fists beneath my chin and breathe deeply in and out. When I speak, I don't even recognize my own voice.

"No. Please... don't go. Don't leave me."

He's eerily still at my back, but when I say that, I feel him relax.

"I'm not going anywhere." His voice is softer than I've ever heard it. "Go back to sleep, princess. We've got a long day ahead of us, tomorrow."

Usually when he says princess, it's laced with sarcasm and derision. An insult, meant to hurt me. Maybe it's because I'm half-asleep, but this time... This time I'd swear it sounds like sunshine as it rasps from his mouth against the thin shell of my ear. Warm and welcome in the chill of the night.

If he says anything else, I don't hear him. I'm already asleep — safe in a set of strong arms.

WHEN I WAKE in the morning, the gale has passed. Pale sunshine basks the world in a warm glow. The fire is blazing merrily. A neat pile of fresh logs and coconut husks are stacked nearby, ready to burn. Sitting beside my backpack I find a ration packet and a soda can, filled to the brim with fresh water.

Someone's been busy this morning.

There's no trace of Beck. No indication he spent the night with his body wrapped around mine, warding off the cold. I'd be damn near sure I dreamed the whole thing, except for a faint indentation in the sand at my back and a strange flutter inside my chest I can't quite rationalize away, no matter how hard I try.

I take slow sips of my water, pretending it's a steaming cup of coffee as I stare out at the ocean. It's truly a spectacular sight. Aqua blue waves crest against the snowy white sand, rhythmic as a lullaby. This beach belongs on the front of a travel magazine or an office calendar. Most people would pay thousands of dollars to wake up to this view.

To me, it's nothing more than limbo. Not quite hell, but certainly not heaven. I'm neither damned nor saved; simply another of those restless souls Dante described, locked in an eternal waiting room. Eyes ever scanning the horizon for an escape route or exit.

It feels somehow wrong to hate a place as gorgeous as this one. To resent something so truly beautiful it makes your breath catch inside your throat and your heart stutter inside your chest. But pretty packaging isn't enough to make me forget I'm not here by choice.

A gilded cage is still a cage.

I finish my water, duck behind some bushes to relieve myself, and strip off my thin button down. In addition to the coffee stain, it now bears several streaks of dirt and grime — as does the rest of my body. I run my fingers through my stiff hair, wishing for a comb or an elastic with which to tame it. Sunburned, salt-streaked, and half-starved, I can only imagine what I look like.

On the other hand, I don't need imagination to know what I *smell* like. My nose twitches as I catch a whiff of myself — caked with sea and sweat and blood and all manner of bodily fluids. It's been a lifetime since the crash, longer since my last shower, an eternity since I've looked in a mirror or brushed my teeth or applied deodorant.

There's a thin layer of gunk growing on my teeth that no amount of swishing with water can remove. I seek out the small bag of toiletries at the bottom of my backpack and dump out the items with excited fingers. There's a travel-sized toothbrush, peppermint paste, several tiny TSA-approved bottles of hair products, a comb, a razor, and even a mini floss dispenser. I feel like a kid on Christmas morning as I squeeze a scant dollop of toothpaste onto the end.

Who knows how long I'll have to make this tube last?

The small act of brushing and flossing brings me more joy than I've felt since we hit the first bump of turbulence three days ago. *Three days.* Can it really only be that long? My whole world has shifted so rapidly in such a short span of time, it's difficult to reconcile in my mind.

With a minty-fresh mouth, neatly combed hair, and a healthy layer of deodorant, I feel like a brand new girl. Later, I'll see about washing my clothes. The thought brings a genuine smile to my face.

Thrilled by the prospect of doing laundry! Mom would never believe it, if she were here.

I brush off the sand clinging to my legs and sweep my eyes across the stretch of dense forest surrounding our camp. There's so much plant life here, I'm certain there's a water source somewhere nearby. A stream, a brook, a waterfall. I'd settle for anything. Hell, even a salty bath in the ocean would be better than another day in this dirty dress. The chiffon blue fabric, which once swished so prettily around my legs, is so sun-bleached and stained I hardly recognize it.

A moan of pain snaps me back into my senses.

Ian.

Shame floods me instantly. I've been so distracted by superficial concerns, so worried about my damn appearance, I've neglected him completely. I curse myself for being so caught up in improving my own quality of life, when there's a man dying a few feet away. As I rush to his side, I'm suddenly happy there are no mirrors here.

I'm not sure I'd like the person I'd see looking back, at the moment.

That girl I used to be — the peppy cheerleader who cared about perfect hair and proper makeup and coordinated outfits — isn't welcome on the island. There's no place for her here. No purpose.

I must shed her like a second skin, shake off the person I once was...

And become someone stronger.

CHAPTER NINE

AGONY

I'M CROUCHED by Ian's side when Beck walks back into our camp. There's no sound, no true indication of his arrival. I sense him like you might a coming storm. The air goes static and I simply know, as every hair on the back of my neck snaps to attention, that he's standing behind me.

I turn in time to see him dump several large coconuts on the ground. He's not looking at me; his eyes are on Ian.

"Good morning," I say haltingly.

His nod is brusque. "Now that you're awake... shall we get this over with?"

I bite down on my lip to keep from snapping at him. "You could've woken me."

"I figured you could use the rest. And—"

"And what?"

His eyes finally flicker up to mine. "I'm in no rush to see how this turns out."

Can't argue with him there.

Heart in my throat, I turn back to our patient as Beck crouches down beside me. He swears colorfully when he catches sight of the leg. I had a similar reaction a few minutes ago, when I pulled off Ian's blankets. The wound is even more inflamed. In addition to the dried blood, there's pus forming at the breaks in his skin. Worst of all, his toes have turned black at the tips from lack of circulation.

Neither of us says anything for a long time. Finally, Beck breaks the silence.

"Violet."

I go still, bracing for whatever he's about to say.

"Look at me," he commands softly.

I glance over, already fighting tears and he hasn't even spoken.

His brow is furrowed as he stares into my face. I get the sense he's weighing his words carefully. "You can't do this."

"Do what?"

"Save the leg. Save... *him*."

A tear trickles out the corner of my eye. "I have to try."

"We don't have the equipment..." He reaches out, as if to touch me, then pulls back at the last instant. "We can't set those bones into place. They're shattered. Even a surgeon might struggle to repair this kind of damage. The leg... it's not salvageable. Do you understand?"

I nod.

He lets out a slow breath. "I'm sorry."

"Why?" I ask, setting my shoulders stubbornly.

He stares at me. "I'm sorry we couldn't save him."

"We are going to save him."

His brow furrows once more, until the scar bisecting his left eyebrow turns white. "Did you not hear a word I said?"

"I heard you. The leg isn't salvageable." I stare him down. "That's why we're going to cut it off."

"The fuck we are," he retorts, looking at me like I've gone mad.

95

Maybe I have.

"You can either help me, or I'll do it myself," I tell him flatly. "But things will go a lot smoother if you help."

"You— this— You can't possibly be serious."

"As a heart attack." I glance around for the supply pack. At the bottom, I find the hunting knife. It's not exactly a Japanese steel chef blade, but it should be sharp enough to get the job done. I walk to the fire and embed it in the hot embers, careful not to singe my fingertips. My eyes scan the ground until I spot Beck's duffle. When I reach it, I lean down and begin digging through the contents without waiting for permission.

"What the hell are you doing?" he snaps, racing to my side and snatching it from my grip.

"The flask. Where is it?"

His eyes narrow. His hands are fisted so tight in the green canvas, his knuckles have gone white. Somewhere in the back of my mind, I recognize this as a fear reaction. He's afraid... of *me*. Of what I plan to do. Perhaps that's what I should be feeling, too — fear. The prospect of cutting off a limb should scare me. Instead, all I feel is grim resolve. It's stolen over my senses, gripped me with unshakeable fingers until I'm filled with nothing except determination to save Ian's life, no matter the cost.

"Beck." I look up at him, imploring. "The flask. Please."

His face is etched with disbelief. "You're serious about this."

I nod.

"You want to cut off a man's leg with nothing more than a Bowie knife and some whisky."

I nod again.

He leans closer. "We have no pain meds. Nothing to keep him from experiencing every excruciating instant of what you're about to put him through. You realize that, don't you?"

My lower lip quivers. I bite down on it until I taste blood and give a terse nod. "I do."

"He may be unconscious now, but I doubt he'll stay that way if we start hacking off his body parts."

My eyes prick with tears. I fight them back. "We have no choice."

"We could let him go!" Beck runs a hand through his hair, exasperation blasting from every molecule of his body. "We could let him die in peace."

"You think he's at peace?" I laugh bitterly. "He's in *pain*, Beck. Besides that leg wound, he's a young, fit, healthy man — he'll take a long time to die, you can count on that. Not just hours of suffering. Days. A week, even." I shake my head. "I can't let him linger in pain. Not when we can do something about it."

He's silent.

"Unless you're still willing to — how did you phrase it?" I sneer. *"Put him to rest."*

At least a minute of total silence passes without either of us speaking a word or breaking eye contact. A staring contest for the ages. His jaw ticks rhythmically, a bomb set to detonate at any second.

"How would you even begin to know what to do?" he mutters finally.

"My mom is a— she's a doctor."

Okay. So, that's technically a lie. But saying *my mommy is a veterinarian* just doesn't carry the same weight.

I hurry on. "She's talked me through more than a few of her surgeries, over the years. Plus, I had basic first aid training as a sailing instructor."

He glances at the sky, as if someone up there is going to offer divine intervention. I think I hear him muttering something about a *damn* sailing instructor who thinks she's a *damn* surgeon under his *damn* breath, but it's pretty hard to make out his low tones.

"Beck."

His eyes return to mine. "Please... Tell me you're kidding."

"I can't."

"God dammit, Violet, you are the most stubborn—"

His words break off abruptly as Ian unleashes a ghastly groan of pain, drawing both our gazes. I watch him writhe on the pallet of palm fronds for a moment, then glance back at Beck. He's already staring at me. Beneath the fear and disbelief in his eyes, I see guilt. And something else.

Acceptance.

Without another word of argument, he reaches into his bag, pulls out the flask, and hands it over. I try to take it from his grip, but his fingers tighten as he leans in to my face. "If we kill him, don't ask me why I didn't try to talk you out of this."

"If we kill him," I snap, yanking the whisky from his grip. "I won't ask you for a damn thing ever again. That's a promise."

WE TALK through the plan three times.

I catch Beck staring at me like I'm crazy on more than one occasion, but I pointedly ignore him. I have bigger things to worry about.

We rub our hands down with whisky to sterilize them, then sponge a few sips of the alcohol down Ian's throat. It's not exactly anesthesia, but I figure it can't hurt if it numbs even a fraction of his pain.

I carefully probe the breaks in his leg. The worst of them is where the metal impales his thigh. By severing the bone, the shard has actually done most of the work for us. Once we pull it out, we should only have to slice through a few layers of ligament and sinew to complete the amputation.

Only.

"Do you want to talk it through one more time?" I ask, pulse pounding.

Beck shakes his head stoically.

"Are you sure?" I'm suddenly flushed with nerves. "I don't know if you have the steps down…"

"Violet."

My wide eyes find his. "Yeah?"

"Breathe."

I pull a deep breath in through my nose and feel some of my panic abate. I was so calm when it came to convincing him to help. Now that he's on board, our roles have reversed. He's remarkably in control; I'm the one spinning out.

"Hey." Beck's big hand lands on my shoulder. "You are not alone. I'm here with you. You got it?"

"Got it," I agree. "But maybe we should sterilize our hands again—"

"They're as clean as they're going to get."

"Right." I steady my shoulders. "You're right. It's time." I glance at him. "You'll hold him steady?"

Beck nods.

"He… he's probably going to wake, and he's probably going to scream." I suck in a breath. "A lot."

"I have the stick for him to bite down on, if necessary."

"It'll be necessary," I mutter grimly.

Reaching out, I check that the tourniquet is still tight, then wrap my hands around the jagged piece of metal protruding from Ian's thigh. When my grip is secure, I look up into Beck's eyes.

"On three."

He nods, adjusting his hold on Ian's shoulders in case he suddenly begins to thrash.

"One… two…. three!"

With one swift motion, I pull straight up on the shard. It slides cleanly from the wound like pulling a stake from the grass after a game of horseshoes. There's less resistance than I thought there'd be, but I don't dwell on that as I cast the jagged debris aside. I'm focused on the blood pouring from the gaping hole I've just created.

Blessedly, the tourniquet holds, preventing him from bleeding out completely. There's still plenty of trauma to contend with. When I see the mangled remains of his severed femur bone, I have to duck my mouth and nose into my elbow, afraid I'll be sick. Thankfully, there's nothing in my stomach to expel.

Ian thrashes in his sleep, his cries of pain louder than ever. Beck's biceps strain as he pins the man against the ground.

"Hold him!"

"Doing my best, princess!"

I grab the sterilized knife from its place by the fire and set about my grim task. I wish I could close my eyes to shut out the sight of my hands sawing through flesh. I wish I could erase the images burned into my mind in those bloody, horrid instants as Ian flails and shrieks for mercy from the pain I'm inflicting on him.

There's hardly anything but skin holding his leg to his body. After a few swift slices, the dead limb falls away. It lands on the sand with a sickening thump and rolls toward the beach. For a few long seconds, I simply stare at it, hardly comprehending what I've just done, unable to rally myself to the remaining task. Continuing seems too awful to contemplate.

It's Beck, who brings me back.

"Violet. Violet! Look at me. Look into my eyes."

My gaze finds his. I focus on his words, instead of Ian's feverish moans of pain.

"It's almost done," Beck tells me, jaw clenching so hard I'm surprised his teeth don't snap. "Just a little more."

"I don't…" I glance down at my hands, slicked to the wrists in blood and gore. The sight of the knife in them makes my stomach turn over. "I don't know if I can…"

"No. You don't get to quit on me now," he hisses, tone ringing with authority. "You will do this because there's no other choice. You will do this because, if you don't, he's going to die." His voice drops an octave. "*Ian* will die. And then, it'll just be the two of us on this godforsaken island, and we both know how much you'd hate that."

I'm so startled by his joke, I nearly let a laugh slip out before I catch myself. It's the most inappropriate thing in the world to be laughing, right now... but I feel unquestionably lighter as his words roll around my mind like marbles, sweeping away the fear. Reassuring me of my purpose. Jolting me back into action.

When I was little, Dad would talk about his time in the war sometimes. He always said the same thing.

You don't stop in the middle of a charge. Even if things get hairy, even if the bullets are raining down, you don't duck for cover before you've reached the trenches. You keep going. You fight. Do you hear me? Never stop fighting, Violet. Nothing in this world worth having comes without some sort of struggle.

My mouth opens and shuts, a shaky exhale slipping out. Without a word, I place the knife back into the smoldering embers of the fire and wait until the tip begins to glow red-hot. When it's ready, my hand wraps around the handle as I look into Beck's eyes. His strong fingers are gripping the ends of the shoelace tourniquet, prepared to undo it on my signal.

"Do it," I whisper.

He yanks the knot until it falls away. A fresh spurt of blood pours from the stump of Ian's thigh, but my hands are already in motion. I grip the knife as tight as I can and press the flat part of the blade across the gaping wound to cauterize the bleeding. There's an unpleasant searing sound reminiscent of steak on a barbecue, but it's quickly drowned out by Ian's screams as he comes fully awake for the first time.

"I'm sorry!" I wail, holding the knife as still as possible. It's only wide enough to cover a portion of his wound. The smell of charred meat hits my nose and I fight off a retch. "I'm so sorry, Ian!"

His screams echo louder. A startled flock of birds bursts from a nearby treetop. He thrashes so violently I nearly drop the knife into the sand.

"You have to hold him still!"

"Doing… my… best!" Beck hisses, laboring from the effort.

Ian may be weak from fever and at least five inches shorter than Beck, but he's putting up an impressive fight. I force myself to hold the knife in place until I'm sure the top half of the wound is completely closed. Returning it to the flames for a few endless moments, I wait until the blade is red-hot once more before I move it down to the bottom portion of his thigh, where the remaining bleeders are still gushing forth in a deadly flood. There's another horrid hiss as I press down hard, singing the rest of the wound shut.

I keep my hand steady as Beck holds Ian to the ground, counting the seconds until it's over. But I know, deep down, it'll never truly be over. Never expunged from my mind or memories. As long as I live, I'll never forget the sound of his agonized screams ringing in my ears.

Eventually, Ian passes out from the pain, for which I'm eternally grateful. It makes it easier to keep the blade in place, those final seconds.

And then, somehow… it's done.

Finished.

I let the knife drop to the sand and stare at the seared stump where Ian's leg used to be. It's red and blistered, uneven and ugly to look at… but it's closed. It's clean of dirt and infection. The bleeding has stopped. Most miraculous of all, the man attached to it is still breathing.

I can't believe I just did that.

I can't believe it worked.

I wrap a clean piece of gauze around the wound, leaving crimson prints on the white fabric as my fingers tie it off, then position a log beneath his thigh to keep it elevated. My hands are stained scarlet. There's a mosaic of blood spattered down the front of my dress.

"Violet..."

I glance up at Beck, where he sits by Ian's shoulders. He looks pale and thoroughly shaken by what he's just seen. *By what I just did.* He's staring at me like he doesn't even recognize me.

Hell, I hardly recognize myself.

I don't speak to him as I stagger to my feet and flee from our small camp down the beach to the water's edge. There, ankle-deep in the shallows, I bend at the waist and dry heave until every ounce of water and bile has vacated my stomach. Until my throat is burning, my eyes are streaming, and my head is pounding.

The physical pain I feel is a flicker next to what I've just put Ian through. And it's nothing at all, compared to the ache in my heart as I stare at my bloody hands and wonder what the hell I've done.

Who the hell I've become.

BECK GIVES me space for a few hours.

I sit at the water's edge, staring out at the waves, mind still ringing with the sound of Ian's screams. The expanse of water seems to stretch out endlessly in all directions. I'm farther from home than I've ever been, not just in distance. I wonder, if a rescue boat appeared on that far-reaching horizon, plucked me from this nightmare, and landed me back in my childhood bedroom, whether I'd even fit there anymore

I've always heard that phrase *you can't go home again* and dismissed it outright. But sitting here, I think I finally understand. The things I've lived through in the span of a few short days have changed me forever. The people I've lost have shaken my ever-optimistic view of the world around me. And... the man still with me, standing at my side through all of this, has left an impression I fear I'll never be able to wipe clean.

Three days.

What will happen in three weeks? Three months? Three years?

I press my palms to my eye sockets, wishing I could summon tears. Crying might release some of these emotions raging inside my head. Might make this burden of horror and heartache inside my chest slightly easier to carry around.

It's mid-afternoon and the shadows have begun to lengthen when I finally feel his presence at my back. I glance over my shoulder and find him sitting in the sand a few feet away, careful not to encroach on my personal space. His eyes scan my face.

He's as guarded as he's ever been, but I've learned to read him better — the tiny furrow of his brow when he's concerned, the slight clenching of his jaw when he's trying to keep himself in check, the infinitesimal narrowing of his eyes when he's overcome with rage. The way his left brow quirks up when he's surprised, and his lips twist at one side when he's fighting back amusement.

Beck's face speaks a whole language, if you take the time to learn it.

"You're red as a beet," he says finally, breaking the silence.

I glance down at my arms. Sure enough, they're sunburned.

"I'll live."

His brows lift at the apathy in my tone. "What you did earlier..."

"I know." I cut him off. "It was awful. Reckless. Bloody and messy and worse than I could've ever imagined. *I know.* You don't have to lecture me."

There's a marked pause. "If you're finished beating yourself up... that wasn't what I was going to say at all."

My heart skips. "It... it wasn't?"

"No. I was going to tell you that, bloody and messy and awful as it was... it was also the bravest thing I've ever seen anyone do in the thirty years I've been on this planet. And I spent three years in the deserts of Afghanistan and Iraq, taking photos of war zones."

Suddenly, there are tears in my eyes. I don't fight them. I let them roll down my cheeks as his words roll around inside my aching chest cavity. There's something almost unbearable about Beck — gruff, grumpy, curmudgeonly Beck — speaking to me with kindness that shatters the last shred of resolve I've been clinging to since I washed the worst of the blood stains from my skin.

This is a man who does not do false praise or fake ego-stroking. He doesn't do flattery. He barely does basic human decency.

The bravest thing I've ever seen.

I recognize these words as a rare gift and feel some warmth creep back into my soul.

Beck watches me weep from a careful distance, his discomfort evident. "I didn't mean to upset you."

"You didn't. I just... I..."

A sob steals my breath. I dash the teardrops from my cheeks, but they continue to fall. I feel completely overwhelmed as all the emotions I forced from my mind while I tended to Ian rush back.

Scooting a bit closer on the sand, Beck reaches out tentatively and pats my hand, as though he's not quite sure whether touching me will make things better or worse. I get the sense he's afraid to make any sudden moves. That comforting a crying girl isn't something in his everyday repertoire.

I look at his large hand covering mine. The stroke of his strong fingers against my skin is lighter than a feather, but I feel it in every atom of my body. Our eyes meet, green on green, and something inside me snaps.

I don't consider my actions. I don't talk myself out of it. I don't give him any warning at all.

In a blur of limbs, I launch myself against his chest and bury my head in the hollow of his shoulder, my whole body convulsing with the strength of my sobs. My arms wind around his neck, my torso aligns with his, my hair splays out in a mahogany curtain.

I don't care that, up until this moment, I'd have considered him the last man on earth I'd ever go to for comfort. He's here, and he's warm, and right now, just for a second, I need someone to put their arms around me and keep me from flying apart into a million pieces.

He goes still, at first, but then... his hands wind their way around me in an embrace, his chin settles against the top of my head, and he holds me so tight, I feel my soul begin to stitch back together.

"You're not alone," he whispers when my tears begin to subside from sobs to sniffles. "And Ian..."

I pull back to look into his eyes, not daring to ask.

"His fever broke a half hour ago."

CHAPTER TEN

HOPE

IAN'S PALLOR changes so quickly, I think my eyes are deceiving me. He's still not awake, but his color is vastly improved. The pale, clammy sheen of fever has faded from his face and, while his breaths are still labored from the pain of his injuries, for the first time since the crash I don't find myself listening intently to his every wheeze, half-convinced the next one might not come at all.

I spend the remainder of the afternoon by his side, watching him sleep, sponging water and whisky between his dry lips in small increments, and checking his pulse. It's definitely stronger than it was yesterday. Another good sign.

Up till now, his health has been our main source of anxiety, as well as the focus of almost all our attention. Now that his condition seems to be improving, there are other things to attend to if we're going to survive here until someone finds us.

Or whatever's left of us.

That starts with food, shelter, and water. Basic needs, but undeniable ones.

The scary reality is, our rations have all but run out. The coconuts Beck collected from beneath the trees were a vast disappointment — we managed to bash them open against the sharp coral rocks only to find dry, inedible pulp inside. The fresh green ones remain far out of reach at the top of the palm trees, and no amount of trunk shaking seems adequate to knock them loose.

My stomach rumbles frequently as I move around the camp, clearing rocks and plant debris from the sand. I long for a rake or a broom to speed up the process. It's shocking, the tools you take for granted when you grow up in the most consumer-friendly country in the world. I can recall very few times in my childhood when I needed something and it wasn't already on hand. If I required an item we didn't own, the absolute worst case scenario was a quick drive to the local superstore. Or, if things were *really* dire, a few clicks on a web browser and free two-day delivery, straight to my doorstep.

Nothing was out of reach. The whole world was at my disposal.

I didn't realize how easy I had it, until I was ripped violently from that reality. How pampered and soft we humans have become, far removed from the struggles our distant ancestors faced in simpler times, before WiFi or medicine or machines. Before microwaves or lighter fluid or flashlights. Before drive-thru meals, ready to eat in five minutes or less. Before shopping malls stocked with every item imaginable.

I grew up in a world of instant gratification, member of a generation that grows impatient when our internet browsers buffer too slowly to stream the latest binge-worthy show. Here, nothing is instant or easy. There are no shortcuts, no superficial struggles. The island has stripped it all away, cut out the gratuitous like a knife paring down an apple until only the core remains.

Food. Shelter. Water.

Breathe. Sleep. Survive.

I've begun to experience bouts of lightheadedness whenever I move too fast. Taking slow sips of water, I tell myself it's an ice cream frappe from my favorite restaurant back home. Thick and creamy and cold.

This would be more convincing if I wasn't sweating so profusely in the intense heat.

Unwilling to stray too far from Ian's side, I replenish our wood stores to keep the fire burning and sort our belongings into some semblance of order. I try not to look too closely at the disturbed patch of earth beneath a nearby palm, where Beck buried the leg.

When the tide goes out, I wander down to the exposed shallow pools at the edge of our cove, marveling at the sight of the tiny ecosystems contained within their rocky limits. Barnacles and mussels stick up like spikes. Crabs bury their bodies beneath the sand, until only their eyes are exposed. Tiny minnows dart in and out of swaying fan coral.

It's a whole world in miniature.

I contemplate borrowing Ian's shoes so I can walk out onto the barrier rocks around the bend of the beach, but it feels wrong to take them without his permission. I'll have to think of something, though, because after all this time barefoot, my heels are cracked and aching. They sting a little more with each step across the hot sand.

Every so often, I glance down the stretch of beach to where Beck works. He's shirtless, skin turning bronze beneath the beating sun. My mouth goes dry, watching the muscles in his back ripple as he drags another heavy log to form the final section of a giant *H*. The letter is at least a dozen feet high. Without an axe or saw, it'll take several more days of scouring the forest for fallen branches to complete the corresponding *E-L-P*. I can see exhaustion gripping his every muscle as he works, but he assures me the effort is worth it in the off chance a plane flies overhead and spots our distress signal.

He doesn't stop until it's nearly dark. When he walks back into our camp, he looks around in surprise at the changes I've made in his absence. In addition to widening the perimeter and clearing away more brush, I've woven palm-fronds into proper sleeping pallets and placed them on either side of the fire. There's a rain-collector strung between two trees, made with spare rope from the raft and one of the thin foil blankets. Next time a storm passes, we'll be ready.

I sit by Ian's side, using the knife, my dental floss, and a needle from the suture kit to hem the black pants from my backpack into a pair of shorts. I've cut the remnants into thin fabric strips — one holds my hair back in a high ponytail, the rest will be used as bandages when we inevitably run out of gauze.

I think Beck might fall over when he spots the bed of fresh mussels cooking slowly in the hot coals of the fire. Nearly done, they've begun to pop open and emanate a mouth-watering odor. My stomach growls at the prospect of a warm meal for the first time in days.

"Honey, I'm home," he murmurs, as though he's walked in on a 1950s housewife with dinner waiting on the table.

I laugh — actually *laugh*. I didn't think I'd ever feel joy again, but there it is. At the sound, Beck's face morphs into a softer version of his typical scowl. If I didn't know better, I'd say he's actually trying not to smile.

"Sorry it's not a meatloaf and mashed potatoes." I shrug. "It was the best I could do, under the circumstances."

"It's..." His Adam's apple bobs. "It's absolutely perfect."

I avert my eyes back to the fabric in my hands. It's safer staring at a needle than his bare chest and bronzed skin. "They should be ready soon. Just a few more minutes."

With a tired exhale, he collapses on the pallet beside mine. I can feel his eyes on me, watching as I cut clean strips of fabric, then fold them on my growing pile. The longer the silence lingers, the harder it is to breathe.

Since we first met, the dynamic between us has altered from animosity to grudging alliance to... something indefinable. I don't dare put a name to it, but I can feel it thrumming in the air between us.

Tension.

Like it or not, things are different now. We've invaded each other's space. Slept side by side, a tangle of limbs. He's seen my tears, absorbed my shivers, heard my sobs, held me close in a moment of weakness. He brought me back, when I feared I'd lost who I was.

Yet... we skipped all the small getting-to-know you stages of friendship. We plunged face first into the deep and, after all we've been through, I don't know how to return to the shallows. How to talk about small, inconsequential things that near-strangers discuss when the silence stretches on too long. I don't know how to ask where he grew up or if he has any pets or whether there's someone waiting for him back home, staring at his picture in a frame with swollen red eyes, praying for a miracle.

I'm surprised how much I dislike that last thought.

"How's he doing?" Beck asks abruptly.

I look at over Ian, still sleeping soundly. "He hasn't woken up, but he's holding steady for now. His pulse is stronger, his fever is down. I'm really hopeful." My face contorts as I add, "But you probably think that's foolish... Me, holding out hope that he'll beat the odds and make a miraculous recovery."

What was it he said before?

You're living in a state of optimistic delusion.

There's a heavy pause. "Quite the opposite, actually. I think having hope is one of the most important things you can do. Once you let go of it, despair takes over. Despair will kill you quicker than hope ever could. So if you're going to hold onto something... I'm glad it's that."

I look up into his eyes and watch reflected flames of the fire dance across his irises. Sitting here with him, it's never been clearer to me that while we may've skipped over that normal phase of simplicity and smalltalk, I'd still very much like to know this man.

How he thinks.

What he feels.

The things that make him tick.

The things that turn him on.

I shove the thoughts to the back of my mind.

"We should eat." Setting down my sewing project, I lean over the coals and examine the mussels. Nestled atop a thin layer of seaweed, they're finally fully open and ready for consumption. I locate the two flat pieces of bark I've been using as serving spoons and scoop them into halved coconut-shell bowls. When I pass a helping to Beck, his brows are so far up his forehead they're about to disappear into his hairline.

"What?" I demand suspiciously. "If you're going to complain about eating with your fingers, save it. I didn't have time to make utensils today. This was the best I could do on a deadline. Maybe if I'd had more time—"

"Violet." He cuts me off, lips twitching as he accepts the bowl.

"Yeah?"

"The only thing I have to say right now is *thank you.*"

"Oh." My cheeks flame. "Well. Whatever. It's just a few mussels. No big deal."

"I don't just mean for dinner." His throat muscles convulse. "Thank you for making a place that could be pure hell feel a bit like... home."

With that, he dives into his dinner. I sit stock-still, processing those words, but after a moment the smell of the mussels hits my nose, my stomach makes its impatience well known, and I dig in. There are no spices or seasonings, no butter or garlic, no slices of toasted bread to eat them with, like Mom and I used to back home in the summertime...

Still, I swear it's the best dinner I've ever had.

We feast like kings, until our stomachs are near to bursting and the sun has dipped below the horizon. Appetite sated for the first time in days, I slump back on my pallet with my elbows braced behind me and stare up at the night sky. I can't pick out a single constellation in the blanket of brilliant stars. The unfamiliar celestial map only adds to the sensation that I've somehow washed ashore on a whole new planet, rather than a new hemisphere.

I hear the metallic sound of a cap twisting and look over in time to see Beck take a swig of whisky. Feeling my attention on his face, he extends the flask in my direction. I'm pulled instantly back to another moment in the dark, on a private plane flying through a turbulent storm, when the same stranger offered me a swallow to settle my nerves.

I turned him down flat, then.

This time, I don't hesitate as I clasp my fingers around the smooth metal of the flask and lift it to my lips. The alcohol burns a fiery path down my throat, then pools in my stomach like a warm cup of tea. Heat sinks into my bones, radiating from the inside out. It's my first sip of whisky, and I enjoy it far more than I ever would've anticipated. I badly want to take another sip, but as I test the half-empty flask's weight in my hands, I know we need to ration the rest for Ian. When he regains consciousness, he'll need it far more than I do.

With a regretful sigh, I pass it back to Beck before I can change my mind. "Thanks."

His eyes move over my face, as though I'm a puzzle he's struggling to work out. "You know, you're incredibly responsible, for..." He trails off.

"For what? A girl?"

He pauses. "No. I was going to say for someone so young."

"Oh." I blush. "Well, I'm not *that* young."

"How old are you?" The softness of the question does nothing to detract from the intensity with which its asked.

"Younger than thirty, you old geezer," I joke.

He doesn't laugh or smile. He's curiously still, his gaze searching. "You don't want to tell me."

"Don't be ridiculous." I snort, avoiding his stare. "I just don't see what the big deal is. Age is only a number, right?"

"And that number would be…?"

I bite my lip.

"Twenty-three?" he guesses lowly.

I shake my head.

"Twenty-two?"

Another shake.

I hear a sharp intake of air. "Christ, if you tell me you're not even legal to drink…"

My eyes lift to his. "We're stranded on an island. I don't think the legal drinking age applies. Plus, we're not even in the US anymore, so technically—"

"Violet."

My excuses dissipate when he says my name. "Yeah?"

"Just tell me."

My teeth gnash into my lip so hard, I'm surprised I don't draw blood. Bracing myself for the worst, I close my eyes and force out the words. "I'm seventeen."

There's a momentary silence. I think, perhaps, he's going to react better than I'd expected. Instead, when my eyes sliver open and lock on his face, I see the same strangled expression he wore when I informed him we'd be amputating Ian's leg.

"Seventeen," he says slowly, sounding out each vowel like he's speaking a foreign language. "You're joking."

Wincing, I shake my head. "Afraid not."

Beck is typically the epitome of self-restraint. So I'm totally unprepared when he vaults to his feet in one seamless motion and begins to pace in front of the fire. His long strides eat up the sand, lapping the whole camp in a matter of seconds.

"Seventeen!" he explodes. "How the *fuck* can you be seventeen?"

"Well… last year I was sixteen… and next year I'll be eighteen… I think that's just how this whole aging thing works," I muse, attempting to lighten the mood.

His glare tells me there will be no such lightening. "Why were you even on that goddamned plane?"

"The Flints needed an au pair for the summer."

"So they hired a child to watch their child? In what world does that make sense?"

My chin jerks higher. "It's really none of your concern at all. My age has nothing to do with you."

"Seeing as we're stuck here together, I'd say every damn thing about you is my concern."

Ugh!

"Well, *I'd* say you're being an ass," I contribute. "But, at this point, I'm starting to realize it's not a temporary state. You're not *being* an ass. You *are* an ass. Always. Constantly. All the time."

He offers no response except a low, predatory growl, still pacing back and forth.

"I don't see what the big deal is," I mutter somewhat sourly as I watch him. "This doesn't change anything—"

"It doesn't change anything?" he scoffs. "It changes *everything*. You— you're a fucking child, for god's sake!"

"I'm not a child."

"Spoken like every teenage girl ever." His laugh is bitter. He runs his hands through his hair, fisting it in angry clumps. "God, what are you, a junior in high school?"

"I'll be in college in the fall." The blood drains from my face. "Or… I would've been."

He stops pacing. His gaze cuts to mine across the fire, and I swear there's more heat in his glare than there is coming from the actual flames two feet away.

"Fuck, Violet," he rasps, sending shivers down my spine.

Fuck, indeed.

"Why are you so pissed?" I ask, narrowing my eyes and ignoring my thundering heartbeat.

"You should've told me."

"You didn't tell me how old *you* were until this afternoon!"

"That's different," he grumbles.

"Spoken like every hypocritical adult ever," I toss back, just to goad him. I rise to my feet, my temper rising along with me. "Tell me why it bothers you so much."

His jaw is ticking. "It doesn't."

My eyes dart down to his hands, curled into tight fists at his sides. "This is you, *unbothered*," I say slowly.

He doesn't respond.

I take a few steps around the fire, closer to him, and he backpedals away like I've contracted the Black Plague. "If it doesn't matter, why can't you look at me?"

He forces his eyes to mine, just to prove a point.

We stare at each other in the firelight as the air thrums with unspoken thoughts. He might not be able to admit it, but we both know exactly why my age is so abhorrent to him.

This tension between us is suddenly laced with a newfound taboo.

I have no explanation for the move I make next. I'd say I'm emboldened by the whisky in my system, but I haven't had nearly enough to use alcohol as a scapegoat. There's no excuse at all for the way I walk toward him, limbs feeling loose, eyes locked on his mouth, lips tingling as I wonder what they would feel like pressed against his.

"Stop," he mutters, rooted in place. Watching me approach like you might watch a venomous rattlesnake slithering your direction. His jaw is ticking again.

"What is it about me being seventeen that's got you so tangled up inside, Beck?" I whisper, sidling ever closer. "Enlighten me."

"Violet, I mean it."

I take another step. I'm officially invading his space. About to cross a line there's no coming back from.

"Beck," I say quietly, trembling with emotions I can barely define. "I want an answer."

"While you're at it," a smooth, southern accent interjects. "I'd like a few answers myself."

Beck and I both whip our heads around toward the voice, identical expressions of surprise on our faces as we stare at the blond man on the pallet by our feet. He's staring back at us, eyes half-slitted with pain and confusion.

Ian is awake.

CHAPTER ELEVEN

ACHE

WE DO our best to explain things to Ian. He reacts about as well as can be expected — which is to say, with a fair amount of shock and disbelief as he stares down at the stump where his leg used to reside. He's equally shocked that so many days have passed since the plane went down. He remembers very little of the actual crash, likely a byproduct of hitting his head in the moments before we struck the water. He has no recollection at all of our time on the emergency raft. The surgery we performed during the height of his fever is a jumble of painful flashes in his mind.

That's probably for the best, if you ask me.

"I suppose I should be thanking you for saving my life," he says after a long moment of silent reflection. "But, if I'm being honest, there's a part of me that would like to kick your ass."

"Ian I—" I start to apologize.

"Unfortunately," he carries on. "I don't think I'll be doing much kicking again anytime soon, seeing as you've chopped off my damn leg."

A startled laugh bursts from my throat before I can stop it. Despite the not-inconsiderable pain he must be experiencing, I can see a mischievous light shining from his light blue eyes. A dimple hints at the corner of his mouth.

"I'm glad your sense of humor is undamaged." Smiling, I brush a few strands of hair from his eyes, then lift Beck's water bottle toward his dry lips. "Now, please drink some water. You're dehydrated. Tomorrow, if you're feeling up to it, we'll try a bit of food."

"Fine." Ian sighs. "But first, in your expert opinion, I must know..."

My brows lift.

"Do you think when we get back home, I'll be able to spin the amputation story to my advantage with the ladies? I mean, being a plane crash survivor is badass enough, but surgery on a deserted island, without any anesthetic... I'm pretty sure I'll be a legend." His dimples pop out. "Really gives me a *leg* up in the dating scene, don't you think?"

Beck snorts behind me.

"Did you..." I blink, stunned. "Did you just make an amputee joke?"

"It was more of a pun, really." Ian yawns and his dry lips crack with dehydration. "Not my best material."

"I'm not sure whether I should be impressed or concerned that you're taking this news in such stride," I murmur.

"In *stride*? Really?" Ian laughs weakly. "Now who's punning, funny girl?"

My cheeks heat as I realize my unintentional blunder. "Oh, god! I didn't mean— That came out totally wrong. Ian, I didn't—"

"We've really gotten off on the wrong foot, haven't we?" he asks, eyes twinkling.

The wrong foot!

"You're incorrigible," I tell him, blushing profusely.

He and Beck both chuckle, equally amused by my discomfort.

"Don't fret," Ian murmurs. "I'm only pulling your leg."

I set my features in a stern expression, but can't quite hide my smile. "Just drink your damn water."

He takes a few sips from the bottle. I urge him to go slow, but he's undeniably thirsty after days without a proper drink. In his weakened state, taking even one sip too fast can send water into his lungs — a fact which becomes apparent when he begins to cough violently.

Grin falling off my face, I watch helplessly as he wheezes for almost a full minute, choking on the trapped fluid in his airway. When he gets his breathing back under control, he attempts a reassuring smile, but I can see how exhausted the coughing spell has left him. These few short moments of consciousness have etched the pallor of exhaustion back over his features.

"You need your rest." I twist the cap back on the water bottle and set it aside. "We'll talk more in the morning."

He nods weakly, eyelids fluttering closed.

"If you need anything, just call out," I tell him, adjusting the blankets more firmly around his body. "I'm a light sleeper."

"Goodnight, darlin'," he drawls in that adorable accent, half-gone already.

"Goodnight, Ian."

He falls asleep a few seconds later. The camp is strangely silent without his cheerful tones. I can feel Beck hovering behind me in the dark, waiting for me to break the silence. I pointedly ignore him as I make my way over to my sleeping pallet.

I can't look at him. I won't.

It's far too dangerous.

Staring up at the stars, I hear him settle in on his own pallet across the fire. He sighs and shifts every few moments, evidently as restless as I am. The phrase *out of sight, out of mind* does not apply when it comes to us. I can't see him, but he's all I can think about.

My earlier words replay in my head on an unending loop.

What is it about me being seventeen that's got you so tangled up inside, Beck?

I torture myself for hours, speculating what would've happened between us if Ian hadn't interrupted at the last moment. I'm still wide awake when the temperature drops and the breeze off the water sweeps through our camp, cold enough to give me goosebumps. Light rain begins to fall and I shiver silently in the dark, trying not to remember how much warmer it was to sleep in the curve of Beck's body, sharing his heat.

He tosses and turns again, clearly uncomfortable. I can't help wondering if his thoughts are aligned with mine.

If they are, he doesn't act on them.

Neither do I.

We shake in the dark on our separate pallets, looking up at the same night sky from opposite sides of a hissing fire. Bound together by invisible strings. Without a single spoken word or stolen glance, I can feel him like an extension of my own body.

I don't see what the big deal is, I hear myself telling him. *This doesn't change anything.*

His sharp scoff still echoes off the walls of my whirling mind.

It changes everything, Violet.

THE FOLLOWING DAYS pass in a blur of activity. If not for the small notches I've started making in the beached driftwood tree trunk at the end of each day, I'd have no concept of how much time has passed since we first arrived on the island. Ian's newfound presence in our camp is a welcome distraction from the strange intensity brewing between Beck and me. I spend my days tending to him in the ever-lengthening periods when he's able to stay awake, monitoring his temperature and checking his wounds. The stump seems to be healing well enough, all things considered. It's swollen and red, but I don't see any signs of sepsis creeping back.

It's beyond frustrating to know that there are probably many plants with medicinal properties in the forest all around us. On our many camping trips back home, Mom used to point out different herbs and trees as we'd walk through the mountains, noting their homeopathic uses with reverence. She had great respect mother nature's natural remedies, and healthy skepticism for big pharmaceutical companies' exorbitantly-priced, mass-produced pills.

Nature provides, she used to say, smiling. *We've just forgotten how to use the things she offers.*

If we were in New Hampshire, it would be as simple as finding a willow tree — making a boiled tea from its bark to reduce his fever, a salve to lessen inflammation. I could use White Pine to treat a cold. Birch for an upset stomach. Comfrey for burns and bruises. Witch hazel as an antiseptic.

I could actually *help*, instead of sitting on my hands, praying for a miracle.

But here, the plants are as foreign to me as their uses. I have no way of differentiating those which would heal from those that would do more harm. So, I sit on my hands. I watch and wait as Ian's broken body attempts to put itself back together unaided.

He must be in an unfathomable amount of pain, but he never complains. His short bursts of lucidity are peppered with inappropriate jokes and personal anecdotes. Over the course of our first three days together, I learn more about him than I have about Beck in triple that time — his childhood growing up in Oklahoma, the hometown honey who broke his heart two days after high school graduation, and the flight attendant program he applied for two days after *that*, lured by the promise of exotic locations and far-flung destinations.

"It started as a way to escape," he confides as I wipe his forehead with a wet cloth. "When you get your heart broken in a small town, there's no outrunning the gossip."

"So you picked a career that would take you as far from home as humanly possible?"

"Pretty much." He blows a puff of air from his hollow cheeks, gaunt from lack of proper nourishment. He still can't manage any food without choking. "I thought I'd do it for a few months, see the sights, then go back for my degree. I didn't expect to love it so much. But the people were nice, the pay was great, and the places I've been... *amazing*." He glances around the island. "Then again, I certainly didn't expect I'd end up here when I lit out of town like a firecracker."

"Trust me, I know the feeling."

His brows lift.

"The need to get out," I clarify. "To escape a small town where everyone knows everyone, where the future seems as set in stone as the past. It can be..."

"Suffocating," Ian finishes.

"Exactly."

I'm surprised by how much we have in common. At twenty-two, he's far closer to me in age than the third member of our trio. There's also the matter of his cheerful disposition and — it must be noted — those charming dimples that flash at me every time I say something even the slightest bit amusing. He never scowls or sneers or mocks me. In his company, I don't feel like I can't catch my breath because the air between us is made of sparks and sexual tension. I don't struggle to control my emotions, or keep myself in check. I don't worry my heart is going to burst from the confines of my chest and leap into his hands if we get too close.

He's the anti-Beck. The cure for a poison that's been slowly killing me.

But if dying is what I've been doing...
Why have I never felt so alive?

"So, what were you running from?" Ian asks, pulling me out of my head. "Or, more importantly, who were you running from?"

"Myself, mostly. The girl I didn't want to be anymore; the woman I didn't want to become. I knew if I stayed in that little town, I'd wind up stuck there for the rest of my life."

"Hence the summer in paradise."

I nod slowly. "I thought, at the very least, I'd see something different. Something exciting, before flying back home and starting classes at the same community college half the kids from my high school attend." I'm so immersed in my own story, I don't hear the muffled footfalls approaching from the beach behind me. "I have this crystal clear memory of my graduation — you know that moment, when you stand on the stage and shake the principal's hand and flip your tassel from one side to the other while the whole crowd claps?"

Ian nods.

"That moment, looking out at everyone I'd ever met cheering my name... I realized I was also looking out at everyone I ever *would* meet. Ever. That moment, on that stage, was *it* for me. The apex of my hero's journey; the climax of my entire life. I'd never do anything more exceptional than cross a stage in a red polyester gown to accept a piece of paper. When I realized that... something inside me snapped." I suck in a sharp breath, lost in the memories, not realizing I've captivated an audience of more than just Ian. "I could see it all laid bare before me, my entire existence stretching out like a jaw-cracking yawn: a timely proposal from my high school boyfriend, Clint, before the ink on our diplomas was dry. Barefoot and pregnant exactly three months after the country-chic wedding I'd plan to perfection with the help of my new mother-in-law, in a backyard barn with a hundred and fifty guests I'd known since birth. Lavender bridesmaid dresses and peony-pink centerpieces. Three pretty babies, with my dark hair and his blue eyes. Poop-filled diapers and high-pitched giggles that would make me laugh, and smile, and occasionally disappear into my room to cry alone after tucking them into bed, weeping into a wine glass for all the things I'd never achieve, all the places I'd never go."

Abruptly, I snap back into the present, mortified by all I've revealed. I was so caught up, I told him far more than I originally planned. I don't know what came over me. Perhaps it's just the fact that, after days of monosyllabic grunts, it's so nice to have someone who's actually interested in learning more about me than my first name.

Ian whistles lowly. "Damn. I've never heard a woman make eternal bliss sound like an alternative to bamboo shoots being wedged beneath her fingernails by a CIA operative trained in torture."

"Okay, maybe I'm being a wee bit dramatic." I try out a laugh, but it's reedy. "I'm sure that destiny, with the perfect husband and perfect children and perfect house, wouldn't be *terrible*. I suppose there's a certain beauty to be found in standing on solid ground, full of unshakable conviction about the world and your place in it. Even a passionless existence would probably be preferable to... oh, I don't know... say... life on a deserted island, unsure of absolutely *everything* for the rest of my days."

Ian opens his mouth to respond, but it's not his voice I hear.

"I wouldn't put my money on that, princess," Beck mutters.

Stunned by his sudden interjection, I whirl around to find him leaning against a nearby tree, taking a break from the midday sun.

"How long have been there?" I demand.

He shrugs. "Long enough."

My pulse is pounding so fast I think I might have a heart attack. "You should've announced yourself."

"And miss that fascinating little speech?" His green eyes glitter with thoughts. "That would've been a damn shame."

"It was a private conversation! You had no right to eavesdrop!"

"Next time I'll be sure to blast off the flare gun before daring to walk back into my own camp," he drawls sarcastically.

"Perfect," I snap, eyes shooting daggers.

I can feel Ian's gaze moving back and forth between me and Beck, but I can't bring myself to look away from the tractor beam in which I'm trapped. We're both breathing a bit too fast.

After a few endless heartbeats, his attention flickers from my face over to Ian's. An indecipherable expression flashes across his face, gone in the span of a blink. Without another word, he turns and stalks back out into the burning sunshine.

I stare after him, a tangle of contradictory emotions warring inside me. I want ask what he meant when he said *I wouldn't put my money on that, princess.* I want to run after him and yell some more insults. I want to beg him to come back and sit with us for a while, telling stories of his own. I want to share my fears and hear his in return.

I want...

I want...

I want...

Him.

Ian lets out another low whistle. "Didn't you just tell me you came on this trip to get *away* from your relationship problems?"

I scowl at him. "Oh, shut up."

I FIND it by chance a week or so later, during a late afternoon walk through the woods.

Half-hidden by an especially dense copse of trees, the secret pool is tucked away at the heart of the atoll. Secluded and still, it's full of crisp, cool freshwater. No more than two dozen feet at its widest point, the thick overhead canopy keeps the brightest sun rays at bay, and the leafy forest ringing the banks lends an illusion of total privacy. As soon as I see it, I'm overcome with one thought.

I can take a bath.

Not a sponge-off with rainwater.
Not a dip into a salty tidal pool
A real, honest-to-god bath.

I can hardly contain my excitement as I race back to camp to grab my toiletry bag, then quickly retrace my steps to the water's edge. With Ian sound asleep, it's the perfect time for me to slip away unnoticed. Beck is off again, scratching another task from the ever-growing survival checklist he's invented to keep himself busy, now that the *HELP* distress signal is complete. One day, he walks the entire island's circumference; the next, he digs a solar still in the hot sand so we have a constant source of water nearby. Over the course of a week, he prepares massive pyres of kindling at several different locations across the island, ready to light in case a ship passes.

If he's not asleep, he's not at camp. I've barely seen him at all; I've spoken to him even less. I try not to take his sudden absence personally, but it's easier said than done. While we've never been what I'd call chummy, we tolerated each other. Leaned on each other, when things were difficult. Now, where there was at least a grudging camaraderie, there is frozen civility. If I were stronger, perhaps that wouldn't bother me so much. But, as I've come to realize, the unfortunate fact is...

I care.

I care so deeply, his avoidance tears at my soul with physical teeth.

For Ian's sake, I've kept a smile on my face and a bounce in my step, doing my best to remain positive. But at night, when the stars come out and my walls come down, I listen to the man sleeping a few feet away from me and wish there was a way to mend things between us. A way things could be different.

He calls me a child, but I'm not entirely naive. I'm perfectly aware that, most of the time, the people we like don't like us back. In the past, I've endured the melancholy ache of unrequited affection with ease.

But things are different on the island.

...things are different with him.

This is no childhood crush I can shake, no unsuccessful flirtation with a cute boy in a coffee shop.

Beck possesses my thoughts the way I wish I could possess his body. And every day that drags by with those desires unfulfilled sends me a little deeper down the rabbit hole of rebuffed feelings. Every time our eyes meet, I grow a little more morose.

Ironically enough, in many ways things on the island have never been better. We don't spend every minute worried about where our next meal is coming from, or whether we'll run out of water again. Ian is still holding on, despite the odds stacked against him. Our shelter is growing more stable all the time as we add makeshift furniture constructed from driftwood. My skin has turned golden brown, no longer sizzling in the sun when I walk along the inlet, ankle-deep in the surf.

We're surviving. Practically thriving.

Yet I'm more miserable than I've been since we first washed ashore.

Finding the freshwater pool is the only thing that's lightened my spirits in almost a week. Stripping to my skin, I carry my dress and underwear with me into the water along with my small bottles of body wash, shampoo, and conditioner. I fall into the sun-dappled surface like it's a featherbed, letting it close over my head in a cool rush. The warm water flows over my dry, sandy skin like a caress. It's absolutely sublime. Heaven on earth.

I float for hours, limbs splayed like a starfish as the sun filters down on me. I examine myself for the first time since the crash, grimacing at the way my hipbones and ribs jut through my skin with new sharpness. I take my time shampooing my hair, allotting myself the smallest dollop imaginable, then lather every inch of my skin with body wash. It has a light, pleasing scent I recognize immediately — gardenias and sage. Feminine without being overpowering. As soon as it hits my nose, the gates of memory are blasted open, yanking me straight back home to our farmhouse, where this same smell saturates every room.

Straight back to my mother.

I haven't allowed myself to think about her except in passing. It's too painful. If I let my thoughts linger on what she'd do if she were here... the things I'd say to her if I could go back to that last moment together at the airport... the pain she's in now, coping with the unexpected loss of a child... I'd probably never get out of bed in the morning. Never stop obsessing over the slew of macabre realizations that accompany that line of thought.

She thinks I'm gone.

Did she buy a casket and hold a funeral service?

Has she already laid me to rest? Turned my bedroom into a shrine of untouched memories, each item exactly as I left it that last day at home?

As far as the world is concerned, Violet Anderson is dead. Lost, somewhere at the bottom of the Pacific Ocean, with all the other unfortunate souls on that plane. It's a strange reality to grapple with.

The water grows chill as afternoon fades to dusk. Still, I float — eyes closed, limbs splayed, worries drifting away with the ripples. I know I should get out, go back to camp... but I can't force myself to leave. In this pool, totally alone, I'm at peace in a way I haven't been for a very long time.

The snap of a twig by the shore jolts me from my reverie. Eyes opening, my feet sink to the silt bottom as I spin around, lift my head... and look straight into a set of wide green eyes.

For one supercharged instant, we're both totally frozen — me, standing naked in the crystal clear water, Beck, stunned silent by the sight of me. Our gazes tangle and hold. For a moment I stand totally still.

Watching him watch me.

He's not touching me — he's not even near me — yet some-how, it's the most erotic experience of my life. The mere weight of his eyes on my skin is more exhilarating than any former boyfriend's rushed hands or sloppy backseat kisses ever were.

The seconds tick on.

I should cover myself.

He should turn his back.

One of us should break the silence.

One of us should tear their eyes away.

And yet...

I can't move. I can barely breathe.

I am a cherry blossom tree hit with the first hints of spring. Something dormant inside me has stirred awake after a long hibernation. Something I'm not sure I even realized lurked there, waiting to be roused, until this breathless instant pinned beneath Beck's gaze.

Now that it's made its presence known, I'm not sure I can banish it back to slumber.

I'm not sure I want to.

Time restarts with the same swiftness it slammed to a halt.

"Shit!" Beck curses, finally turning his back to me. "I'm sorry, I didn't realize you were..."

Naked.

Totally, completely naked.

Cheeks flaming red, I fold my arms over my chest and wade toward the opposite bank, where I laid my dress and underwear out to dry in the sunshine several hours ago. My hair streams in a damp curtain around my shoulders as I scramble onto the sandy shore.

"What are you doing here?" I ask quietly, yanking my dress over my head with haste. I'm so focused on the taut muscles cording Beck's back, I can't even enjoy the sensation of clean clothes against my skin. He holds himself so still, he looks carved from marble in the filtered blue-green light of the forest.

"I came looking for you," he says, voice a half-octave lower than normal.

"Well, you certainly found me."

"I didn't mean to intrude on your privacy."

"Then why did you?" I can't help scoffing. Fully clothed, I begin to pick my way around the pool toward him.

There's a long pause, as if he's choosing his words with great care. "You've never been away from camp for this long. Ian had no idea when you'd left or where you'd gone. I was worried something had happened to you."

"Oh, now you're worried?" I snort, coming to a stop a few feet away, eyes on his broad shoulders. "That's rich. You've been ignoring me for a week. You look straight through me half the time. I'm surprised you even noticed I was gone."

He whirls around to face me so fast, my eyes can barely track him. Whatever apologies he'd been prepared to offer are discarded as he takes two strides into my space, bringing us within inches of each other. My heart stops beating. For a split second, I think he's going to do something totally crazy, like crush me against his chest or slam his mouth down on mine.

"Believe me, things would be a fuck of a lot simpler if I could look straight through you, Violet."

My heart stops beating.

He leans in. "Next time you decide to leave for half a day, a heads up would be appreciated. I've spent three goddamned hours searching the forest for you."

"No one asked you to come looking for me."

"You didn't have to ask. Like it or not, I'm responsible for you."

I jerk my chin, outraged. "How many times do I have to tell you — I am not a child! You are most definitely not my father! So do us both a favor and stop acting like it."

"Oh, princess, I'm perfectly aware I'm not your father," he growls, voice shaking. His eyes scan me up and down, scorching into my skin as though he remembers exactly what I look like beneath this dress.

With a sound of disgust, I push past him and run back to camp, toiletry bag clutched tight against my aching chest. I hope the image of me floating naked in that water haunts him for the rest of his days. I hope he can't close his eyes without seeing me on the back of his eyelids, burned in like a brand.

It would serve him right, the jerk.

CHAPTER TWELVE

FLYER

"I can't stand it," Ian wheezes.

Dropping everything, I fly to his side. "What? Are you in pain? Where does it hurt?"

"No..." His eyes are crinkled at the corners — not with agony, but amusement. "I just can't stand. Literally."

I groan. "Your jokes are getting worse."

"You try thinking up unique leg-related humor all day long, it's not as easy as it looks."

"Alternatively, you could stop altogether."

"Nah, not a chance." His dimples appear. "Have to make you smile somehow. Why so glum today, sourpuss?"

"I'm not glum."

"Yesterday you disappeared for hours, today you've been moping around like a pre-teen at Hot Topic whose debit card got declined."

"Harsh!"

He shrugs. "Calling it like I see it."

"Well, you must be going blind because I'm perfectly fine."

"Uh huh."

"Let's talk about someone with real problems. You, for instance." I eye his gaunt face. "You're not eating."

"Menu here isn't to my taste. Lots of seafood and, gotta be straight with you, I've always been more of a steak guy."

"Uh huh. I'll get right on that," I say wryly. "In the meantime, how about you try some fruit? Those weird melon things on trees with the red flowers are actually pretty good. I don't know what they're called, but they taste like a cross between a mango and a papaya…"

"No," he cuts me off. "I'm not hungry."

I chew my lip worriedly. "You really should try to keep your strength up. The fruit…"

"Violet. Unless it's Kobe-beef-flavored fruit, I'm not interested."

"Fine." My hands lift in submission. "Is there anything else I can get you?"

"A margarita would be nice."

"I realize it's a struggle for you to take any of this seriously, but I need to know about your condition."

"My condition? Hmm, let's see. Single. Sagittarius. Stunningly handsome. Recently lost about thirty pounds, all in the lower extremity region. Enjoy long hops on the beach at sunset, followed by fluorescent-lit dinners at the International House of Pancakes."

I choke down a laugh.

"Oh, come on," he drawls. "Not even a chuckle for *IHOP*? That was a good one."

I lose the battle for composure and giggle helplessly. "Fine! If I admit it was funny, will you agree to tell me how you're actually feeling?"

"Yes."

"Ha. Ha. Ha. You are oh so hilarious," I deadpan. "They should give you your own late night show. That guy Jimmy has nothing on you."

He grins. "Thanks Violet. That means so much to me, especially knowing you were blackmailed into saying every word."

"Quit stalling. How are you feeling?"

"Never better."

I stare him down.

He sighs deeply, then finally relents. "Lightheaded. Dizzy. The leg pain is intense, and the burns itch so bad, I'd scratch them raw if I knew it wouldn't do more nerve damage. I'm tired all the time. Physically, emotionally. Tired of sitting under this damn raft tent, tired of not being able to move, tired of pissing into coconut shells and handing them to you to take care of for me. I am a grown ass man, weak as a fucking kitten, withering away in hundred-degree heat. Worse, I'm a burden on you. Just being here, I make things doubly hard, because you have to take care of me in addition to yourself. You've got enough to deal with already without me bogging you down."

"Ian… Why didn't you tell me you were feeling this way? I had no idea." My stomach flips at the thought of him being in so much pain. I reach out, grab his hand, and give it a tight squeeze. "You have to know, it's not true. You're not a burden. You're just about the only good thing on this entire island."

His eyes drift over my shoulder to Beck, where he sits on the crest of the beach attempting to lash together a fishing trap using sticks and vines. I'm not sure whether he's within earshot. I don't care, at the moment — I'm too focused on Ian.

His lips twitch when he takes in the sight of my expression. "That look on your face right now? That's exactly why I prefer to joke and laugh. Talking about this stuff isn't nearly as fun."

"Maybe. But your health is more important." I place the back of my hand against his forehead to check his temperature. "You may be running a low-grade fever. You feel a little warm."

"We're in the tropics."

"Thank you, Captain Obvious." I roll my eyes and reach for his bandages. "Now, let's have a look at the leg."

"Not right now," he says, pulling away. "I've just gotten myself into a comfortable position."

"Fine. But we're changing those dressings before you fall asleep tonight. It's been two days and in this heat, the longer they stay on, the greater the risk of an infection."

He nods, a spark of fear flaming in his eyes. For all his wise-cracks, I'm sure he's horrified by everything that's happened to him... and terrified by the prospect of everything that still could.

"Hey." I wait until his gaze meets mine. "I don't think I can manage a margarita, but would you settle for some fresh coconut milk? It's all the rage here on the island. All the cool kids are drinking it."

The fear fades from his expression and his dimples return. "All the cool kids, huh?"

I nod gravely.

"Well, then I guess you'd better fetch me one of those coconuts. I have a reputation to maintain, woman!"

Ten minutes later, I find myself balanced precariously on a stack of logs, praying they don't give out beneath me. I stretch up onto my tiptoes as my fingers dig into the trunk of the palm tree, grappling for purchase against the smooth, ringed bark.

"You are going to fall on your face, and I am going to laugh at you," Ian calls up to me from his pallet. "There must be a better way to do this, Violet."

I ignore him, attention focused upward. Come hell or high water, today is the day I will finally get one of those damn coconuts.

"I mean it," Ian drawls. "Don't expect sympathy from me when you break your ass."

I gasp, faux-offended. "After all I've done to nurse you back to health..."

"Just looking out for you."

"I appreciate the concern, but I think I can manage to climb a stupid tree."

Hell, I'd climb to the moon if it meant getting Ian to drink something with nutritional value.

I lift my right foot and plant it flat against a small wood knot. "If I can leverage myself up, maybe I can make a flying leap and grab one..."

"Who do you think you are, Nastia Liukin?"

My nose wrinkles in confusion. "Who?"

"Olympic Gymnast," Ian clarifies. "A super hot one, too, so take it as a compliment."

I snort. "I may not be a gold medalist, but for your information, I was the head flyer of my cheerleading squad. Three-time Northeast Champions. Contenders for the national title."

"You were a cheerleader?"

"Go Sasquatches!"

"Your mascot was the *Sasquatch*?" He sounds dubious. "What the hell kind of hick town were you raised in?"

"New Hampshire has a strong affinity for yetis." I shrug. "Also, winter sports, leaf peeping, Tom Brady, and tax-free purchases. We're wicked awesome."

"Remind me never to visit you in this hell dimension you call home."

"Too bad, my mother would adore you."

"Oh, wow, bringing me home to meet the parents already? Seems like this relationship is moving a little fast, but..."

I roll my eyes. "In your dreams, pretty boy. Now, hush. I'm going to jump."

"Did I mention this stunt appears to be a terrible idea? Especially from this vantage point?"

"Don't get excited — I have shorts on under my dress."

He sighs heavily.

Eyes locked on the dangling coconuts at the top of the palm, I flex my arm muscles and take a deep breath. It's now or never.

I choose now.

I'm a half-second from catapulting my frame into the sky when two giant hands wrap around my waist and pluck me from my perch. Lifting me like I weigh no more than a bag of flour, he sets me back on the ground without a word.

"HEY!" I yell as soon as my feet hit the dirt. "What the hell?!"

Beck's hands drop away instantly, but he doesn't move out of my space. When I spin around, I find myself nose-to-nose with him. It's a jarring experience, being this close to those intent eyes.

We stare at each other for a long moment. When I can't take it anymore, I shatter the silence.

"Why did you do that?"

"Ian was right. You would've busted your ass." He shrugs lightly. "Figured I should stop you before you could."

"As I already assured *Ian*, I'm perfectly capable of doing this. I can pull off a flawless scorpion pose with a one-man base, for Christ's sake."

Beck's brows lift, but otherwise he gives no indication that he understands a word I've just said.

"A bow and arrow," I offer.

The blank stare persists.

"A needle. A tick tock. A liberty."

His lips twitch. "Either you've had a stroke or I've missed a crucial piece of information."

"I'm pretty sure she's just making things up, at this point," Ian adds.

I scowl at them both. "I was a varsity cheerleader. A flyer. That means I was always the one at the top of the pyramid of girls."

"Oh. Let's pause here. I think we need to discuss this pile of women," Ian murmurs wolfishly. "Preferably in as much detail as possible."

Beck cuts him a severe look.

I ignore them both. "If I can stand on one foot, being held over a spotter's head by a single hand, I'm damn sure I'll be able to reach those coconuts by myself. Hell, if one of the guys from my cheer team was here, we'd already be drinking them instead of standing around talking about it."

"There were *guys* on your cheerleading squad?" Ian snorts. "And here I thought it was tough being a male flight attendant..."

I roll my eyes.

"I could do it," Beck offers quietly. "I could... be your base."

My eyes widen. "Seriously?"

He nods. "Just tell me what to do."

STRIPPED down to just my bra and the thin black shorts, I stand pressed as close to Beck as I've ever been. So close, I can feel each of his breaths stirring the wispy hairs at the back of my neck. I swallow hard and try to gather my composure.

"Ready?" His voice is a rumble, rolling over me like thunder.

"Yes." Dear lord, I'm already breathless and we haven't even started the stunt. "Let's go for it."

His hands encircle my waist, each finger digging into my bare flesh. The rasp of his calluses against my sensitive skin is almost too much to bear. I try to put it from my mind, so I can focus on the task at hand, but there's an undeniable lump in my throat as he bends low and lifts me up onto his shoulders in one smooth motion. Settled with my thighs sandwiching his head, I ignore the butterflies swarming in my stomach and position my bare feet in his hands. I almost moan at the sensation of his thumbs brushing against the balls of my feet.

There is something seriously wrong with me.

When he straightens his arms up over his head, I lock my knees and engage my core muscles to keep from toppling over. Fully extended, I can just reach the top of the tree. Plucking a dozen coconuts from the hanging bunch, I toss them down onto the sand. I'm still grinning like an idiot when Beck lowers me back to earth.

"YES!" I exclaim, giddy with success.

Victories here have been few and far between. I needed a win, a single moment of triumph after all the darkness and defeat. Maybe we all did. Ian cheers riotously, as though I've just landed a perfect Double Arabian that would make even his beloved Nastia turn green with envy. And Beck looks down at me with an honest to god grin lighting up his features. The effect is intense — I feel my heart skip a beat at the mere sight of all those white teeth, this close to my face.

"Thank you," I tell him sincerely.

"You're welcome."

For a while we stand there grinning at each other like idiots. Perhaps we're leaning a little too close, playing with gasoline near a sparking power line, but I can't force my feet to move away from him. It's amazing to feel joy zipping through my bloodstream again as we laugh together.

"Tell the truth," Ian calls. "Beck, you were on an all-male cheer squad. It's okay, you can tell us. We won't laugh." He pauses. "Nah, I take that back, we'll definitely laugh."

"You caught me," Beck jokes, shaking his head. "But it was actually rhythmic gymnastics. I'm quite light on my toes."

"Downright dainty," I quip, eyes on his large feet. He must be at least a size twelve. "How ever did you find ballet slippers that big?"

Ian cackles.

Beck snorts in amusement as he steps away from me, walking over to sit by the fire as I collect the coconuts. I'd be lying if I said I didn't miss being in the circle of his arms as soon as I stepped out of them, but I push those thoughts aside, determined to hang onto the light mood of the past few moments.

The atmosphere conspires to aid me on that front — it's a clear night with no breeze, so we stoke the fire higher than we've ever dared before. Showers of sparks dance upward and dissipate as we watch, clacking our coconut shells together in a celebratory cheers as the sky turns jet. They're not margaritas, but they're not half bad.

Over a dinner of fire-roasted crab and sea clams, Ian entertains us with endless stories of terrible flight passengers, until all three of us are in stitches. Before I know it, the moon is high in the sky and my eyes are drooping closed. Ian's face splits in a giant yawn, mid-tale.

"So, I told her, 'I'm sorry ma'am, I don't know what you thought your first class ticket entailed, but I can assure you what you've just done in the bathroom with the gentleman from seat 3C is *not* on the menu.'"

I giggle until there are tears gathering at the corners of my eyes.

"You should get some rest," Beck tells Ian, when our laughter tapers off. "Save your energy for tomorrow."

"Ah yes, another big day spent sitting in this same spot."

"Actually, if you're feeling up for it, maybe I can carry you to the pool Violet found the other day — get you washed up, give you a change of scenery."

Ian's throat works rapidly, and I can tell he's moved by the offer. "Thanks, man. I'd like that."

"Also, there's this." Beck rises to his feet and walks to the edge of camp, where his things are stacked. When he returns, there are two long wooden branches in his hands, their tops shaved smooth.

Crutches, I realize. *He's made Ian crutches.*

My eyes well up. I have to look away to keep the tears from falling. Ian is similarly affected, judging by the thickness of his voice when he thanks Beck.

"Least I could do." Beck shrugs. "They're not finished yet, but they will be by the time you're ready to use them."

"Means a lot, man," Ian says shakily. "Appreciate it."

Beck merely nods. As if it's no big deal that he's just given a man trapped by pain and circumstance something to look forward to. A reason to get up in the morning.

I am a grown ass man, weak as a fucking kitten, withering away in hundred-degree heat.

Worse, I'm a burden on you.

I think perhaps Beck doesn't know what he's just done, but as I catch his eyes I read awareness on every plane of his face. He heard our conversation earlier, heard how disheartened Ian was becoming... and he did what he could to rectify it. Not using a method I would've chosen, not in a manner I would've even considered... In his own way, on his own terms.

That's simply... *Beck.*

He shows up. He saves people. Not because he wants praise in return. Not for credit. Not for notoriety. It's just who he is, beneath the cutting commentary and blunt rebukes.

Hidden deep below that caustic exterior is a heart of solid gold. I'm sure of it.

"Why are you looking at me like that?" His voice is barely a whisper, so as not to wake Ian.

I give a start. "How am I looking at you?"

"Like..." His inhale is audible. "I might not be the biggest asshole on the planet."

"Ah. I feel confident saying you're *probably* not the biggest asshole on the planet." My head tilts. "You're *definitely* the biggest asshole on this island, though."

His grin is a bolt of lightning in the dark. "I guess I deserve that."

I don't contradict him.

"I'm sorry I was such an asshole, yesterday. Actually, I'm sorry I'm an asshole all the time... but yesterday especially. When I got back and you weren't here, when I couldn't find you... I thought you were hurt. Or worse." His head shakes, as though he can't bear to contemplate that thought. "In my mind, as I searched the water and the woods, I kept imagining what this place would be like without you. Waking up without you here singing under your breath as you tidy the camp, smiling at the damn hermit crabs who steal our breakfast every morning, grinning at the baby birds who live in that nest over by the boulders. All those tiny moments of life you bring to this place... gone."

My heart clenches as I realize I've been wrong about something.

He doesn't see straight through me.

He sees my every detail sharper than a telephoto lens.

"I know it doesn't excuse how I've been acting." Beck's voice grows so soft, it's hard to make out his next words. "But the thought of losing you... I about lost my damn mind. And my temper was quick to follow, I'm afraid."

How on earth am I supposed to respond to something like that?

"I know I'm not like Ian. I know things between you and me are... complicated," he says carefully, sidestepping an atomic bomb. "But I'm hoping you'll give me a chance to prove that I can do better. *Be* better. I—" He breaks off abruptly. "Look, I'm no good with words. We both know that. But I also don't make false promises. I don't commit to things and back out when it gets tough. So, when I tell you I'll be there, I will. No exceptions. If you let me... I'll show up for you. I'll be your support system, whenever you need me. You can count on that." He pauses. "Always. Even when I'm being a dick about it."

My eyes are watering. I lie to myself that it's caused the fire sending smoke into my face, instead of the apology I've just received. I don't know whether to be stunned Beck can, in fact, own up to his own arrogance, or awed that the peace treaty I've been praying for has manifested without my lifting a finger.

As I contemplate his words, I look at his face, cast in contradictory hues from two angles — the moonlight above, the firelight below. A true dichotomy, much like the man before me.

Unapologetic curmudgeon.

Unfaltering caretaker.

In cheerleading, there's no greater trust than that between a flyer and her base. You can't reach the top of the pyramid without a solid foundation beneath your feet. Beck may not have phrased it as eloquently as my cheer coach, but the concept still applies. What he's saying — what he's offering — is clear as day.

I'll be your support system.

Always.

When we eventually fall asleep, we don't move to opposite sides of the fire, as we have for the past week. We lie side by side, not quite touching, but close enough that I could reach out and grab his hand with a simple flick of my wrist. There's a warm glow inside my chest I cannot seem to suppress, even after my eyes have closed and Beck's breaths have slowed to the steady rhythms of sleep.

It's been a good night.

A *great* night.

I never would've predicted I'd find myself saying that again, so long as we remain on this island.

Basking in the warmth of the fire, I slip unconscious with a smile on my face... in my lingering joy, completely forgetting that I never got around to checking Ian's leg bandages.

Later, I'd look back at that moment of bliss and wonder if it was possible to hate myself more.

CHAPTER THIRTEEN

BREAK

IT'S AMAZING how much can happen in eight hours.

A speeding car can cross New England in its entirety. A person can work a full day shift, or catch a total night's sleep. A space satellite can complete an orbit. A single cell can replicate exponentially until one unit of bacteria becomes a hundred, a thousand, a million.

Until it spreads enough to do irreversible damage.

As soon as my eyes open, I know something's wrong. Ian isn't propped up on his pallet, drawing inappropriate things in the margins of the children's coloring book with our stock of crayons to keep himself entertained. He's huddled low, shivering like it's eight below zero rather than eighty and rising. I spare a single glance at Beck, sleeping soundly at my side, as I sit up and make my way to Ian.

"Hey," I murmur, pulling his foil blankets down so I can see his face. "Are you—"

My mouth goes dry. My eyes widen as they trace over his skin. The fever is back, that's immediately obvious. There's a clammy sheen to his face that wasn't there last night.

Or, maybe it was... and you were so focused on enjoying yourself, you simply didn't see it.

Selfish, selfish, selfish.

I press my hand to his forehead and wince when the heat of his skin nearly scalds me. He's burning up.

"Ian? Can you hear me?"

"What's up, doc?" he murmurs, eyelids fluttering as a grin tugs at his lips. It quickly morphs into a grimace. An insuppressible groan of pain hits my ears. "*Christ,* it hurts."

"What hurts?"

"My leg."

All traces of humor are gone from his voice. This is no pun. I don't wait for a punchline or a lighthearted twist. With trembling fingers, I reach for the fabric wrappings around his stump and slowly unwind them. My heart pounds a sharp staccato inside my chest.

The smell hits me first. Decay and death. I breathe through my mouth as I pull away the final piece of bandage, nearly fainting when I take in what's become of his leg in the short time since I last saw it. Patches of black, necrotic tissue are no match for the angry red streaks of infection. Beginning at the seared burn site, they stretch toward his groin, disappearing beneath the edge of his boxer shorts. Creeping toward his heart.

"Oh, Ian," I breathe, horror overtaking me when see the extent of the blood poisoning. "Ian…"

There's no reply. He's unconscious. Delirious. Lost in the throes of fever dreams as his skin trembles with cold.

Why didn't you tell me? I want to wail, shaking him for answers. *Why didn't you say anything?*

He must've known. This did not happen over the course of a

few hours. To spread this far, he must've been feeling the effects for days.

My mind whirls as I consider our options. They are grim indeed, from where I sit. With no medicine and precious little remaining alcohol, we can hardly sanitize our hands of germs, let alone kill an aggressive bacterial infection. I've begun to study the trees around our camp, but I don't know nearly enough to start blindly shoving them down Ian's throat — not without testing their effects on myself first. Picking the wrong plant could kill him even faster than this infection.

My desperate eyes sweep the camp, snagging on the smoldering fire. It's hard to believe mere hours ago we were all laughing together around a magnificent blaze. Hard to believe things could change so swiftly from fun to fear. Discarded coconut shells litter the ground like party favors.

Coconuts! The thought clangs loudly inside my skull, inspiration striking like a blow. *Coconuts have medicinal properties!*

I used to tease some of my more health-conscious friends about their obsession with the thick white oil. They'd put it in food, on their skin, in their hair. Over the past few years it's become such a fitness fad, I've heard claims about curative benefits ranging from fat burning to wrinkle reduction to hormone balance to blood pressure. It's been linked to treatments for everything from Alzheimer's to cancer to heart disease.

The Tree of Life — that's what they call coconut palms, here in the South Pacific.

There must be some truth to that claim.

There must be. Please, God. Please.

As gently as possible, I prop up Ian's damaged leg and turn, calling out for Beck as I run for the closest palm.

"Beck! Wake up! I need your help!"

I need a miracle.

THE NEXT TWO weeks are the hardest of my life.

I spend every waking moment by Ian's side. I neglect food, ignoring my own bodily needs in favor of his. I barely sleep, afraid to close my eyes for longer than a moment in case he wakes in need of help. Not that there's much I can do at this point, besides hold his hand and wait for him to... to...

I can't even say the word in my own head.

Night and day, I lie by his side on the sleeping pallet, in the off chance he wakes. At best, he's conscious for a few scant moments before falling back under the pressing weight of fever. At worst, he does not wake at all.

Each day, he slips a little farther from us; I fear, soon, he'll be entirely out of reach.

He doesn't speak to me, except to murmur feverish nonsense under his breath, the meanings of which I cannot fathom. Sometimes, he calls out for his mother, his father, the girl who broke his heart back in Oklahoma. I hold his hand and assure him they're here with him, hoping he can't hear the devastation in my voice. His cracked lips form more incoherent syllables, babbles of a man lost to the world.

Beck stares worriedly at the ever-darkening shadows beneath my eyes and the ever-shrinking margins of my waistline, but I avoid his stare. He brings a constant supply of food and fresh water, stacks our cache of firewood so high there's no chance I'll ever have to leave Ian's side in search of more. We communicate in wordless gestures and loaded glances, hardly speaking aloud at all as the days pass rapidly.

You should eat something.

I'll eat when he does.

Stubborn girl.

Bossy man.

I change coconut-infused bandages and sponge hot broth down Ian's throat, until there comes a point he can't swallow even the smallest beads of moisture without choking. I look up, eyes moving to the edge of our camp where Beck is lashing yet another tree trunk into place. The first section of our log-cabin is nearly complete. Within a month or so, he should be able to construct the remaining sides, until we have a real, actual house with walls and a roof.

It's impossible to believe Ian won't be here to see it. And yet...

I'm beginning to doubt he'll see the other side of tomorrow.

Listening to his labored breaths, I wrap his cold hands within mine and squeeze. There's fluid in his lungs. Pneumonia, most likely. Each inhale is a struggle, each exhale rattles from his emaciated throat like death itself, whispering in my ear.

Beck appears at my side, somehow sensing I was about to call for him. We're so attuned to each other at this point, I wonder if he can hear the private thoughts inside my head.

I hope not. I still have few secrets I'd like to keep to myself.

Green eyes find mine. His brows arch. *How is he?*

I shake my head. *Not good.*

My heart is so heavy inside my chest I can hardly catch a breath. I turn my head away from Ian, so he won't see the tears trickling down my cheeks if his eyes crack open. I thought I'd cried every tear left in my body, that eventually the well would run dry, but still more come — an endless waterfall of grief seeping out over hours and days and weeks.

A big hand reaches toward me, as if to brush them away. I freeze. He halts a few centimeters from my cheekbone, catching himself just before his fingertips make contact.

There's an apology in his eyes.

I turn my gaze out to sea, so I don't drown in him. It's stormy today. A rare overcast afternoon. The ocean is riled up with waves. I watch them crashing against the reef break a hundred yards offshore and wonder what we'll face when hurricane season arrives in the fall. I can't quite summon the energy to care what happens to us. Whatever we must face, at least we'll still be *here* to face it. We'll still be alive.

The tears flow faster.

On a normal day, with the bright sunshine turning the Pacific into a vast sheet of cerulean, it's impossible to make out any details on the horizon, with the exception of the occasional heat mirage or optical illusion. But today, under the dim cloud cover, my eyes snag on an incongruous shape. A white block, drifting at the farthest limits of my vision.

"Beck."

He flinches. It's the first time I've spoken aloud in days and my voice sounds torn to shreds. Clearing my throat, I try again.

"Beck... is that a ship?"

I hardly dare speak the hope aloud, half-afraid just acknowledging it will make the vessel disappear from view. I never shift my eyes from the horizon as I slowly rise to my feet.

"Where?" He's right by my side, hand lifting to shield his eyes. "I don't see anything."

I extend my arm, index finger shaking as I point to the tiny blob. "There."

"Your eyes must be better than mine," he murmurs. "I can't see anything."

"It's there." I jerk my chin stubbornly. "It's a ship."

He takes a few strides down the beach, eyes cast outward. I can almost hear the thoughts whirring around inside his head.

She hasn't eaten in days.

She's desperate to save Ian.

Maybe the ship isn't there at all.

"It's there," I say, mostly to myself. "It has to be there."

Beck turns to look at me, conflict warring in his eyes. "Violet. We only have two flares. We may only have one shot at signaling for help. If you say there's something out there, I'll believe you. But... you have to be sure. Damn sure."

I sway on my feet, so exhausted I can barely stand. Tears trickle down my cheeks.

Is my mind playing tricks on me? Am I so desperate for rescue to arrive — not just for my sake, but for Ian's — that I've conjured up the thing I most want to see?

The shape is getting smaller on the horizon. Fading from focus, the longer we stand here deliberating. I hear Ian struggling to drag in another ragged breath and, just like that, my decision is made. Brushing the tears aside, I sprint to the supply kit and grab the flare gun off the top.

"Violet, wait!" Beck yells, but I'm past listening.

I run down the beach to the water's edge. Before he can stop me, I shove a cartridge into the barrel, snap it into place and cock back the hammer. My arm lifts from my side as I aim straight overhead. My eyes slam shut as my finger squeezes the trigger. There's a loud bang as the firing pin strikes the back of the flare. The gun recoils in my hand with an intense jolt as the shell explodes from the tip of the barrel, shooting up into the sky several hundred meters overhead. I watch it light up the afternoon, burning red like a Fourth of July firework. It arcs through the air, sinking slowly over the course of about thirty seconds before burning out.

Please, I pray, dropping to my knees in the sand, the gun still gripped in my hand. *Please, tell me someone saw it. Tell me someone's coming.*

But... no one does.

An hour ticks by, then two, without so much as a flicker of life on the horizon. Whatever I saw... it wasn't a ship. It wasn't our salvation. I'm flooded with shame and despair. I sit unmoving in the sand, full of loathing. For the island, for our fate... but mostly for myself.

I can feel the weight of Beck's stare on me, but I don't dare look up. I don't want to see the stern set of his jaw, the disapproval blaring from his eyes. I'm already disappointed enough. After a while, I hear him sigh heavily. He crouches down in the sand a few inches away and waits until I glance at him.

I expect nothing short of fury. Instead, I'm greeted with

compassion. His eyes are soft on mine, practically glowing in the fading twilight. There's a furrow in his brow, but it's not angry — it's concerned.

"I'm sorry," I whisper brokenly. "I thought… I really thought…"

"I know." His big hand finds mine, slowly pulling the flare gun from my grip. "It's okay, Violet."

"It's not okay! I wasted one of our flares on *nothing*. An optical illusion. A desperate hope. You tried to stop me, but I couldn't face the possibility that I might be wrong." My eyes lift to his, watering once more. "I couldn't face the reality that, in a few hours, Ian is going to die, and there's nothing I can do to stop it. Nothing but hold his hand and say goodbye."

It's the first time either of us has said the truth out loud.

Beck, ever stoic, nods gravely as he sets the flare gun aside and reaches for my hand. His hold is tentative, as though he's not sure, even now, that he's allowed to touch me. Our fingers twine together like vines, clinging in a tight grip I feel over every inch of my skin.

"You've done everything you can. You've stayed with him through it all. Every spasm, every cough, every fever dream. You've fed him and washed him and kept him as comfortable as you possibly could." Beck's voice is rough as coral. "He knows exactly what you've done for him. And, if he could tell you himself, I'm sure he'd thank you for it."

My tears leak faster. "I wanted to save him. I wanted so badly to keep him alive."

His jaw clenches tight as he watches me weep. His free hand lifts and, with a tenderness that splinters my already bruised heart, he brushes my tears away. "I know you did, princess."

The pet name is spoken with what I can only describe as reverence. I can't believe I used to bristle whenever I heard it. Now, the sound is enough to mend my soul… or maybe it's the look in his eyes when he says it, that inspires such a reaction. Maybe it's just him.

All of him. Every facet.

Before I can figure it out, he tugs me to my feet.

"Come on." He supports me when I start to sway, waves of exhaustion coursing through me. "Let's get you back to the fire. It's getting cold, and you're shivering like a leaf."

I don't tell him my shakes are more from the storm of emotions raging inside me than they are a sign of hypothermia. I don't have the energy to form the words. He leads me by the hand back to our encampment and settles me by Ian's side. He disappears for a moment to put the flare gun away.

When he returns to me, the black sweatshirt from his duffle is wadded in his hands. Like a child, I allow him to manipulate my limbs as he tugs the garment over my head and pulls the sleeves down my arms. It's so large on me, I can fold my legs up to my chest inside it. Fully cocooned, I'm truly warm for the first time in days.

"Better?" Beck asks.

I nod, even though it's a lie. How can I be better — how can I be anything but ruined — as I watch the frail rise and fall of Ian's chest, wondering how many more breaths he'll take before his last. How many more heartbeats until his pulse stutters into silence.

A soft moan draws my attention to his pale face. Instantly, I'm crouched close, fingers stroking his cheekbones.

"Ian?"

There's a long silence. I brace for another string of feverish babbling, but miraculously, his voice rasps into the night.

"Violet?" He sounds like a child — fragile and afraid. Nonetheless, he's conscious. He's *lucid* for the first time in days. His eyes sliver open and find mine. "I...I want..."

"What?" I ask instantly. "Name it, it's yours."

"Want to say... thank you." He wheezes, face contorting in pain. "Not your... fault. You... did... your best."

"Shhh. You don't need to thank me now."

"Now... or... never." He coughs wetly, the fluid gathering in his lungs making breath nearly impossible.

"Never? Don't be silly," I say, blinking away tears. "There'll be time later, once you're better."

"Doc... we both know..." His eyes struggle to focus on mine. I think I see a glimmer of his old humor, lurking beneath the pain. "One foot... in the grave... already."

I attempt to laugh at his awful joke, but it quickly morphs into a sob. My eyes stream like faucets and my breaths turn to hiccups.

"Beck?" Ian asks.

"I'm right here."

I look up and see Beck's position mirrors mine. Crouched directly across from me, he holds Ian's other hand in a white-knuckled grip.

Ian's strength is fading. I can see it in his every breath, feel it in the thready pulse at his wrist.

It won't be long, now.

"Take... care of her. Promise... me," he demands, staring up at Beck.

"You have my word."

Ian gives a tiny nod. His eyes move back to my face. "You..."

I can't get out a single word, I'm crying so hard.

"When you... get home... you tell your mom..." He shudders as a wave of agony grips him. "Tell her... I wish I could've met her. Tell her... if things were different... would've been my honor... to call her family."

I lean forward, tears falling onto Ian's face as I press a soft kiss to his lips. They're chapped and still beneath mine.

"Go to sleep, Ian. When you wake up, we'll be on a rescue boat. On our way home. You hear me?"

He nods weakly.

I press my cheek to his and whisper into his ear. "You'll get better, and then I'll bring you to New Hampshire to meet Mom.

You two will have so many inside jokes, I won't be able to keep up."

"Sounds... perfect."

I nod, barely keeping myself together. "It will be. We'll build a big house. By the lake, not the ocean — I think we've spent enough days looking at crashing waves to last a lifetime, don't you? We'll get married in a big ceremony. Your whole family will come. Your ex will be so jealous, when she finds out."

He tries to chuckle, but it turns to a jagged cough.

"We'll have a bunch of kids. Loud ones, with your sense of humor. You'll all tease me constantly, but I won't mind, because we'll be so happy. The kind of happy that makes total strangers smile on the street, and turns the closest friends green with envy, wishing they had a life like ours. The kind of happy they write fairy tales about."

A small sound escapes him — half sigh, half exhale. His chest goes still beneath mine. No breaths move from his parted lips.

I cling tighter to his shoulders, pressing in as if to keep him with me one more second. There's no denying the truth, though.

He's gone.

I reach up and close his unseeing eyes.

"We'll be so happy," I whisper again, feeling hollow.

I doubt I'll ever be happy again.

CHAPTER FOURTEEN

PARTINGS

WE BURY HIM AT DAYBREAK, on a jagged cliff on the east side of the island where the dirt is soft and the views are spectacular. It's the first spot the light hits every morning when the sun creeps up over the horizon. Here, Ian will always be warm, always bathed in the same light he carried inside his soul. Here, he'll finally be out of pain. At peace.

Beck smooths the dirt flat with a crude wooden spade as I watch dawn slowly bask the world in a swathe of red. At the sight, an old adage pops into my head.

Red sky at morning, sailors take warning. Red sky at night, sailor's delight.

A storm is brewing.

Good.

It'll match the one inside me. As far as I'm concerned, the weather can tear me to pieces. My soul is already shredded beyond repair.

Finished with his bleak task, Beck rises to his feet and moves to my side. I lift my empty eyes and watch his face contract with worry when sees how haunted they are.

"Violet..."

"Don't." My head shakes swiftly. "Don't say anything kind. I can't bear it."

He's silent for a long moment. "Are you ready?"

My brows lift.

"To say goodbye."

I suck in a sharp gulp of air. "No. But I'll never be, so we might as well get it over with now."

His gaze is searching. "Do you want to say something?"

"I don't really believe in anything specific," I whisper. "I don't know if Ian did, either. We didn't talk about religion."

"I don't think it matters," Beck murmurs. "Whatever words you choose... it's the meaning behind them that carries true weight."

I stare at the patch of disrupted earth, thinking about what Ian would want me to say if he were here. Nothing sounds right inside my head. Probably because saying goodbye to him feels so utterly wrong. In the end, I simply speak from the heart and hope it's enough.

"I knew the moment we met that you'd be a friend for life," I murmur. "I just didn't realize that life would be cut so short. I wish I had words eloquent enough to convey how much I'll miss your bad jokes and constant smiles. I wish you were here to make fun of me one more time. But I know you had to go." My voice breaks. "I'll miss you so much, Ian. I hope, wherever you are, you're at peace now. If there is a heaven up above, I'm certain you're already in it, making the angels laugh."

I close my eyes, feeling the first true sunbeams of the day break over the horizon and bask me in warmth. I might not be totally sold on the existence of a higher power or an afterlife...

but in my heart, I'd like to believe those rays of light are Ian, shining down on me.

One final farewell.

Beck clears his throat. "Ian. I hope you're somewhere with plenty of steak, endless margaritas, and zero pain." His tone turns somber. "You were a better man than I'll ever be. You brought so much heart to this place. You faced the end with the kind of courage I've only ever seen from soldiers on a battlefield. You were a fighter. A warrior, fearless right till the end. It won't be easy, filling the shoes you've left behind." He pauses. "Of course, if you were here, you'd say *the shoe, Beck, singular* and we'd all have a good laugh."

A snort-sob catches in my throat. "You're right. He totally would say that."

"He was one of a kind."

I nod, unable to speak.

"It won't be the same here without him."

My eyes move to Beck's face, still streaked with dirt from digging Ian's grave. He looks impossibly young in the weak morning light. More boy than man, shaken and sad. I'm stunned to see tears glossing over his eyes.

Beck Underwood, stone pillar of masculinity, unshakable mountain of a man... crying.

I dig my fingernails into my palms, trying to get myself under control, but it's no use. I've always seen Beck as indestructible; watching him begin to unravel is simply too much to bear. My own seams begin to come apart.

"*Violet.*"

It's a plea and a promise. A benediction and a burning wish. We move at the same time. I think we both need it desperately — the connection of skin against skin. The heat of his firm chest seeps into me like a drug. After this seemingly unending ordeal, I crave contact like a junkie in need of her fix. It's the only reminder that I'm still alive, that I haven't disappeared into thin air never to be seen again, a balloon without a string.

His arms loop behind my shoulders, grounding me unquestionably in reality. I'm crushed so tight to his chest it's difficult to draw breath, but I don't mind because that feeling — the one that I might float away — begins to dissipate as soon as my arms wind around his back.

You're still here.

You matter.

I've got you.

I cling to him as he buries his face in my hair. After a moment, I feel the distinct smattering of his tears against the strands near the crown of my head. My own eyes leak onto the bare skin of his chest, turning the dirt and dust clinging there to a muddy paste. I can feel it smearing against my cheeks, dripping down my neck in rivulets, but I don't care. I'm already filthy after two weeks without a proper bath. In this instant nothing in the world, especially not a bit of dirt, could convince me to shift out of Beck's embrace.

We stand together on the cliff for a small eternity, until the sun has ascended far past the water's edge. The tears have stopped, but still we cling. I wonder if he's as terrified to let go as I am.

What if we never touch again?

What if we can't ever stop?

Both alternatives shake me to my core.

We both know things are going to change, now that Ian's gone... whether we want them to or not. There will be no more third party to break the tension with quick quips, no buffer zone between the two opposing hurricanes raging within Beck and me, on an indisputable collision course for a natural disaster.

Change is coming. I can feel it in my bones, sense it in the air. I'm just not sure if it will be for better or worse.

Intertwined, we lend each other strength until I feel my legs begin to tremble. It's been weeks since I've properly slept; longer since I've eaten a full meal. Without Ian here, there's no longer a need to keep up the illusion of composure I've been maintaining for so long. My body officially hits its breaking point when my knees buckle completely.

Beck catches me as I fall. Without a word, his arms shift and he scoops me up against his chest. Cradled like a child, I rest my head on his shoulder as he carries me away from the gravesite, eyes on the glorious morning sunshine that stains the clouds with silver linings. The last thought I have before they slip closed is of Ian.

Goodbye, sweet friend. I miss you already.

I THINK he's going to carry me back to camp, but he brings me to the hidden pool instead. I'm glad for it — I don't think I could keep it together if I had to look at the spot where Ian took his last breath. Not yet, anyway. I need a little distance.

Beck seats us by a bend on the soft bank, near the sun-dappled shallows. The water is so clear I can see straight to the bottom. He steers my limbs without resistance, reclining me back against the firm planes of his body. My toes skim the water's edge.

I feel hollow, heart cleaved from my chest. No vital signs. Scoured clean of everything that's ever mattered, like the seashells I've spent so many hours collecting since we arrived here a month ago.

A month.

Has it only been that long? The tallies I scratch into the tree trunk each day concur with that timeline, but it feels vastly inaccurate. I have aged at least a thousand years since we arrived. By all rights I should be wrinkled and arthritic, an old crone bent at the waist as she walks the beach, barely able to remember the life she lived before.

Back home, they'll be celebrating Independence Day in less than a week, ringing in the true start of summer with backyard barbecues and screaming bottle rockets. Mom will be especially devastated I'm not with her. I turn eighteen on July 4th and, before this trip, we'd always planned to spend the day riding around in her Jeep Wrangler with the doors off and that Jason Mraz song blasting from the stereo.

'Cause you were born on the Fourth of July, freedom ring.

We'd eat lunch by the lake, then Mom would take pictures to record the moment as I legally purchased my first scratch ticket. After winning MegaMillions, in accordance with tradition, she'd recite the story of my birth... and the way I got my name.

I held you in my arms at the hospital, watching the fireworks explode in the distance, and as they lit off a whole series of purple ones, your little hand curled around my finger for the first time. I looked over at your father and he looked straight back at me and we just knew.

Violet.

Our little firecracker, right from the start.

My eyes press closed, as if to hold onto the memory a little tighter, until it's burned into my brain. Her face is still clear in my mind. How long until it fades? How long until I can no longer recall the sound of her voice or the cadence of her laugh?

I tremble, and Beck's arms tighten around me. He doesn't say a word, doesn't attempt to console me. We both know there's nothing he can do to lessen the steady ache beneath my ribcage.

The sun climbs higher in the sky, but even the harshest midday beams are hard-pressed to find us in this secret, shady place. Looking around, it's easy to believe the world outside this ring of trees does not exist.

The mud on my cheek itches as it dries. When I scratch at it, chunks of dirt fall like snowflakes onto Beck's arm. Moving slowly, he shifts to dunk one cupped hand into the water. Half-sprawled in his arms, I crane my head back to watch as he brings it close to my face. His eyes are startlingly green as he lets the handful trickle across my cheek. The water droplets pour down my neck, pool in the hollow of my throat, curve across my chest.

Handful after handful, he removes the dirt from my skin in slow degrees, washing away the grime of the past two weeks and with it, some of the lingering ghosts of this morning. He is so cautiously tender, so tenuously sweet, I can hardly stand it. I sigh and close my eyes, a cat stroked into compliance with careful hands.

Eventually I fall asleep, propped half-upright against him. I'm too tired even for dreams. When I wake, I can tell by the sun's position overhead that several hours have passed. We're horizontal on the bank, tangled together in a single form, our sandy limbs totally intertwined. Beck's chest moves rhythmically at my back, his heart as steady as a drum beating in my ear. I do my best not to wake him as I untangle my body from his and drag myself to the edge.

I feel marginally better after a few swallows of cool, crisp water.

Chasing the sensation, I wade into the shallows on my knees, until my dress floats up around me. I keep going until the surface covers my breasts. My neck. My mouth. Until it closes overhead completely.

My hair drifts around me as I sink, numb, toward the silt bottom.

There's comfort in the darkness. It calls to me with a siren song. In that broken moment, I don't care whether I ever breathe air again. I don't care about anything, except escape.

My chest tightens, lungs beginning to scream for air. I ignore them, fascinated by the black spots that have begun to dance in my visual field.

Fireworks.

Two hands close over my forearms and heave me bodily from the depths. Spluttering, I'm dragged ashore and practically thrown down against the earth. Beck towers over me, hands curled into fists, jaw clenched tighter than I've ever seen it. He's seething with rage. The violence brewing inside him is boiling over.

"What the fuck, Violet!"

I stare at the ground. It's too hard to look at him.

"What the hell were you doing in the water?" he growls, voice shaking with such fury I think he might spontaneously combust.

"Nothing," I murmur.

"*Nothing?*" he explodes, hands flinging out. Water droplets fly in all directions. "You call trying to drown yourself *nothing?*"

My eyes jerk up. "I wasn't trying to drown myself. I'm not suicidal."

"From where I was sitting, sure as shit looked like you were. If I hadn't woken up when I did..." He runs his hands through his hair. The rage fades and a shattered look creeps into his eyes. Seeing his pain, knowing I'm the cause, sends a lance straight through me.

"I'm sorry. I wasn't thinking. Honestly I just..." My voice is small. "I needed it to stop for a while."

"God, Violet. I know today feels dark, but that's not the answer. That's *never* the answer."

"I know."

He falls to his knees, head bowed, breathing hard. His shoulders are shaking. Before I can stop it, my hand lifts from my side and lands on his skin. With sandy fingertips I stroke the strong tendons at the juncture of his neck and shoulder. He goes stiller than stone.

"You can't leave me," he whispers, anguished. "I need you here."

I suck in a sharp breath. My fingers press harder into his skin.

Beck's eyes find mine. "He's gone. But you're still alive. *We're* still alive." His hand reaches up and drags mine from his shoulder down to rest over his heart. "Feel that?"

I nod at the steady *thump-thump-thump* against my palm.

He bends my elbow, forcing my hand flat against my own chest.

"Feel *that*?"

I nod again.

"That's a gift, Violet. You can't punish yourself for what happened to Ian. You have to let him go." He shakes his head. "You know how pissed he would be at you for throwing away your life after you just worked so damn hard, trying to save his?"

"Tried," I say bitterly. "And failed."

"You did your best."

"My best?" My eyes widen. "I didn't do my best. What I did... it's damn near criminal. Everything that happened to him is my fault. They should lock me up for murder and throw away the key."

"What the hell are you talking about?"

"The leg! The fever. The fear. All of it." I hunch in on myself. "If I'd just let him go at the beginning, he'd have been spared weeks of pain and suffering."

"You don't know that."

"You're right, I don't. I don't know anything. Maybe that's the point I'm trying to make here." My words are thick with disgust. "I'm selfish. I see something I want and rush at it with blind conviction, regardless of who I hurt in the process."

"That's not true."

"Isn't it, though?" My tone is bleak. "My mom didn't want me to go on this trip. My friends were unbelievably pissed when I said I'd be gone for our last summer before college. My ex-boyfriend tried to talk me out of it on more than one occasion. Did I listen? *Nope.* Violet does what she does, damn the rest. And look where we are. Look at the consequences."

"Princess... you may be all powerful, but I don't think even you can take credit for our plane crashing, unless you're going to tell me you're some kind of sea goddess who summoned the storm that night."

His soft words work their way under my skin like a healing salve, soothing me, easing some of the blame from my shoulders. I feel the self-loathing slipping out of my hands, and clutch ever tighter rather than feel the other emotions crowding in behind it, eager for their chance to occupy my mind.

The sadness. The grief. The pain.

Can't I just stay numb?

"Well?" Beck prompts impatiently. "Are you a descendant of Poseidon or not?"

"Fine. So I didn't bring down the plane," I admit. "You want to hear a real gem? *My mom isn't even a doctor.* She's a veterinarian, for god's sake! I lied so I could convince you to help me cut off Ian's leg. I was so sure of myself, I didn't care if it meant manipulating my way to get there. What we did to him... What *I* did to him..." I laugh without humor. "Christ, the closest thing my Mom's ever done was treat a horse with a broken leg. And after all the pretty splints she made, the owner still came outside, took one look at the poor beast, and shot it dead."

"Let me get this straight." His eyebrows furrow until his scar turns white. "You think you manipulated me into helping? You think I sat there that day and said to myself, *'Huh, this babysitter has a few years of CPR certification under her belt, seems petty qualified to amputate this guy's limb!'* Give me a little credit, Violet. I knew you were making it up as you went. I was right there by your side, the whole time. You want to blame someone? Blame me. I could've talked you out of it. I could've said no. But I looked into your eyes and I saw the same thing that's there every damn time you look up at me. Blind courage. Raw strength. I don't know where it comes from, or how you keep finding deeper reserves within yourself, but you do. Anyone else would've fallen apart long before this. And I don't just mean any *teenage girl* — I mean anyone. The toughest soldiers in the Afghan army, the baddest special forces guys in the desert. You put them all to shame without even trying."

"But..." I'm breathless, nearly hyperventilating. "You told me to let him go, Beck. You told me to let him be at peace. Did I listen? Of course not. I *never* listen. I *never* learn. Because I'm a selfish—"

"Hey." His hand cups my jaw, stopping me mid-criticism. I'm stunned as he pulls my face up to his until we're a half-inch apart, breaths mingling, eyes catching. "I was wrong. Not you. *Me.* I let fear get in my head. And then, against my will, I found myself learning a hell of a lot about courage from a girl—" He corrects himself. "—a *woman* who refused to falter, even in the face of a pretty terrifying situation."

"But I—"

"Violet. Do you truly think you'd feel any better if we'd never tried? If we'd let him die weeks ago, when he was nothing but a stranger on a raft?" His fingers flex against my cheeks. "Because I don't. Losing Ian would be horrible no matter when it happened — two weeks ago, tomorrow, seventy years from now." His exhale is sharp. "You gave it a shot. That's all you could do. Sometimes you win, sometimes you lose. The important lesson is, no matter the outcome, you *live.* You *carry on.* And you keep fighting."

Suddenly, my Dad's voice is in my head, blending with Beck's.

Never stop fighting, Violet. Nothing in this world worth having comes without some sort of struggle.

Beck is still holding my face, his strong fingertips tracing the fragile skin beneath my eyes, skimming my temples, stroking my jawline. Taking a tactile inventory of my every feature, as if he's not sure he'll ever have the chance again. It takes all my self-control not to nuzzle my cheek against his palm and surrender to the sensation.

"You have to know," he rasps intently. "I wouldn't have survived this — any of this — without you."

"You would have. You'd have found shelter, and figured out the food thing, and—"

"No."

My eyebrows lift at the finality in his tone.

"I'm not just talking about the island, Violet. I wouldn't have survived without you. Period. You make me stronger, better, tougher, kinder. You've kept me going through all of this. Every day, every moment, every fucking beat of my heart." He's panting as his eyes drop to my lips. "You have given me purpose, blinded me with light in a world that once held only darkness. You have altered my life in a way I never expected. And I don't know how to go back. I don't know how to—"

He never finishes his sentence, because I can't take it anymore. I can't go another moment without knowing what his mouth will feel like crushed against mine. So, I close the last shred of distance between us, slamming my body up against his chest as my lips claim his in a kiss.

A kiss that changes everything irrevocably.

CHAPTER FIFTEEN

FIRE

I AM on fire beneath two callused hands.

They roam my skin relentlessly — running down my sides, splaying across my back, shoving impatiently at the straps of my dress until they slip over my shoulders. The fabric falls to the earth, but I pay it no mind. There's no room in my head for thoughts of anything but the man setting off explosions in my every nerve ending.

Beck's mouth — that lush, luxurious mouth that's captivated me from the very first moment I saw it — is finally on mine, and it's better than I ever imagined. His stubble scrapes my face, my neck, my collarbones as he flurries kisses across every inch of skin within reach. I cry out when he buries his face between my bared breasts, hands tangling in his wet hair as his mouth closes over one of my nipples.

Sand coats our limbs like a layer of grainy white paint as we kneel on the shore of the pool, wrapped so tight together it's hard to tell where his body ends and mine begins. My spine bows as desire sings through my veins. I am burning up beneath the sensation of his hard muscles and devouring lips, combusting like a solar flare off the surface of the sun as his towering frame wraps itself around mine.

My fingers turn to fists in his hair when I feel a scrape of teeth against a spot of hyper-sensitive skin. I tug his face back up to eye-level. His gaze is hazy with heat, his mouth parted as pants of desire slip out. Shaking, my hands slide to his jaw as I bring our lips back together. I can hardly breathe, but I'd rather die from oxygen deprivation than stop kissing him. Not now that we've finally succumbed to the tension that's saturated our every glance since that first instant in the airport.

His tongue demands entrance. I open for him willingly, more than happy to let him wreck me. I drown in the sensation of his mouth moving over mine. My world dwindles, every life experience I've ever had fading out of focus, my very identity stripping away until I can't recall my name or this place or how we wound up here, together. None of that matters. Here, in his arms, I am precisely where I need to be, my tattered soul made new again, bolstered by his own.

His hardness juts against my hip through the fabric of his shorts, and I lose my ability to breathe. To move. To think. Pressed against me is irrefutable evidence that my days of stolen glances and nights of dark-cast fantasies did not go unshared or unrequited. He has burned for me just as I've burned for him. Struggling in silent desperation as the pressure slowly built to this moment, here and now, with our mouths laying claim to each other and our bodies perfectly aligned.

He pushes me back against the bank and stretches out over me, delicious weight pressing me into the earth. Our mouths never break contact. Our hands never pause. There is not a shred of hesitation in the way we trace and memorize each other. Not a single beat of awkwardness.

There is only joy. Heart-pounding, euphoria-inducing joy.

In these stolen, sun-streaked moments on the shore, being kissed as I've never been kissed before, I taste true happiness for the first time in my life. My heart fills to bursting as I'm hit with the sensation of something very right finally falling into place, after an eternity of breathless expectation.

We belong together.

It's as simple as that. We are a perfect match, his hard edges absorbing my soft ones as my hands splay out across his skin. He buries his face in my neck as I trace the muscled planes of his back with hurried fingertips, exploring all the bits I've dreamed about from afar. It's been sweet torture, wondering about the taste of his lips, the feel of his hips digging into mine, the sound of his groans when I stroke my hands low across his abdomen, tracing the thin strip of hair that leads down into his shorts. My imagination is not half as satisfying as the real thing.

My fingertips are skimming the elastic strap of his black boxers when his mouth rips itself from mine.

"Stop." He's on his feet before I can blink, backing away from me like I'm a bomb with ten seconds left on the timer until detonation. "We have to stop this."

I scramble up, eyes locked on his, confusion clawing at my insides.

"What? *Why?*"

He doesn't answer. His eyes are on my bare chest, scanning my naked body up and down. The expression on his face is full of such acute torture, I feel my heart skip a beat; he's in physical pain, not being able to touch me.

"Beck..." I whisper. "If this is about my age... I'll be eighteen in a few days. The Fourth of July. Frankly, I don't think it should matter how damn old I am—"

"It's not your age." His voice is so tight, I could pluck his words from the air and snap them in two.

"Then what?"

He stares at me across the bank, tension emanating from his skin like steam off the water. There's an unreadable expression on his face, but I know him well enough to recognize the pain brimming over in his eyes. "There's something I need to tell you."

"You can tell me anything."

His fists clench and unclench rhythmically at his sides.

"Beck..." I take two steps toward him, certain if I can just put my arms around him again, this — whatever it is — will all be cleared up. Certain there's nothing in the world that can keep us apart, now that we've finally smashed the wall between us into dust. "Beck, please, whatever this is about... we'll fix it."

He cuts me off before I can take a third step. His words are the sharpest blades, cutting the world out from beneath my feet until everything I thought I knew shifts to something unrecognizable.

"I'm married."

MARRIED.

Married.

I can't stop saying it. Can't stop thinking it. Can't stop feeling it twisting around inside my stomach like a poisonous snake, its venom spreading a little farther through my system with each passing moment.

Married. Married. Married.

I murmur it under my breath like a curse, until it loses all meaning. I can feel his eyes on me as I pace back and forth, dress whipping around my legs, feet creating divots in the sand with each furious stride. I'm angry at him for not telling me, angrier at myself for not figuring it out sooner.

And heartbroken beyond belief that I've fallen in love with a man who wasn't free to claim.

Were there signs?

Did I miss them somehow?

I rack my brain for any indications he gave me that he was someone's husband, but come up short. I'm certain he never mentioned any woman, even in passing. Not a mom or a sister or even a distant female cousin. I would've remembered.

Then, of course, there's the small fact that he doesn't wear a wedding band. The only time the subject of marriage ever arose was the day he overheard me talking to Ian about the perfect life. I'd said maybe a passionless existence with the perfect husband, house, and kids would be preferable to life on a deserted island... and he'd snapped something back at me.

What was it he said?

I wouldn't put my money on that, princess.

"Violet—"

"Shut up." I cut him off, throwing out a hand to silence him. I don't want to hear his explanations. I don't even want to look at him. The only thing I truly want to do is hurl a coconut straight at his head.

"If you'd just let me—"

"SHUT. UP."

He falls silent.

I pace some more, trying to sort out my emotions. It's hard to focus on anything with his eyes tracking my every step. I feel them like a physical weight, skating across my skin in a featherlight caress. It was difficult enough to ignore him before today. After our ten — or was it twenty? — minute make-out session, earlier, I fear I'll never be able to focus on a damn thing again. The memory of his mouth is inked permanently on my brain. I can't expunge him. He's embedded deep under my skin, an irreversible tattoo.

I'm going crazy just standing this close to him. Angry as I am, my body calls out to his, desperate for his touch. Reedy breaths slide from my mouth as a dangerous thought enters my brain.

So, he has a wife.

She's not here.

I shut it down so fast, my world spins. Clearly, I need a little distance to sort through my unraveling emotions. A few days apart, to get some perspective. Halting a fair distance from him, I'm careful to keep my gaze averted. I clear my throat and do my damnedest to hold my voice steady.

"I need some time to process this. Time... and space." I swallow. "I realize that'll be difficult, since we share a camp. That's why I'm going to bring my things here for a while. You can keep the beach."

I hear him suck in a shaky breath. "How much time?"

"I don't know, Beck." My voice breaks on his name. "I don't know anything anymore."

"Violet—"

"Just don't, okay?" I curl my hands into fists, eyes on the sand at my feet. "You've done enough."

A long exhale escapes him, an indication of his deep frustration. I can feel his impatience, tangible in the air between us. The inability to explain himself, to justify his actions, is tearing him apart.

Good, a small, vindictive part of my psyche whispers. *I hope it hurts like hell.*

"I'll go get my stuff. When I get back here... I'd like it if you weren't." Heart aching, mind reeling, I pivot on my heel and walk away from him without another word.

Being away from him right now is for the best, I tell myself. *Even if it tears you apart.*

It sounds like total bullshit, even to my own ears. Apparently, Beck thinks so too, since I only make it about three steps before a hand closes over my arm and he hauls me back toward him.

"Beck!" I snap. "Did you not hear a word I just said? About needing time and space to process?"

"Fuck time. Fuck space. Fuck that whole idiotic plan, Violet."

"Excuse me?"

"You heard me perfectly fine." He leans close, eyes spitting fire.

"You don't get to set all the terms of our relationship and then storm out of here without giving me a chance to explain."

"We don't have a relationship," I hiss. "Because you have a *wife*."

A growl rumbles in his chest.

"Let me go!" I yank at my arm, but he's holding fast. "I mean it, you unbelievable asshole!"

"No."

"*No?*" I blink, amazed at his audacity. "I'll... I'll scream!"

"No one to hear you but hermit crabs."

"Then I'll smash you over the head with a coconut."

His lips twitch. "That's your prerogative, princess. Not my favorite plan, but if it'll calm you down enough to listen, I'm all for it."

"Beck... please." I can't hold on much longer. My resolve is cracking, my fury fading into a deep despair that threatens to pull me under. "Let me go."

"Like I said — *no*." He stares at me, fingers flexing against the flesh of my arm. "Today alone, you've lost a friend, nearly drowned, and had a bombshell dropped on you."

"You skipped my favorite part," I mutter. "Let's not forget how you nearly deflowered me without bothering to mention you've got a wife waiting for you at home!"

He flinches as if I've landed a physical blow, but his eyes glitter with resolve. "You can try your best to piss me off so I'll let you storm out of here, but it's not going to work. If you think I'm letting you wander into the woods by yourself, feeling the way you're feeling right now, you don't know me a damn bit."

"You're right," I say, tears of rage and hurt springing to my eyes. "I don't know you at all."

"You know me, Violet. You know me better than anyone."

"I thought I did, but apparently I was wrong. Because I don't know where you grew up, or where you went to college. I don't know where you lived before this island, or why you agreed to shoot photos for the Flint Group if you're such a damn good photographer. And I sure as hell didn't know about *her!*"

"You want to know about my life before? That's what this is about? You want details to flesh out some backstory that's no longer relevant to the man I've become?" His eyes flash. "Who I was, who you were, where we came from… none of that matters, Violet. Don't you see? We're here now. And we both know there's a pretty fucking good chance we're going to spend the rest of our lives on this island."

"God forbid!" I snap, just to be cruel. "I don't think I can stand to be trapped here another second with someone who lies as easily as you do."

"I have never lied to you," he growls in a lethal tone.

"You omitted. It's the same thing and you know it."

"It's not the same at all." His pissed-off expression now rivals mine. "Tell me… what would've been the ideal time to share my marital status with you? During the crash? On the life raft, dying of thirst? While we were cutting off Ian's leg? Or maybe when I found out about the thirteen year age gap that made all the things I was feeling for you completely null and void? Forbidden, unequivocally, no matter how much the thought of never touching you tore me apart?"

My heart clenches at those words.

He leans closer. "And while we're on the subject, how many details have you revealed to me about yourself? How much have you offered up about your past? Snippets of overhead conversations with Ian don't count."

My mouth goes dry.

He's right. I've never told him a thing. Never volunteered any meaningful information about who I used to be.

"Violet…" The pain in his voice makes me tremble. "The truth is, it's never been about who we were before. I don't know that girl from that tiny New Hampshire town. Maybe I caught a glimpse of her at a Los Angeles airport one afternoon. Maybe I thought, fleetingly, that she was beautiful, with a smart mouth I wanted to slam against mine the first instant she opened it and called me an ass. But if circumstances were different, if we'd never boarded that plane... that girl wouldn't have ever crossed my path again. We'd have gone our separate ways, lived totally disconnected lives, and never even had an inkling of what we were missing."

"Maybe that would've been better," I murmur, feeling broken. "Maybe we weren't meant to meet. Maybe all this is one giant mistake."

"I don't believe that, and neither do you. You and I... the people we've become, though all this struggle... it's the one thing I understand with perfect clarity. Maybe it's wrong, maybe it's unconventional, maybe no one else would even begin to accept it. But that doesn't make it a lie, Violet." He sighs. "If you want details, I'm happy to share. Eventually, I'd love to hear yours as well. But I think we both know, this connection between us runs a hell of a lot deeper than trivial details about favorite colors and college majors and how you take your coffee in the morning. What I feel when you look at me, when your hands touch my skin —" He physically shudders, as though the effort of keeping himself in check is damn-near killing him. "I've been looking for that feeling my whole life, in everyone I've ever met, half-convinced it didn't exist at all. Never thought I'd find it on a deserted island, of all places. Never would've guessed I'd find it with you."

The tears gathering in my eyes threaten to spill over. All those words — more than I've ever heard him speak in a single stretch — are tumbling around inside me, filling up the vacant chambers of my heart, taking the pressure off my lungs until I can breathe again.

Beck's eyes lock on the single tear that's escaped down my cheek. He reaches out to brush it away with his left hand, moving cautiously, as though he's afraid I might flinch back from him. I hold myself perfectly still, staring at his empty ring finger.

"You don't wear a wedding band."

"Does this mean you're ready to hear the story, now?"

My hesitation is relatively brief. With a nod, I settle a few purposeful paces away from him on the sand, not trusting myself when he's within reach. I watch as he paces by the water's edge, struggling to find the right words. My heart thunders inside my chest as I wait for him to begin.

"I met her in D.C. — that's where I'm from, where I went to school, where my whole family lives. We were young, still in college, when we met. I was studying photography; she'd signed up to be a model in one of my portrait classes. She was a beautiful foreign exchange student from Paris; I was a starstruck shutterbug in need of a muse. We hit it off immediately. We both wanted to see the world — I thought we'd see it together. Join the Peace Corps, teach English classes in Spain, anything we could think of, so long as it took us far from the bubble of political prosperity I'd been raised in." He swallows roughly. "When we graduated, her student visa expired. She gave me an ultimatum: either we got married, or she was going back to France and I'd never see her again. I was so young, barely twenty-two, and she was the first woman I'd ever been crazy about. I thought I was in love. I didn't want to lose her."

"You gave her a ring."

He nods. "We were married a few short weeks later. The first year was fine. The next two were not." A grimace contorts his features. "Turns out, all those things she'd told me about seeing the world, experiencing new cultures, traveling to far off destinations... All lies. She'd filled my head with exactly what I'd most wanted to hear, spun her web of exaggerations so thoroughly I didn't know I was trapped until the life began to leech from my bones. Instead of a partner, I found myself married to an aspiring fashion model, consumed entirely by her looks. A woman who wouldn't leave the Virginia suburb she'd insisted we move to as soon as we signed the marriage certificate. The only trips she'd go on were to the posh resorts her friends frequented for spa treatments, or expensive hotels the night before callbacks for modeling gigs she never landed."

I'm hardly breathing, awaiting his next words with bated breath.

"I tried to make it work. Surprised her with plane tickets to Africa on our second anniversary so we could spend the summer on safari, fixing our marriage while volunteering with an organization that protects endangered elephants. She turned me down flat. Resented me for asking. Wouldn't even consider going." Pain crosses his face at the memory. "Suddenly, I was a twenty-five-year-old man, stuck in a marriage I didn't want to a woman I no longer recognized."

"I'm sorry," I whisper, meaning it. "That sounds awful."

"It wasn't ideal, that's for sure. Neither of us was happy the way things were. She thought a baby would solve all our problems, I thought bringing a child into an unhappy marriage would make things worse, not better. I was getting ready to ask her for a divorce when an opportunity fell into my lap. The newspaper I'd been doing freelance photography for was sending a team to Turkey, to cover the migrant crisis and the increasing threats of terrorism to the region. It was the perfect opportunity to escape, and I jumped at it."

"And...your wife?"

"To say Monique was unhappy would be a grave understatement."

"She didn't want to lose you."

He shakes his head. "She didn't want to lose her *citizenship*. Why do you think she was so eager to have a baby, when she could barely stand the sight of me?"

My heart aches for him.

"I took the job. She begged me not to file the paperwork right away, told me we'd be free to live separate lives, but she needed time to apply for permanent resident status. I was so tired of fighting with her over every damn thing, from the mortgage payments to the exorbitant upkeep costs of her nonexistent modeling career. I didn't have it in me to argue anymore. I just wanted *out*. So, I agreed." He shrugs. "I was gone a week later, half a world away, and she was free to do whatever the hell she pleased without me there to hold her back or finance her expensive life-style." He stops pacing and his eyes meet mine. "Violet... I am married, legally. On paper. But in every way that counts, I'm divorced. Separated. Whatever you want to call it, I've been living as a single man for more than four years."

"You... do you still love her?" I ask, voice small.

His face goes soft and he falls to the sand at my side. He's careful not to touch me, but his eyes never shift away. "I don't think I ever loved her."

I release a breath I didn't know I was holding.

A flare of hope moves through his eyes when he sees the relieved expression on my face.

"Violet." His voice goes gravelly. "The truth is, I never loved anyone... until I met you."

CHAPTER SIXTEEN

TYPHOON

"Happy birthday, princess."

I smile in my sleep, rolling over onto my back. I blink up at Beck, haloed in the early morning light as he leans down to brush his lips against mine in a soft kiss.

"It's morning already?" I ask, voice groggy.

He nods.

I've slept straight through from yesterday afternoon. The instant I finally closed my eyes, I was out like a light. I suppose I shouldn't be surprised. It was the most emotionally draining day of my entire life — neither best nor worst, but both at the same time. A true rollercoaster.

The grief of burying Ian could not be erased by the joy I felt at Beck's revelation, nor was the love burning within me untempered by heartache. The two emotional extremes did not cancel each other out, but rather multiplied twofold, piggybacking in intensity until I was fraying like a bolt of over-stretched fabric.

I look around, eyes latching onto Ian's empty pallet, and a pang of pain grips my heart.

Goodbye, sweet friend.

I look up at the man leaning over me, butterflies bursting to life inside my gut.

I never loved anyone... until I met you.

It's hard to reconcile feeling such joy and sadness in tandem. With difficulty, I set Ian aside and focus on Beck. There's been so much darkness, so much pain. I know, for my own sake, I have to let myself bask in the light for a while. I have no doubts the grief will be back — in waves, undulating through me for weeks and months and years every time I think of Ian. But for now, just in this instant, I let lust and longing fill me to the brim as I crane my neck to kiss the man I love.

The man who loves me back.

Beck Underwood loves me.

It's hard to fathom, given the place we started out. Strangers, enemies, allies, friends, soulmates.

Yesterday, after he spoke those three little words that changed everything, he didn't even give me a chance to echo the sentiment back to him. Reading the sheer exhaustion on my every feature, he lifted me into his arms and carried me back to camp. Back *home.* We collapsed onto one of the sleeping pallets before the sun had begun its western descent, dead to the world the second our eyes closed.

For the first time in a long time, I slept with his strong arms around me, feeling warm and safe through the long hours of the night.

"Wait." I sit up, finally processing his wake-up call. "It's my birthday?"

"It is." He nods toward the tallies in the tree trunk a few yards away. "I counted back from the date of the crash. Today is the Fourth of July."

"Happy Independence Day," I murmur. "Too bad we don't have any fireworks."

He stares at me, his heated gaze on my face setting off an entirely different kind of fireworks inside my chest. I lean forward to kiss him again, reveling in the heart-stopping feeling of his mouth on mine. It's still hard to believe we're finally here, finally *together*.

I deepen the kiss, tongue seeking his as my hands wind around his neck and I press myself flush against his chest. He indulges me for a long moment before his hands wrap around my wrists and, with a groan, he gently pushes me back to create some distance.

Still panting, my mouth twists into a pout.

"Why won't you touch me?" I whisper, wondering if he's changed his mind about us in the few hours since we fell asleep. *Maybe he doesn't want me anymore.* The tortured look of restraint on his face removes those doubts almost as soon as they enter my head.

"There's no need to rush this." He tucks a strand of hair behind my ear. "I want to take my time with you. I want you to feel safe. Secure. Especially now that I know..."

My brows lift. "What?"

"That you've never done this before," he says carefully.

"My virginity didn't seem to slow you down last night," I mutter, cursing myself for ever telling him about my sexual inexperience. "I don't see why it changes anything. I want you. You want me. Unless... you've changed your mind."

"Violet. Believe me when I tell you that I want you. *Badly.*" There's stark desire in his voice. "But I also want to do this right. I want your fist time to be special."

"Deflowering seems like a perfectly special birthday gift, if you ask me," I grumble.

He laughs, a flash of straight white teeth amidst his thick stubble. It's been a while since he shaved. "Be that as it may, we're going to wait. Not forever. But... until I know it's right."

With that, he leans in and kisses me again, a lingering brush of his lips that leaves me breathless and aching all over again. "Come on," he murmurs. "We didn't eat dinner last night and I'm starving."

"Let me guess — crab for breakfast. Again."

His eyebrows waggle playfully. "If we're really feeling crazy, I was thinking we'd try to catch a fish with the traps I made."

"A fish!" I throw my hand over my heart with an exaggerated gasp. "You really know how to show a girl a good time."

"I know. Pulling out all the stops for you."

"Think we can make a birthday cake out of clams?"

"Oh sure. Topped with seaweed icing. A true delicacy."

Rolling my eyes, I allow him to pull me to my feet. I put on a show of reluctance, but the truth is, there's nothing but happiness inside my chest as we walk hand in hand toward the tidal pools. It may not be the eighteenth birthday I'd imagined, but it's the best one I've ever had.

The man by my side... he's a gift beyond my wildest dreams.

———————

THE NEXT FEW months mark the happiest I've ever been — not just on the island. Ever.

It's odd to admit that, even odder to feel it... but there's no denying the overwhelming sense of joy that consumes me from the instant my eyes spring open each morning to the moment they close as I snuggle against Beck's chest each night.

When we landed here, I was so certain that my life, for all intents and purposes, was over. As it turns out, it hadn't even begun. Not until I met him.

We're rarely apart, doing everything together as a team whether it's improving our camp, scouring the island for untapped food sources, exploring the small network of caves we discovered on the western side of the island, or thinking up new ways to entertain ourselves as summer passes by in a haze of unbearably hot days.

I become a master at coconut collecting, going so far as to teach Beck proper cheerleader posture so he can lift me without pulling a muscle. If Ian were here to witness that lesson, he'd have laughed until tears streamed down his face.

Beck successfully catches small fish in the shallows with his traps, which offers some much-desired variation to our diet. He's quite proud of himself for his invention... until the day I fashion hooks made from soda-can tabs onto string from the suture kit. Armed with a proper lure, I can't help crowing with victory when I reel in a massive mahi-mahi on my first fishing attempt. It's almost too pretty to eat, its brilliant green and aqua scales flashing in the sun as we wrangle it from the water. When I mention I might set it free to Beck, he looks at me like I'm crazy before cracking it over the head with a rock.

That night, as I fill my stomach with deliciously flaky filets, I somehow find it in my heart forgive him between moans of contentment. My guilt is no match for a well-sated appetite.

Our log cabin grows larger every day, the lashed-palm walls ascending toward the sky until they tower overhead. By the fall, we'll be able to start the slow process of thatching a proper roof from woven fronds.

My dress, tattered and bloodstained beyond repair, has been officially retired. I use the salvageable parts to fashion a new outfit — a bralette and breathable shorts — before burning the rest in the fire. My stomach, leaner than ever from our limited diet, turns deep tan. My hair, once a rich mahogany brown, bleaches with blonde streaks from our many hours in the sunshine.

As the height of summer fades, the days pass in a blur of laughter and love. We're content — more than content. We're *happy*, stealing kisses in the shallows, body surfing in the warm waves, walking the beach at sunset collecting shells and whispering secrets. We tell each other stories and slowly fill in all the blank spaces we skipped over, at the beginning.

He's in stitches laughing at some of the things Mom and I have gotten up to over the years: the day she turned the living room floor into an indoor ball pit, the time she scolded the head of my high school PTA for daring to imply cheerleading wasn't a credible sport, the morning she forgot to put the oars in the dinghy and we got stranded in the middle of the lake until nightfall.

I just about keel over when Beck tells me, at my age, he was a total nerd who never would've gotten close to a cheerleader like me unless he was taking a picture for the school paper. I wonder if the girls he went to high school with have followed his rather illustrious career... or seen what he looks like now...

If so, I bet they're kicking themselves for being so uppity.

He talks about his work, his favorite pictures ever taken, his photojournalist heroes — Robert Capa, James Nachtwey, W. Eugene Smith. He tells me about his life growing up in the nation's capital, grandson of a former Attorney General, and how his parents always expected he'd seize their many political ties with both hands. Their disappointment was great indeed when he became a photographer instead of the President of the United States. I assure him, if they can't be proud of three Pulitzer Prizes, they're the ones with the issue.

The one thing we never discuss is Monique.

As far as I'm concerned, dredging up details about his wife will only rock the boat we've thus far managed to keep on such a sunny course. Anything he says about his former French-model love is likely to make me feel insecure; anything I say runs the risk of stirring long-buried drama to the surface. So we avoid her completely, a tacit agreement that suits us both just fine.

The more days pass, the more comfortable we grow with each other; the more nights that slip by, the harder it becomes to pull away when dawn breaks. He's still adamant that we wait for the *right time* to finally surrender to each other, body and soul... to consummate our relationship in that most final way… but I can feel his resolve crumbling as the desire between us crescendoes from a whisper to a scream.

There's a magnetic current charging the air even when we're a dozen feet away, separated by a stretch of white sand beach. Just the weight of his eyes on my body makes me want to writhe. Every time our hands brush, sparks electrify my skin, kindling a fire inside me that threatens to rage out of control.

One night in late August, as we lay beneath a bed of stars in our open-roofed hut, our kisses grow so fervent I think I might shatter from just the press of his lips, the scrape of his teeth, the rasp of his stubble against my cheeks as his mouth trails down to the valley between my breasts. I hear him sigh painfully and know what's coming — he's about to pull away. My body is already tensing with the ache of impending separation.

No, I think, a firm denial. *Not tonight. Not again.*

Before he can stop me, my palms shove up against his shoulders and I buck, flipping him onto his back in one smooth motion. Straddling his waist, I take control, wrapping his wrists in my hands as I slam my mouth down on his. My hips slide back until his length is nestled perfectly between the junction of my thighs, so hard it makes my eyes water with sheer desire.

"Violet," he growls against my lips, a warning. "We decided to wait…"

"No, *you* decided. And my patience has officially…" My hips roll deliciously and we both gasp at the feeling. "…*expired.*"

His forehead hits mine as he wrestles his wrists from my grasp. A few seconds later, he cups my cheeks gently with both hands. Our breaths mingle. "Your patience will be rewarded," he pants softly. "I promise."

"When?"

"Soon."

"So, like, in ten minutes? Tomorrow? How soon is *soon?*"

His laugh is laced with torment. "You are going to kill me."

"That's the idea."

"If I'm dead, you'll never get what you want."

A sound of discontent rumbles from my mouth. "Did you take a vow of celibacy or something? Please tell me. I'm beginning to think you're a monk."

"Not a monk. A saint," he mutters. "Or, at least, a man with the self-control of one."

"Please... feel free to be less saintly." I undulate my hips again, rubbing against his length until I see stars. "...and..." I gasp into his mouth. "A little more *sinful*."

"Do you want me to go sleep on the beach?" he threatens, fingertips digging into my hips to keep them still. "Keep that up, and I'll have no choice."

With a grumble, I slide off his chest and roll away from him, creating a buffer of cool air between our heated bodies. I'm quaking with lust, aftershocks of an almost-orgasm rolling through me in mini waves of pleasure. I was close. Teetering on the brink.

I could feel it.

Beck lets me sulk for about thirty seconds before he reaches out and hauls me against his side. My head rests against his chest as he loops one powerful thigh over both of mine. His arm hooks around my back as my hands tuck beneath his armpit, tracing the indentations of his ribcage. The sharp sting of disappointment fades as he strokes my hair and presses a soft kiss to my forehead. I let my eyes drift closed and remind myself he's not dragging this out for his own benefit. Hell, he's suffering a perpetual state of blue-balls because he truly believes it's what's best for me.

Because he loves me.

There's a smile on my face as I drift into slumber.

THE HOWL of the wind wakes us.

Like a pack of wild dogs, it sweeps off the water and up the beach with stunning force, a precursor to a far greater threat. Beck's wild eyes meet mine in the dark as we stumble from our cabin into camp. His hand wraps around mine, keeping me tethered to him as the frigid wind whips into our faces. It blows hard enough that I have to shield my eyes in the crook of an elbow, hard enough that the nearby palm trees creak precariously with each gust.

"Fuck," I hear Beck mutter, the word snatched away by the breeze a second after it leaves his lips.

I follow his line of sight out over the white-capped water. What I see there makes my blood run cold. There's a dense wall of rain moving toward us, pouring straight down in a sheet as the storm-front makes its approach. The sky above churns with clouds, moving clockwise like a deadly carousel. It's maybe a mile offshore, two at the most. And from the looks of it...

It's headed straight for us.

These gusting winds are merely the first claws of the beastly typhoon bearing down on our island. Lightning flashes, illuminating the swirling clouds from the inside like a cat-burglar in a darkened house. As a little girl, whenever an electrical storm would light up the mountain range just beyond my backyard, I'd count Mississippis in my head before thunder shook the sky, trying to gauge the storm's distance from my bedroom window.

I do the same thing now.

One Mississippi.

Two Mississippi.

Three Mississippi.

Boom.

The whole earth seems to tremble. If it's this intense while the storm is still a few miles offshore... I can only imagine what that same thunder will feel like when it's directly over our heads. Apparently, Beck has the same thought. Without another moment's hesitation, his hand tightens on mine as he turns and starts dragging me back toward the cabin.

"Come on!" he barks, increasing his pace. As we run, I watch the wind tear our raft to ribbons, the thick plastic shredding like a piece of tissue paper. Coconuts begin to catapult from the branches overhead like bombs, crashing against the beach with an explosive shower of sand.

"Duck!" I scream as I watch one fly straight for Beck's face. We only just manage to avoid the hurling projectile. I've always thought that statistic *'Falling coconuts kill more people than shark attacks!'* was total bullshit until this moment, when I find myself dodging them like bullets, my heart hammering against my ribs so hard I'm sure an arrhythmia is imminent.

We burst through the entryway, a momentary reprieve from the lashing wind. Beck drops my hand and beelines for his duffle bag. As I watch, he starts shoving items in at random — the knife, the water bottle, our fishing line, the first aid kit, our flare gun. Anything within reach that seems at all important is deposited roughly into the green canvas.

"What the hell are you doing?!"

"We have to leave!" He yells over the roaring wind, tossing my backpack in my direction.

I barely manage to catch it. *"Leave?!* And go where?"

"The caves, on the west side — we'll be protected there!"

My head shakes in swift rejection. "We can't abandon our home, Beck!"

"This isn't a discussion. We're going, *now.*"

"You can go, but I'm staying!" I snap, digging my heels in.

"Like fuck you are!"

My next argument is cut off by a loud creaking sound. I watch with wide eyes as the left wall of the cabin we've spent the past three months building — log by log, lash by lash — is shorn cleanly from the rest of the structure. Beck hurls himself on top of me, flattening us against the earth as the remaining walls cave in all around us. It happens so fast, there's not even time to scream.

Someone up there must be looking out for us, because we're untouched when the sand clouds lift. Raising his head, Beck glares down into my face. "You can come willingly or I'll carry you. But we aren't staying here another second."

I stare into his eyes, then around at the remnants of our home, reduced to rubble. Everything we've worked so hard to piece together... gone in a single gust. My eyes sting from more than the whipping winds as I give a tremulous nod.

"Let's go."

As we scramble to our feet, Beck grabs his duffle and I sling my backpack over one shoulder. Lacing our hands together, we start running as fast as we can. I throw a glance back at the beach and see the typhoon is even closer now, roiling black and purple as it prepares to make landfall. As I watch, a tornado funnel descends from the clouds to form a waterspout. Two more appear in the seconds after.

Fuck.

We increase our pace as we sprint down the beach, the wind at our back spurring us onward. My backpack bangs between my shoulder blades with each stride. We pass the tidal pools, completely submerged by frothing surf. Beck's fishing traps are scattered in pieces on the beach, smashed to bits by the ocean's punishing assault. When a massive swell crashes a bit too close for comfort, we dart beneath the tree cover.

Calling it *cover* might be a stretch, at the moment. Palms are stripped bare as strong blasts of wind rip away branches. Low-lying bushes are pulled up by their roots and sucked into the sky. More coconuts fly through the air, smashing into the sand like deadly mortar shells, a tropical version of D-Day at Normandy.

We keep our heads down as we race west, in the direction of the caves. My feet slice to shreds against the rough coral rocks littering the ground. Wincing with pain, I wish I'd had the forethought to pull on Ian's shoes before we left camp. There's nothing to be done about it now. No time to stop, no possibility of a break.

Much as I initially wanted to deny it... Beck was right. This storm will kill us, if we don't reach shelter soon.

By the time we burst from the trees by the western cliffs, I'm breathless and bleeding. There are scratches all over my arms and legs from racing through the thicket. Each step across the rocks leaves a bloody footprint as I limp toward the dark mouth of the cave. We stagger inside without preamble, leaning on the rock walls for guidance in the pitch black. There's no light, nothing to see by. Every surface drips with moisture.

"Beck?" I whisper, fear coursing through me.

"I'm here."

I feel his hand lace with mine, squeezing to offer reassurance. Slowly, my eyes adjust to the dark. I can make out only the most basic of shapes — Beck's silhouette, the closest wall, my own hand five inches in front of my face. The rest of the world is a mere shadow.

Thunder rattles the thick stone around us a scant instant after a flash of lightning splits the sky. The wind whistles louder than a banshee scream. I hear an unfamiliar rumbling sound and for an instant, I fear the rocks are caving in around us. I quickly realize it's merely the sound of heavy rainfall, pummeling the roof above in an incessant onslaught.

The storm is here.

Sinking to the frigid stone ground, we hold each other in the dark as the wind howls ever louder, feeling desperately fragile in the face of mother nature's wrath.

"I love you," I whisper, the first time I've ever said the words aloud.

"I know," he returns, kissing me blindly.

CHAPTER SEVENTEEN

SYMPHONY

AFTER THREE HOURS, the storm shows no signs of letting up. Huddled together for warmth, we shiver in the shadowy cave, frozen to the bone as the minutes tick by without any source of light or heat. The damp stone walls act as an icebox. I blow on my fingertips, flexing them to keep the blood circulating.

A few more hours of this, and hypothermia will set in.

"It'll pass soon," Beck assures me periodically. I can't help noticing he sounds a shade less confident every time he says it.

Robbed of my sight, I explore the contents of my backpack by touch. The fringed, flat-edges of the coloring book pages. The waxy tips of the crayons. The saw-toothed metal of my toiletry bag's zipper. The toothpick-thin wood of our two remaining waterproof matches.

Two.

Not nearly enough to keep the cave awash in light for hours on end. The paper coloring book would do well enough for starting a fire, but without driftwood kindling or dry leaves to keep it burning... we'd be back at square one within a matter of minutes. Marooned in the dark once more.

"Unless..." I murmur under my breath.

"What?" Beck asks.

"I think I have an idea."

I remove the contents of my backpack one by one. My numb fingers tingle as I grip the crayon box. Pulling a color out at random, I pass it to Beck.

"Hold this for a moment."

His voice is wry. "Violet, as much as I'd love to color with you, this doesn't seem like an opportune moment to explore our creativity—"

"Do shut up."

He laughs in the dark.

Gripping one of the matchsticks between my fingers, I make sure I've got a steady hold on the side of the box before I strike. There's a flash as the friction causes the tip to catch. I squint against the sudden brightness as the smell of sulphur drifts up into my nostrils. Before the match can fizzle out, I hold it to the tip of the crayon in Beck's hand. It takes a moment to light, but eventually the waxy paper wrapping flares with heat and begins to burn like a taper candle.

Beck shoots me an amused look as I gently take the flaming magenta stick from his grip. Tilting it at an angle, I let a few drops of melted wax fall to the stone floor, then press the flat end of the crayon into the pink puddle. After a few seconds, the wax dries and I pull my hand away, pleased when our makeshift flame remains upright.

"Did you know?" I ask, grinning broadly. "Crayons make perfect emergency candles."

He grins back at me. For the first time in hours, I can clearly make out his chiseled features in the flickering light. The view lifts my spirits immediately.

"Each one burns for about thirty minutes, if I remember correctly. And considering I invested in the jumbo pack…" I look down at the container. There are at least a hundred crayons of all shades stacked in neat rows. "We should be good for a while."

We grab a few more and position them strategically around the space, until there's enough light to see by. I can't stop smiling as I watch the tiny lights burning merrily. It's true what they say — everything really is more romantic by candlelight.

Even a cave.

"Where'd you learn that trick?" Beck asks, sprawling against the flattest wall with his feet outstretched. "Summers at sailing camp?"

My head shakes as sudden sadness flares through me. "My mom taught me, actually."

"You miss her."

"I do." The lump in my throat makes it difficult to breathe. "She's — she was — my best friend."

"She still is."

I settle against his side, craving heat and contact. My head hits his shoulder as his arm slides around my waist.

"Past tense feels appropriate," I say, when I've found the strength to keep my voice somewhat steady. "She thinks I'm dead."

"You don't know that for sure."

"Maybe." I sigh and close my eyes. "But I just feel so guilty. She must be going through hell, back home."

"That, I can believe." His head comes down to rest against mine. "If I lost you, I'd be in hell too. You may not know this about yourself, Violet Anderson, but you're not the kind of person people simply move on from. You're rather… unforgettable."

We're silent for a long stretch, just watching the flames dance. They cast strange shadows on the cave walls all around us as the rain patters on overhead, a muted staccato. If I believed in ghosts, this is exactly the kind of place they'd dwell. Ancient spirits at the edge of the world, in a place untouched by human hands.

Until ours.

"Do you ever think about what would happen if we actually made it home?" I breathe, half-afraid to ask the question aloud. It feels safer, here in this place of shadows and secrets, to voice the deepest fears of my heart. The ones that whisper things I don't want to hear late at night, about ex-wives and age gaps and societal norms. The ones I push away with every ounce of strength I possess, refusing to accept any other ending than one in which Beck and I end up together.

At my question, he tenses almost imperceptibly — just the slightest stiffening of his muscles before he regains control. If I wasn't so attuned to his every detail, I wouldn't notice it at all. His voice betrays none of his inner turmoil.

"No. I don't think about it."

He volunteers nothing more than that... but I know him.

I know how his mind works, how his heart beats. I know the sound of his sighs and the break in his laugh. I know him like the breath in my lungs, the blood in my veins. And so I know... I am not the only one who wonders, in the small hours of the night, whether there is any world outside the one we have built from scratch on this island in which a future for us exists. I know I am not the only one who questions if the salvation we've been praying for these days and weeks and months will ultimately be our undoing.

His lips hit my forehead. Not kissing, just breathing. He does that often — breathes me in, as if he might pull me into his lungs and hold me there, beside his heart, forever.

"Me neither," I lie, feeling my eyes prick with unshed tears.

No past. No future.

Only now. Only us.

I slide my palm against his and knit our fingers together.

We are here. We are happy. That's all that matters.

Moving in slow motion, I slide my leg across his body and shift onto his lap. He makes a small sound as his hands find my hips, tugging me closer. Face to face, my arms draping around his neck, I stare into his eyes in the mellow light. He's so gorgeous, sometimes just looking at him too closely takes my breath away.

Arching my neck, I lean in and kiss the scar that bisects his left eyebrow. My mouth lingers for a moment before moving to the bridge of his nose, across the sharp slope of his cheekbones, down the firm line of his jaw.

I take my time. Kissing, tasting, teasing.

His fingers are digging into my skin by the time my lips finally make it to his. I keep them an inch away, close enough to breathe his air, careful not to brush. The longer we hover there, poised on the edge of a kiss like a swimmer on a diving board twenty feet above the pool, the more potent the tension becomes.

This is the moment before the fall. The last, breathless instant of toe-curling deliberation before the dive.

My tongue darts out to wet my lips, and that's all it takes.

The tension snaps.

With a growl, Beck's mouth crushes mine. My hands slide into his hair as his arms band around me like steel, plastering me against him so tight it's difficult to draw breath. He holds me like a promise, his body whispering everything we're both afraid to admit out loud.

Mine is speaking the same language.

The bralette disappears over my head in Beck's hands, so fast I hardly notice him removing it until my bare chest brushes against his muscular one. My teeth sink into my lip. I catch a fleeting glimpse of a wolfish grin before his mouth drops lower, laving one of my nipples with his wicked tongue until I am no more than putty in his vastly capable hands.

"Beck," I beg, barely able to form the word.

I don't know exactly what I need; I just know I need *more* of it.

Lips, teeth, tongues.

Him.

His hands are infinitely gentle as he lays me back against the cold cave floor. I feel them shaking as they trace sensual patterns on my skin and know what this display of restraint is costing him.

"Touch me, please," I breathe, staring up into his face. "I promise I won't break, Beck."

"*You* might not. Maybe I'm afraid *I* will." His voice is a growl. "I don't think you know what touching you does to me."

"I don't know," I admit, watching the firelight flicker across his skin. "So… why don't you show me?"

His eyes flash with such intense heat I think I'll burst into flames. I thought, after so many months, I'd memorized his every expression but now, as his mouth parts on a shaky exhale, I watch his features rearrange into a look I've never seen before. It's as though he's taken off a mask to reveal the true man beneath — his edges a little sharper, his needs a little stronger, his hands a bit less gentle.

Yes.

Finally, yes.

My heartbeat quickens to a mad tattoo I can't control as he strips off the rest of our clothes. His drugging kisses melt my bones into rubber as his mouth moves down my neck and across the planes of my stomach. Head bowed, he maneuvers my calves up onto his shoulders.

I watch him move in the semi-dark, barely breathing. When our stares tangle once more, I see his need to possess every inch of me warring with his desire to make my first time as pleasurable as possible.

"Violet," he rasps, a question and plea.

"Please," I breathe, an answer and a prayer.

With a violent buck of his hips he thrusts into me, tearing through the last traces of my innocence in a single stroke. I cry out at the unfamiliar pressure, eyes stinging with tears, my mewls absorbed by his mouth as it claims mine in a relentless kiss. He moves within me, pace increasing in smooth strokes, and after a few moments, I begin to adjust. The ache of pain and shock morphs into something entirely different as my body finds a matching rhythm beneath his weight.

So this is what all the fuss is about, I think, beginning to spiral into bliss. *It was worth every second of that torturous wait.*

Pleasure grows in steady increments, a drumbeat inside my veins growing faster and faster as I stare up at Beck, seeing nothing but pure wonder reflected back at me. As if he too is awed that our bodies could come together to create this whole symphony of euphoria, flowing from him to me and back again in perfect harmony. There is music in my veins, a melody between my legs I'll never forget no matter how much time goes by, no matter where we end up — together or apart, uncharted or back on solid ground.

Beck Underwood sings the song of my soul.

For the next few hours, as the typhoon rages on outside, we gasp and cry and sigh, creating a storm all our own within the circle of each other's arms.

THE WALK back to camp the following day is slow for many reasons — not the least of which involves the tinge of pain that flares deep inside me with each step, a constant reminder of Beck's thorough possession last night... and again this morning as our candles burned low and the rain tapered to a drizzle overhead. As much as we'd hated the cave at first, by the time the storm passed I could hardly bring myself to leave.

I smile absentmindedly at the memory, squeezing Beck's hand tighter as he helps me over a particularly large fallen palm. He grins back, more joy on his face than I've ever seen.

We are bursting with life and love, surrounded by utter desolation.

The total wreckage of the island cannot be overstated. Any paths we'd forged through the brush have been obliterated by the typhoon. Elephant ear plants wave like tattered flags of defeat on a deserted battlefield. Bushes lay upside down, roots exposed to the sky. Scattered rocks litter every surface, coral confetti from an unwanted party guest.

I step on something sharp and wince. After yesterday's bolt toward the caves, my feet are a tattered mess, covered in welts and scrapes that make even the slightest pressure unpleasant. Beck hears my muffled sound of distress and, without a word, drops to his knees to offer up his back. I roll my eyes as if he's ridiculous, but that doesn't stop me from looping my arms around his neck and my legs around his waist. I cling like a baby koala bear as he carries me along, picking our way slowly toward our camp.

Or, whatever remains of it.

My hopes aren't high by any means. Witnessing the devastation on this side of the island, it's hard to believe there'll be anything left at all in our unsheltered lagoon. We will have to start anew, armed only with the few possessions in our bags and the clothing on our backs.

Somehow, that challenge doesn't seem quite as dire as it once might've. I think that has a lot to do with the fact that, this time, we're unquestionably together. A single unit, forged by time and trauma. I know in my soul that we are stronger than whatever hurdles an unexpected typhoon can throw at us. No matter what the future holds, we will weather every storm and come out stronger on the other side, hand in hand.

It takes nearly an hour to find the beach. When we finally hit white sand, Beck sets me down. My eyes swing in an arc, taking in the whole span of coast, from the rainbow cresting over the distant horizon to the newly exposed bed of coral, stripped bare by the crashing waves.

It's just as well I've prepared myself to find our camp reduced to rubble. It is. Unfortunately, it's something else, something I haven't prepared for in the slightest, that makes my feet turn to stone and my heart clench into a fist.

Oh my god.

Is that...

It can't be...

I hear Beck moving around the remnants of our cabin, searching for anything that can be salvaged, but I don't look at him. I stand stock still, afraid to blink. Afraid to move. Afraid it's another mirage.

But, most of all, afraid that it's actually real.

"Hey, princess did you hear me?" Beck calls. "Your fishing rod is still in one piece!"

When I don't answer, he moves to my side. I feel his hand at my elbow, hear the concern in his tone, but I can't bring myself to acknowledge it.

"What's wrong, Violet? Is it the camp? I know it looks bad, but we'll make it right—"

"Beck."

He stops short at my grave tone. "What is it? What's wrong?"

Shaking like a leaf, I lift my hand and point down the beach, past the other side of our inlet, to the exposed bed of reef. There, embedded on its side in the coral, mast snapped in two, is a wrecked sailboat.

I hear Beck gasp.

My eyes lift to his, wide with worry and hope.

"You see it too, don't you?" I ask, unsure which answer I'm most hoping for.

It doesn't matter.

I get neither.

He's already running away from me.

CHAPTER EIGHTEEN

SAVED

THE SAILBOAT IS ABANDONED.

There are no footprints in the sand around the hull, no signs of life at all. Whatever poor souls once dwelled aboard are long gone, likely victims of the typhoon. As we approach, picking our way across the coral bed with care, I notice the life ring is missing from the stern — not a good sign. Someone went overboard, a rescue was attempted.

Clearly, that attempt failed.

There's a snapped harness tether dangling from the steering wheel, as if the sailor at the helm was simply torn away and tossed into the waves. Guilt and sorrow spiral through my chest. I wouldn't wish that fate on anyone.

The boat is canted at an angle, but with a slight boost from Beck I'm able to scramble aboard. It's not a particularly large vessel — only around forty feet — but it's equipped for blue water sailing. The impressive panel of navigational instruments by the helm is a dead giveaway, as are the solar panels affixed to the tattered dodger that covers the cockpit.

Beck moves behind me like a shadow as we make our way down three steep, ladder-like steps into the cabin. The space is so disheveled it looks as if a tornado has picked up the boat and used it as a cocktail shaker. Then again, remembering the waterspouts I saw, I'm not fully confident saying one hasn't.

Every cushion is overturned, every item scattered across the floor. We sort through piles of clothing, foul weather gear and spare rope. A solar-powered camping lantern. Countless boxes of unopened matches. Bottles of water. Rolls of plush toilet paper. A full stockpile of canned food.

So many things we could've used to survive.

So many things I would've killed to get my hands on.

I nearly lose it when I spot the perfect fishing lures, manufactured by an assembly line, glinting at me from a clear tackle box. My heart aches when I stumble across an orange pill bottle full of emergency antibiotics, months too late to do Ian any good.

If only, if only, if only.

I know I should be celebrating. Doing cartwheels at our good fortune. The wreck has provided an unexpected windfall. These items will make survival far easier than it's ever been. We'll have a supply of food and plenty of warm clothing. A bona fide tool kit with hammers and wrenches and a handsaw. There's even a miniature charcoal grill.

Yet… there's a strange, inexplicable heaviness inside my chest I cannot shake off. Instead of a triumphant conquest, this feels like a pyrrhic victory — the first rotation of a crash course about to spin entirely out of my control.

"Violet. Look at this."

My eyes swing to Beck. His eyes are on his hands, and his hands are shaking.

He's holding a portable VHF radio.

I don't think either of us breathe as he lifts his fingers to twist the power button into the ON position. With a beep and a quick buzz of static, the screen lights up and the antenna begins searching for a signal.

Suddenly, something that once seemed desperately out of reach solidifies into a firm reality beneath our feet.

We can call for help.

The thought has barely entered my mind when Beck lifts the radio to his mouth and presses down on the transmit button.

"Can anyone hear me?" he says into the speaker. "Is anyone out there? If you're listening... this is an emergency SOS call..."

<hr />

WRAPPED IN A WARM WOOL BLANKET, I sit on my favorite drift-wood tree trunk tracing the many tallies I've carved into its surface over the past few months. There's a can of half-eaten peaches by my side, steaming in the sun. A freshly-applied coat of red polish glitters on my toenails. My body has been scrubbed head to toe with an unfamiliar body wash that reeks of roses. A stranger's t-shirt drapes me like a dress.

I am a princess on her throne, reveling in the spoils of war.

It's been five days since the sailboat washed ashore.

Five days of waiting.

Five days of watching Beck pace ever-deepening trenches in the sand before bed each night, calling for help into the damn radio on every channel imaginable. He allows himself only fifteen minutes per day, terrified the batteries are going to run out at any given moment.

I want to grab him by the shoulders and shake him until he realizes this obsession is going to drive him insane. I would, if I thought he'd listen.

To me, the sailboat is nothing but a twist of fate. Seems that spiteful bitch had one final game in store for us — dangling the tantalizing hook of rescue, only to snatch it out of reach at the last moment.

I've begun the slow process of sorting through the wreckage, taking stock of the damage to the hull. There's a pretty serious hole in the fiberglass after being bashed repeatedly against the reef. Water has flooded the entire bilge. I doubt, even if we could repair the engines or re-rig the mast, she'd make it more than the length of a football field before filling with water and plummeting to the bottom of the Pacific.

When I reveal this news to Beck, his nightly radio calls become even more frenzied.

Every time he catches me carrying something from the boat to the site of our former camp, I see a bit more despair creep into his eyes. He's delayed his efforts to rebuild, convinced someone will hear our distress calls and charge full-throttle to our rescue.

Over a dinner of saltine crackers and cold tomato soup, I broach the topic.

"I was thinking, tomorrow, we should start collecting wood for a new cabin. Maybe this time we should build it closer to the caves. The beach on that side isn't as pretty as this one, but it's definitely more sheltered. If another storm comes, we'll be safer there."

Beck is silent.

"Hello?" I wrinkle my nose at him. "Did you hear me?"

"I just don't think we need to start rebuilding yet. I still think..."

"That help is coming?" I say, voice a bit sharper than I intended. I soften it before adding, "I know you believe someone is on their way as we speak, but maybe it's time to face reality."

Brows lifting, he stares at me for a beat. "You're the one who's been telling me since day one that I need to have hope. That I need to believe, in spite of the odds, some things actually work out."

"And *you're* the one who told me to stop thinking that way!" I throw back at him. "I believe your exact words were, *you need to prepare yourself for the possibility that this story might not have a happy ending.*"

"That was before."

"Before what?" I yell, exasperation bleeding into my tone.

"Before I fell in love with you!" He yells right back. "Before everything changed! Before you taught me that some things are worth fighting for, worth *dying* for."

"I don't..." I shake my head. "I can't..."

"Violet. *Talk to me.* Tell me what's going on. You haven't been yourself since that ship washed ashore."

"I'm fine."

"You aren't fine. You're distant. You're distracted. You're even sad. But you're definitely not *fine*." He runs his hands through his hair, at a loss. "The thing is, for the life of me I can't figure out why. Seems to me, the possibility of getting off this damn rock — the *real* possibility, not some faint flicker of a mirage on the horizon — should be something you're a little more invested in."

I try to conjure a denial, some sort of distraction to keep him from seeing through me to the shameful truth, but it's too late. He knows me too well. He cares about me too much to let this slide without unearthing the source of my discontent.

"Beck..." I start. Horrifyingly, I can't get out more than his name before emotion overwhelms me. Burying my face in my hands, tears explode from my eyes. I try to staunch their flow, but it's no use.

"Shit! Violet!?" A few seconds later, Beck is at my side, his arms sliding around me. His mouth hits my temple. "What's the matter? Are you okay? Are you hurt?"

Hurt.

What an inconsequential word to describe such a feeling.

"No, I'm not hurt," I murmur.

"Then what is it? Tell me."

I shake my head. "I can't."

"Violet. You can tell me anything. You know that by now."

Looking up at him with watering eyes, I force out the words that have been haunting me for days. Words that have been tearing my insides to shreds since the instant I spotted that sailboat. Words that claw up my throat and threaten to burst forth every time he turns on that damn radio and starts to pace.

I can't hold them in any longer.

"I don't want to go."

His face flips through a series of expressions so fast I can hardly keep up. Confusion. Rage. Disbelief. Sadness. Shock. Love. When he speaks, his voice is carefully empty.

"What did you say?"

"I said I don't want to go!" I reach up and dash the tears from my eyes, pulling out of his arms in one violent gesture. "I don't want to leave the island."

"How can you say that?" He sounds baffled. "Violet, you're not thinking straight."

"I am! I am thinking straight." I whirl around to face him. "Would it be so bad? Staying here together? Would you hate it so much if this, you and me on this *rock*, as you called it, was the sum total of the rest of your life? Would you feel just as trapped by me as you did…"

As you did by her.

I see realization click into place. "Oh, Violet. You think, if we're rescued…"

"It'll be over." My voice breaks. "This. *Us*. As soon as we leave, as soon as we go back… I'm terrified you and me will cease to exist. That there's no place for us there — not together, at least. So forgive me if I'm not doing cartwheels at the prospect of a ship on that horizon. You may be thrilled beyond belief, but me?" My voice cracks. "The constant thought of losing you hasn't been a fun way to spend the past few days."

My voice fades out on a tattered breath, leaving us in total silence. As we stare at each other, listening to the rhythmic crashing of waves, I rack my brain trying to think of a way to bridge this sudden distance.

Before I can open my mouth to try, Beck starts moving. He stalks toward me, closing the gap between us in two long-legged strides, and grabs me firmly by the shoulders. Glaring down into my face, I can see how pissed he is before the first syllables leave his lips.

"That's what you think of me? Of *us*? You think what we have will disappear, just because we go back home?" He gives me a small shake. "Haven't you been listening to a damn thing I've said for the past few months?"

"I...I..." I hiccup.

"Violet Anderson, you utter madwoman. You crazy, stubborn, complicated, awful, wonderful, beautiful girl. You lovely, charming, wretched, funny, sweet, strong woman." He releases my shoulders to take my face between his hands. "I love you. *I love you.* And I will keep loving you until I take my last breath, whether that's here on a deserted island with only hermit crabs to witness it, or back home in civilization, with the rest of humanity. I told you a long time ago — I'm here for you. I'll be here for you. *Always.* Even when I'm a dick about it." His lips twist. "Even when *you're* a dick about it."

I can't help smiling at that amendment.

His eyes soften. "We may've been lost on this island, but I found myself in you. And I'm never letting you go. Not now. Not ever."

His lips land on my cheeks, kissing away the tears still streaming down my face, then moving to claim my mouth. The kiss is one for the record books — an indisputable underscore to the emotions he's just laid bare at my feet. I feel like I might float up out of my body as we stand interlocked on the beach, both trembling.

When he finally breaks away, my tears have stopped and there's a lightness in my chest that's been missing for days. He's brought me back, yet again. My ever-present guardian, hauling me bodily from the brink.

From the depths of a swallowing ocean.

From the clutches of a scorching thirst.

From the embrace of a still, clear pool.

From the midst of a pit of despair.

He has saved me over and over and over again. Without faltering. Without failure. In the darkness, he leads me back, a guiding star illuminating my way home. In the glaring light of day, he is my solid foundation, letting me fly but always there to catch me when I need to return to earth.

I hear my pulse pounding in my ears as I look up at him. They say the average human heart beats 2.5 billion times over the course of a lifetime.

2.5 billion heartbeats.

And every one of mine belongs to him.

"I love you," I tell him, kissing him again with every ounce of passion in my bloodstream. We're both breathless when we finally break apart.

Beck's eyes never shift from mine, emerald surfaces shining with light as he holds me close.

"Going home won't be the end of us, Violet. It'll be a chance at a real beginning. A future together, carved out in whatever pattern we want." His nose nuzzles mine in a stroke of reassurance. "I don't give a fuck what anyone else thinks about that. About *us*. The world can go to hell, for all I care. I've been there and back already. And if, when all is said and done, I walk out with the love of my life at my side... I guess I can't really complain about a damn thing."

IN THE END, it happens rather quietly.

There are no waving flags, no blaring trumpets. No armored

knight on a white horse, charging in to save the day. A helicopter does not swoop down at the last second to air-lift us to safety. Men in black flak jackets don't storm the beach, guns blazing, as though we're hostages in a standoff with the island keeping us against our will.

It's a sun-drenched morning. I sit with my feet in the shallows, watching minnows dart by with preternatural speed as Beck re-builds his fishing traps in the sand nearby.

One minute, the horizon is clear. The next, there's a large luxury cruiser gliding into view.

Beck speaks rapid-fire into the radio as I throw wet leaves on our fire, sending a plume of thick black smoke up into the sky, to lead them straight to us. It's far too shallow for the hundred-foot ship to approach our reef-ringed atoll. We stand on the beach, hand in hand, watching as a hard-bottomed inflatable dinghy is lowered from the upper deck with rope pulleys. It hits the water with a splash.

A few minutes from now, they'll be here.

A few minutes after that... we won't be.

This is our last moment alone together, I realize. *Our last moment on the island.*

I turn from the shore and glance around at the dense trees, the white sand, the azure sky overhead, taking it all in with fresh eyes. All the beauty and the devastation, all the love and the heartache. This place has been the battleground that tested my mettle; the fire that tempered me to steel; the landscape that altered me from girl to woman. I can't help a bolt of sadness that shoots through me at the thought of leaving it all behind.

Well...

Not *all* of it.

I'll be bringing the most important piece home with me.

"Are you ready?" Beck asks lowly, squeezing my hand ever tighter.

Whispering one last goodbye to Ian beneath my breath, I turn my back to the island and look ahead, toward the future, prepared to face whatever comes next. As long as we're together, we can face anything.

Craning my neck, I plant a lingering kiss on Beck's mouth.

"Let's go home."

THE END

...or is it the beginning?

ACKNOWLEDGMENTS

So, funny story.

I never planned to write this book. I mean it! It started as an inside joke.

A bit of background...

At the end of 2016, I wrote a two-book series called **THE GIRL DUET**. In that story, the main character is an aspiring actress who lands the role of a lifetime starring in a movie about two people stranded on an island in the South Pacific after their plane crashes.

Their names: *Violet and Beck.*

The movie: *Uncharted.*

Sound familiar?

Nearly a year after publishing THE GIRL DUET, I sat down and gave Violet & Beck their own story. It was supposed to be a creative exercise between manuscripts. Instead, it turned into a full novel that touched my heart in so many ways, that made me grow my craft, that challenged me to try something radically different from my previous work.

I truly had the most magical time writing this story. I love it. Every sentence. Every character. Every scene.

I hope you love it too!

I'm so blessed to be able to write for a living, and when I get the chance to do something crazy — *like write a book based on the fictional movie within one of my other books* — I'm reminded just how cool my job is.

Thank you for coming along for the ride with me, these past few years. I can't wait to see what else lies ahead!

Much love to my family and friends for all their help throughout the writing process, whether it's assisting me with edits or easing me out of deadline-mode with an extra large margarita.

Thanks a million to my reader group THE JOHNSON JUNKIES for always brightening my day, to the book bloggers who tirelessly spread the word about my novels, and to my fellow authors who offer amazing support and guidance whenever I find myself lost.

Lastly… thank **you**.

Whether or not we've ever met in person, whether this is your first #JJbook or your tenth… THANK YOU. Your support means the world to me. xx

---

Keep reading for an excerpt from **THE MONDAY GIRL**

ALSO BY JULIE JOHNSON

STANDALONE NOVELS:

LIKE GRAVITY

SAY THE WORD

ERASING FAITH

––––––––

THE BOSTON LOVE STORIES:

NOT YOU IT'S ME

CROSS THE LINE

ONE GOOD REASON

TAKE YOUR TIME

––––––––

THE GIRL DUET:

THE MONDAY GIRL

THE SOMEDAY GIRL

ABOUT THE AUTHOR

JULIE JOHNSON is a twenty-something Boston native suffering from an extreme case of Peter Pan Syndrome. When she's not writing, Julie can most often be found adding stamps to her passport, drinking too much coffee, striving to conquer her Netflix queue, and Instagram-
ming pictures of her dog. (Follow her: @author_julie)

She published her debut novel LIKE GRAVITY in August 2013, just before her senior year of college, and she's never looked back. Since, she has published five more novels, including the bestselling BOSTON LOVE STORY series. Her books have appeared on Kindle and iTunes Bestseller lists around the world, as well as in AdWeek, Publishers Weekly, and USA Today.

You can find Julie on Facebook or contact her on her website www.juliejohnsonbooks.com. Sometimes, when she can figure out how Twitter works, she tweets from @AuthorJulie. For major book news and updates, subscribe to Julie's newsletter: http://eepurl.com/bnWtHH

Connect with Julie:

www.juliejohnsonbooks.com
juliejohnsonbooks@gmail.com

NEXT UP...

Want to read the story that started it all? The inspiration behind
Violet & Beck's story in UNCHARTED?

Pick up **THE GIRL DUET** today!
Both parts now available.
Continue reading for an excerpt from **THE MONDAY GIRL**,
Book #1 in the duet.

THE MONDAY GIRL

CHAPTER ONE

"I'm just not looking for anything serious right now."
- A guy who's about to start a long-term relationship... with someone else.

I sit alone in the darkness, watching bugs fly one by one into the glowing fluorescent zapper machine my neighbors installed to keep the mosquitos away from their balcony. Every few seconds, like clockwork, the pervasive quiet that seems to wrap the world in wool at three in the morning is interspersed by the unsettling buzz of tiny winged kamikaze pilots meeting their maker.

Zap, zap, zap.

I am transfixed, entranced by the sudden flare of the bulb each time it claims a new victim. There is something morbidly fascinating about these insects, drawn against all natural instinct to their deaths by the lure of this warm, bright killer. Can't they see their brothers and sisters before them, incinerated like birds flying too close to the sun? Don't they recognize danger as they sail straight toward it?

Zap.

Apparently not.

I press the damp surface of my beer bottle against my cheek, closing my eyes at the cool sensation. It's humid tonight. Sticky heat. The kind that makes you sweat through your clothes just sitting there still as a statue, doing nothing more exerting than pulling breath into your lungs.

The sprawl of downtown is a distant glow from out here on my narrow cement balcony, which overlooks a parking lot full of crappy old cars and cracked asphalt. This neighborhood is about as far from the glitz and glamour of the Hills as you can get while still calling Los Angeles home. Cynthia, my mother, hates that I live here almost as much as I hated living under the roof she pays for with an overly-generous alimony stipend from her third husband. Moving out last year with nothing but the thin wad of cash in my wallet, my broken-down Honda, and whatever clothes I managed to stuff into a duffle bag in the hour-long interval she vacated her beach-front condo in Manhattan Beach for her yogalates class was the best decision I ever made, even if she refused to speak to me for six months after she realized I'd gone.

Cynthia — which, for the record, is what she's asked me to call her since I was in diapers— still hasn't quite forgiven me for maneuvering my way out from under her thumb, but she can't shut me out completely. After all, I'm the star on which she has pinned her every hope and dream for fame and financial security. And a trainer doesn't let their prized racehorse just *quit*. Not before they've won the damn Kentucky Derby — or at the very least been turned into glue for profit. I'll be auctioned off for parts before she willingly loses her return on investment.

I did not pay for fifteen years of dance and vocal lessons to have you flush it all down the toilet.

Bringing the bottle to my lips, I drain the dregs of my beer in one long gulp. I set it beside the six other empties lined up like fallen soldiers at my feet and tilt my head up to look at the faint stars overhead. They swim before my eyes like fireflies in the hazy LA heat.

Everything is a bit fuzzy around the edges.

Maybe I shouldn't be drinking by myself, but I live alone and right now *not* drinking is not an option. I could call Harper, but she's got work in the morning and dragging her out of bed to deal with my drama in the middle of the night would only make me feel worse. I sure as shit can't call Cynthia. She'll never let me hear the end of it.

Drinking on the night before your big audition? You'll have bags under your eyes! You're competing with perfect little seventeen-year-old sluts for this part. We can't afford mistakes like this, Katharine.

If my ancient twenty-two-year-old ass can't land this shitty part because of a few beers, I'm sure my darling mother will still manage to spin it to our advantage. She's a pro at it. I'll be enrolled in rehab for a nonexistent drinking problem before I can blink, in some elaborate scheme to rebrand me as a bad girl and "broaden my image" — something she reminds me at least twice a week is in severe need of a makeover if I want to land any kind of steady role during pilot season.

I snort at the thought and lean back on my elbows.

There's very little allure in the prospect of securing the lead as a teenage airhead on some vacuous new network television show — a last-gasp effort at appealing to a generation much more inclined to binge-watch on their laptops than tune in every Tuesday at eight for yet another vampire show. That's not my dream — hell, that stopped being my dream about six years ago, when I realized my stint on a short-lived kids' show called *Busy Bees* was not going to impress the casting directors of edgy indie films or big Hollywood blockbusters.

Frankly, I'd like nothing more than to fade quietly into my mid-twenties, working nights as a bartender at Balthazar, the trendy nightclub downtown where I regularly serve bottles of champagne that cost more than my rent, and slowly scraping together enough money for college tuition.

Unfortunately, Cynthia is not quite so eager to relinquish her dreams of stardom. Despite my apathy, she remains doggedly determined to make her only daughter into an A-list celebrity, come hell or high water. Hence the audition tomorrow.

Another role I won't get, another disappointment she'll bear with all the grace of a blunt battle axe.

If you'd just smile more enthusiastically, Katharine...

If you'd just put in a bit more effort, Katharine...

If you'd just...

If you'd just...

If you'd just...

A deep sigh rattles out between my teeth as I rise, collect the empty bottles at my feet, and head through the sliding glass door into my dingy kitchen. The glowing green numbers on the microwave panel inform me it's nearly three thirty. Going to sleep now will probably leave me groggy and exhausted when my alarm blares to life at seven, but with the beer humming in my system I can't quite work up enough energy to care much.

If I manage to make it to the audition, it's sure to be a disaster.

Cynthia is going to be livid.

I smile in the dark as I collapse onto my lumpy mattress.

Self-sabotage is my middle name.

A psychiatrist would have a field day with me.

My Honda makes a scary noise as I punch the gas and hurtle toward downtown LA — a death-rattle, of sorts. Fitting, since this will go down in history as the day Kat Firestone finally managed to kill her acting career. Twenty-five minutes late, with last night's mascara still caked beneath my eyes and hair that hasn't seen a brush since well before my little balcony-bender last night, I know I'll probably miss my audition slot and, even if by some miracle I get there in time, I'll look more like a crack addict than the "fresh faced All-American girl-next-door type" they're looking for, according to the call sheet.

I press the gas pedal harder, wincing when the Honda begins to shudder, and pray I don't hit traffic. Though, not hitting traffic in LA would mean something ghastly has happened.

The nuclear apocalypse, perhaps.

Or, worse... *rain.*

I am self-aware enough to admit the irony of my race to read for a part I don't want, my headlong flight to salvage a career I severed all emotional ties with long ago. Yet, here I am. Hurtling down the freeway full-speed toward the demise of something inevitable. Racing toward an ending I don't necessarily want to reach.

That's life though, isn't it?

We're all in such a damn hurry to grow up — to turn eight and strap on a big-kid backpack and declare yourself too old for naps and dolls and dress up; to turn sixteen and get angry because, *god,* Mother, I'm old enough to stay out until midnight with my friends; to turn twenty-five and squeal *yes,* honey, of course I'll marry you and settle down in a suburban house far from the city lights in a marriage I'm not sure I'm ready for because, well... what's the alternative?

We move. We rush. We run.

Sharks in the water: stop swimming and you die.

And then quite abruptly we are old and wrinkled and frail, lying on our death beds looking back at a life we didn't even pause to enjoy. We are so busy speeding toward that damn finish line, trying to keep up with everyone sprinting alongside us, we forget sometimes that the finish line is death and the trophy is a coffin six feet beneath the earth.

I press the pedal a little harder and the Honda groans precariously. A strange smell has begun to emanate from the vents in my dashboard. By the time I screech to a stop in the parking lot of the talent agency holding the casting call, it's a quarter-past eight and my head is aching from the fumes. At a run, I drag my fingertips through my dark tangled mane and scrape it up into a pony-tail at the back of my skull. The weight of it tugs at my temples, exacerbating a headache from a hangover that hasn't even properly hit me yet.

I skid to a halt just inside the doors. They slam shut at my back with a bang loud enough to make me flinch, drawing the gazes of nearly everyone in the starkly decorated waiting room.

There are a few dozen girls scattered along the aluminum seats lining the wide hallway, waiting for their turn inside the thick double doors — biding time until they get their shot to read lines they've likely memorized and rehearsed a thousand different ways, for a character with the emotional complexity of a hamster. They all look nearly identical — glossy blondes in sweater sets and heels. A few of them are wearing pearls for god's sake, which says something about the role we're reading for. Between my mussed, chocolate brown waves, thready jean cut-off shorts, and faded *Ramones* t-shirt, I don't exactly blend with the crowd.

Damn Cynthia to hell for signing me up for this.

A wave of smug condescension crashes over me as sets of eyes coated with two perfect swipes of mascara scan my disheveled appearance from top to toe. Immaculately-lined lips purse in amusement and self-affirmation. Their thoughts are thinly-veiled as they examine me like a wad of gum stuck to the bottom of a Manolo Blahnik slingback.

I may not get the part, but at least I don't look like her.

Grabbing a script off the stack on a table by the door, I sigh heavily and collapse into the closest aluminum chair.

I probably should've read the call sheet Cynthia emailed me last week, accompanied by a terse note reminding me that I am not getting any younger and haven't had a steady role since I was wearing training bras a full decade ago. As is the case more often than not, her admonitions fell on deaf ears. I haven't exactly bothered to prep — unlike the perfect, pretty, petty girls littering the room around me like mannequins in a store window. Heads buried in cue cards and hand mirrors, they run through last minute lines and check their makeup.

My eyes drop to the phone clutched between my fingers. I scroll through a week's worth of backlogged spam emails until I find my mother's message. I pick absently at my chipping black nail polish as my gaze sweeps the casting call. It's a recurring guest role on a new pilot set during high school, featuring vampires or fallen angels or some other incomprehensible shit. Beth or Becky or some equally non-threatening name suited for a sidekick. A best friend.

Not the lead. Those were cast weeks ago.

I snort and the girl in the chair closest to mine makes a deliberate show of scooting away from me, as though my unkempt state is contagious and I'm liable to lessen her chances by sheer proximity. Twin spots of color appear on her high cheekbones when I waggle my fingers at her in a teasing wave.

"Don't worry, sweetie," I confide in a whisper. "I don't want the part. But if *you* do, I think we both know what kind of *qualities* the casting director is really looking for."

I make a crude pumping gesture with my hand and push out the inside of my cheek with the tip of my tongue.

With an indignant huff and a resolute shake of her slim shoulders, she turns her attention to the phone in her hands and attempts to ignore my existence.

That suits me fine.

The double doors at the opposite end of the room swing open and every head pivots to watch, faces etched in various expressions of critique, as a production assistant wielding a clipboard steps out, trailed closely by a girl who's just auditioned. Looking a bit green around the gills, the girl makes her slow march through the gauntlet of aluminum chairs on which her competition sits, her eyes never wavering from the exit. Judging from the way her hands are shaking and the thoroughly bored look on the PA's face, it's clear she won't be playing Becky.

A new name is called. A girl clamors to her feet and vanishes into the inner sanctum. I read through the script sheet briefly, grimacing at the cheesy lines. It's even worse than I imagined, and not just because my headache has evolved into a migraine. This is bad writing, even by network television standards.

After a few moments of painful study, I close my eyes and lean back in my seat, wishing I'd had time to grab a bagel in my mad rush to get here. The thought of composing myself enough to walk through those doors and say the words, "What do you mean, Stefano is a... a... a *vampire?*" in a tone of breathy incredulity is almost more than I can bear without any carbs in my system.

Every few minutes, I hear the sound of the doors swinging open, of girls exchanging places, of heels clicking against tile floors as those who have failed to impress the producers escape eagerly into the parking lot where they will sit in their cars and cry until their perfect mascara is smudged beyond recognition. The hopefuls — those who still cling to this impossible dream of "making it" — always take rejection the hardest.

I should know. I used to be like them. I used to give a shit.

Slumping down so my neck is braced against the curved back of my aluminum chair, I fight the waves of nausea coursing through my veins. God, I'm hungover. I haven't felt this crappy since last April, when Harper and I did mushrooms at Coachella. Fun at the time; not so fun the next morning, when I woke up naked in a stranger's tent covered in glitter, missing both my panties and my dignity.

An abrasive tapping sound intrudes on my recollections, followed shortly by an impatient cough. I open my eyes to find the stony-faced PA staring down at me, her clipboard clutched so tightly it's a wonder her acrylic fingernails don't pop off with the force of her grip. When our stares meet, her lip curls in a hint of disdain.

"Katharine Firestone?"

I blink. "Guilty."

"You're up," she says coolly, turning on a heel and marching toward the double doors without another word. I push to my feet and follow her at a leisurely pace, feeling the heat of glares from the rest of the girls in the room burning into me from all sides, an inferno of female contempt. Just before I reach the doors, I turn and blow them a goodbye kiss.

"They're waiting," the PA informs me testily, tapping her pencil again.

I push down the urge to reach out and break it in half. Denying her a snappy retort will spoil her dramatic little power trip, so I simply arch my brows and wait patiently, a small smile playing on my lips, until she shoves open the doors and ushers me inside.

There's a table set up across the room, about twenty feet from where I'm standing, its surface littered with empty iced coffee cups and stacks of notes. Sitting behind it are three people, none of whom bother to glance up when the door closes behind me with a resounding click. I hear the PA take a seat somewhere out of sight.

"Stand on the X in the middle of the floor, please," one of the women says in a tired voice.

I walk soundlessly to the spot marked with masking tape.

"Name?"

The woman at the center of the table is speaking again. She seems to be in charge. There's something insectile about the way she moves that reminds me of a large praying mantis — too thin, too jerky, highly inclined to bite your head off. Every strand of hair in her bleached blonde bob stays perfectly in place when she tilts her head to scan the sheet in front of her.

"Katharine," I say, my voice parched and cracking. Cynthia

always says I have a voice made for radio, but my hangover has made me sound even huskier than usual. I clear my throat and try again. "Katharine Firestone. But I go by Kat."

The man on the right looks up when I speak, interest written plainly on his angular features. He's in his early thirties and strikingly handsome — tall with an athletic build, his blondish-brown hair pulled back in a man-bun. I usually hate that look, but he somehow pulls it off effortlessly. I suppose, if you're attractive enough, it doesn't much matter what you do with your hair.

He looks like a Viking. Or maybe an Instagram model.

His eyes rake me from my messy pony-tail down to my battered Doc Martin boots. Surprise flickers in his dark blue irises as he takes me in.

"You're here to read for the part of Beth?"

There's an unmistakable note of incredulity in the question, fired at me from the other woman at the table — a middle-aged brunette with an air of superiority wrapped around her like an afghan. It's clear she's wondering what a girl like me, who sounds like a sex-line operator and dresses like a punk rocker, is doing here.

"Yes."

"I see." She glances down at the sheet in front of her and I see a flash of comprehension on her face. "Oh. *Firestone*. You're Cynthia's client."

"I am," I agree, forcing myself not to fidget under their unwavering stares. I'm not sure what's more humiliating — the implication that my mother had to make a call to get me this audition, or that she is so eager to be seen as my manager instead of the woman who physically pushed me from her womb twenty-two years ago.

The brunette murmurs something under her breath. It sounds suspiciously like *I should've known.*

"Why do you want this part?"

This time, the man is speaking. There is none of the brunette's arrogance or the blonde's apathy in his tone; he radiates a quiet intensity that commands attention. His voice is crisp and clear — it hits me like a splash of water and trickles down my spine in a sensation that's not altogether unpleasant.

I jerk my chin in his direction and hold his gaze. I contemplate mustering up some false enthusiasm, giving a fabricated answer about my passion for the role, but when my mouth opens I find myself answering honestly.

"My rent is due in two weeks and I currently have seventeen dollars and twenty-three cents left in my checking account."

The blonde titters, as though I've made an uncouth joke. The brunette pretends I haven't spoken. But the man shifts in his seat, the curious look in his eyes intensifying.

I try not to let it bother me. Men have been giving me that look for as long as I can remember. Like I was bred for sex and sin — a creature who exists only in the hours between midnight and dawn, when proper girls are sleeping. I'm not sure what makes them see me in that light, have never quite been able to pinpoint what part of me screams out to be degraded and deconstructed down to my basest parts.

Daddy issues?

Lack of self-esteem?

Fear of commitment?

Some other bullshit psychological diagnosis that reaffirms my deep-seated emotional damage?

Oh, who the hell knows.

Back in my elementary school days, boys used to tease me about the natural rasp in my vocal cords, about my too-large lips and masculine jawline. Funnily enough, when they hit puberty and started imagining how that rasp might sound if I were breathing out their names in the back seat of their cars, how my bee-stung lips might feel pressed against their own, the teasing came to an abrupt end.

There's a moment when they just sit there, the three of them, blinking at me. It's quite clear whoever they were expecting, it was not me. Likely another cog in the wheel of sweater-set wearers who came before. Pearls and pumps and well-practiced introductory speeches.

"Well, then... I'll prompt you with Angelica's lines," the praying-mantis woman says in a voice that sounds like air hissing from a balloon.

I nod and say nothing.

Sure, I should probably spend a bit of time trying to convince them why I'm suited for this part, but frankly... I'm not. I know it; they know it. Hell, even the bitchy PA knows it.

"Okay." The brunette woman slides her glasses down the bridge of her nose and stares at me like a pigeon who's just crapped on the hood of her freshly-waxed Mercedes. "Whenever you're ready, then."

It's clear before I ever open my mouth that there's very little point in even trying. There's a greater chance of this woman asking me to go tandem bicycle riding with her this afternoon than actually giving me the part. But I wasted a quarter tank of gas getting here, and then there's the small matter that Cynthia knows everyone in this industry; if I walk out without reading a single line, she'll hear about it — and I'll never hear the end of it.

Clearing my throat once more, I glance at the lines on my script as the blonde starts to speak.

"Oh, Beth! You'll never believe it... Stefano..." Her hand flutters to her heart and I try desperately to bury a laugh. "He's... he's..."

"What is it, Angelica?" I croak in a strangled voice. "I'm your best friend. You know you can tell me anything."

"But *this*...Oh!" The blond is quivering with passion. "This is not my secret to tell. I cannot betray the trust of the man I love..."

I gasp in an unconvincing show of surprise. "You *love* him?"

"Yes! I do!"

"But you barely know him," I choke out, gripping the script so hard my fingertips turn white. "How is that possible?"

"Beth, *anything* is possible when it's true love! Stefano is my soulmate..."

A snort of laughter slips out. I can't help it — this is cheesier than fettuccine alfredo. I try to cover it with a coughing fit, to maintain a serious tone as we make our way through the rest of the lines... but, judging by the cold glare darkening the brunette's face, I don't think I convince anyone in the room that I'm taking this seriously. My suspicions are confirmed a few moments later, when she cuts the audition short.

"That'll do." The brunette's eyes slide to the PA, who leaps to her feet and appears at my side, more than eager to escort me out. "Thank you for coming in. We'll reach out if we're interested in a call-back."

"Right." I grin ruefully. "I'll wait by the phone, night and day."

The women have already tuned me out, fixing their attention back on the papers in front of them, but the man shifts in his seat as his eyes scan me again. I swear his lips are twitching as he watches me turn and stride toward the exit, a jaunty bounce in my step because, as shitty as the audition was, it's *done*. Even the prospect of walking through the gauntlet of bitchy girls outside the door is not enough to dampen my spirits.

Now I can go get tacos.

I'm halfway to my car when I hear the sound of footsteps trailing close behind me in the long shadows cast by the building. Twenty-two years of possessing ovaries in modern-day America has taught me that, no matter the time of day, there is a fifty percent chance you are about to be raped if you hear someone walking behind you in an empty parking lot, so I reflexively position my keys between my fingers like little blades before whipping around to confront my stalker.

"Listen, buddy, I don't know what you—Oh." The words dry up on my tongue as I recognize the male producer from the casting session. He's slightly out of breath, as though he's run to catch up to me. "It's you," I finish lamely.

"It's me," he echoes, his eyes crinkling up in amusement. "Were you planning to key me to death?"

I glance down at my hand and find the keys still clutched tightly in my grasp. "Only if you were planning to rape me."

"I'm not."

"That's comforting."

His head tilts. "Are you always like this?"

"I assume by *like this* you mean charming and delightful."

"I was going to say abrasive and caustic, but I'm not one to judge." He leans in conspiratorially. "My therapist says I'm chronically distant and damaged."

"Well, shit, mine says I use humor as a defense mechanism for deep emotional pain." I shrug. "I told him I don't have any deep emotional pain. Maybe I'm just a bitch."

He laughs. "What are you doing right now?"

I glance around. "Standing in a parking lot with a stranger, contemplating the possibility that I'm an asshole by nature. Also contemplating the likelihood that my favorite food truck is serving tacos at this time of day."

He laughs again. "What are the chances of you putting your taco quest on hold?"

"I don't know. I'm pretty serious about tacos." My eyes narrow. "Why?"

"I want you to come with me somewhere."

"I don't even know your name."

"That ever stopped you before?" he asks.

I grin in lieu of a reply.

"It's Wyatt." He reaches out a hand and I slowly shake it. "Wyatt Hastings. And yes, I do mean *that* Hastings."

I feel my mouth gape a bit. The Hastings family owns half of Hollywood, controlling majority shares in AXC — one of the largest media conglomerates in the world. Their family fortune makes most A-list celebrities look like paupers.

"My father runs the network. That's why I'm here," Wyatt explains, jerking a finger toward the building behind us. "He likes to have someone from the family supervise casting calls for our newly green-lit shows, make sure everything is running smoothly before they start filming."

"Well... *shit.*" I blink at him, feeling lost for words.

His grin widens. "Does that look of stunned disbelief mean you'll come with me?"

"You're not going to have me read for that role again, are you? Because, I'm sorry... Hastings or not, I don't think I'm cut out to play Biffy the best friend on your new vampire show."

"I don't think you are either," he says, stunning me. "In fact, I don't think you're meant for television at all. I've got something else in mind."

"Oh."

"Just get in the car, please." He turns and walks toward a shiny black Audi convertible parked a few spaces down from my decrepit Honda.

"Is this, like, a sexual thing?" I tilt my head curiously as I watch his retreating back. "Because, honestly, I'm confused."

"Sexually confused?" he calls, clicking a button to unlock the doors.

"No. Just the regular kind of confused."

He pulls open the driver's side, grinning at me over his shoulder. "No, this is not a *sexual* thing. I'm old enough to be your... well, not your father. But maybe, like... your cool uncle. The one who buys you a keg after prom and beats up your boyfriends when they cheat on you."

"I'm twenty-two," I point out. "And this is LA."

"Your point being?"

"Most men date women at least two decades younger than them. I'd peg you at thirty-five, tops."

He looks affronted. "And here I thought I was passing for thirty-three. My life is a lie." He pauses. "Actually, it may just be my personal trainer who's lying."

I snort. "My point still holds. Walk into any coffee shop in this city, you'll spot a loving father-daughter duo having breakfast... until he starts to feel her up beneath the table and you realize he's just another sugar daddy treating his whore-of-the-week to crepes."

"That may be true. But we're getting off topic." He pulls his door fully open and pins me with a serious look. "I promise my intentions toward you concern nothing but your career. Now get in the damn car, Katharine, before I decide you aren't worth the hassle."

I arch a brow. "You're going to help my career?"

"No." His eyes gleam. "I'm going to change your life."

Manufactured by Amazon.ca
Bolton, ON

21310343R00141